GRAVEDIGGER

by

JC JAYE

Copyright 2021 by JC JAYE and Hot Pot Happenstance LLC. All rights are reserved. No part of this book may be used or reproduced in any manner without written permission except in the case of brief quotations used in articles or reviews.

Gravedigger is a work of fiction. Names, characters, places, and incidents are products of the writer's imagination or have been used fictitiously and are not to be construed as real. Any resemblance to persons living or dead, actual events, places, incidents, or organizations is coincidental.

ISBN- 978-1-7360583-1-2

Cover design by CT Cover Creations

Edited by Elaine York, Allusion Publishing

Formatted by Self-Publishing Services LLC.

Dedication

To all the souls in all the cemeteries I've visited
in my backyard and around the globe.
Rest In Peace.

🪦 🪦 🪦

Acknowledgements

Huge hugs to all my romancestagrammer buddies
for the shares, the reposts, and the sisterly support.
I keep finding you, you keep finding me…
It's a beautiful thang.

Gravedigger Playlist

"Dig Gravedigger Dig," Corb Lund
"The Bottomless Hole," The Handsome Family
"Headstone," Whiskey Myers
"Ain't No Grave," Tom Jones
"Fixin' to Die," Black Mountain Whiskey Rebellion
"Hell's Half Acre," Robbie Robertson
"Tombstone Blues," Bob Dylan
"Hip Boots," Deep Purple
"It Ain't All Flowers," Sturgill Simpson
"30 Days In the Hole," Humble Pie
"God & the Devil," The Surreal McCoys
"Angel Dream (No.2)," Tom Petty
"Two Hearts Down," The Black Lillies
"Late For My Funeral," Mike Stinson
"Diggin' My Own Grave," Artists of Dark Country
"Rock That Says My Name," The Steel Woods
"The Dirt Been Calling 'Em Home," Justin Tapp
"Golden Rails," Kasey Chambers
"Gawd Above," John Fullbright
"Fire In the Hole," Blackberry Smoke

Busted!

Wincing, Sunshine paused with glass halfway to lips, looking concerned.

"Ouch, your voice. All that hollering you did earlier, charging down that hill… You sound really scratchy, Clint. Better stop and get some lozenges to suck on before you get home."

Say wha? Suck?

Once again, a pair of porn star lips was shaping a word that wasn't helping matters any below the belt. *Christ, lady, have mercy!* Trying not to moan out loud, I choked down a cooling slug of hops, shrugging.

"I'll be okay."

Mumbling the dismissal, I fantasized about something else I'd much rather be sucking on than a nasty, menthol-flavored pellet.

Or, to be more specific, fantasized about two something elses.

Do not look at her tits, tool. Do not. Do not. Do not.

Being a huge pig-beast when it came to this woman, I did look, and none too subtly. Thankfully, Sunshine didn't catch my despicable lack of restraint, seeing her nose was buried in clear liquor.

Goddamn my life, such firm little tatas. So lush and round, the absolute perfect fit for my greedy, itchy hands.

Beneath half-mast lids, my eyes burned, honing in on two sweet mounds as I silently posed the $64,000 question that had been dogging me for hours.

Is she wearing a bra under that thin dress? Or are those gorgeous tits free and unfett—

"Boy, I hope you're not coming down with a summer bug, Clint. First your throat, now your face is all flushed. I will say it's pretty warm in here, though. Shall I run to the bar and grab us two more libations and some waters, and ask that bartender to crank up the A/C a notch?"

Busted!

TABLE OF CONTENTS

DIGGER: ONE	1
CASEY: TWO	17
DIGGER: THREE	34
CASEY: FOUR	53
DIGGER: FIVE	68
CASEY: SIX	87
DIGGER: SEVEN	100
CASEY: EIGHT	119
DIGGER: NINE	134
CASEY: TEN	151
DIGGER: ELEVEN	167
CASEY: TWELVE	183
DIGGER: THIRTEEN	200
CASEY: FOURTEEN	220
DIGGER: FIFTEEN	239
CASEY: SIXTEEN	257
DIGGER: SEVENTEEN	276
CASEY: EIGHTEEN	295
DIGGER: NINETEEN	317
CASEY: EPILOGUE	327
More by JC	334
Contact JC	335
About the Author	337

DIGGER: ONE

They call me Gravedigger.

That's right, just like it sounds. Grave. No space. Digger. Period.

Zero prettiness attached, zippo chance for misinterpretation. The moniker cuts right to the chase, describing my post-military career in three succinct syllables. Short, not too sweet, and unsettling to most.

It is what it is, folks. No sugarcoating necessary.

How does a big, semi-reclusive fucker like me earn my daily crust? I dig deep and tidy graves for recently departed stiffs; that's how. Furthermore, anywhere from six to eight months running (depending on Mother Nature), I till the earth by hand, the old-fashioned way. Not how the suits in the office want it done, but I negotiated that part when my PTSD counselor landed me the gig many moons ago.

Nuts? Maybe. But I figured a surplus of manual labor might help muffle the battlefield blasts in my head.

Outcome? Fair at most.

GRAVEDIGGER

Dubious success on that score aside, I got my way, and in accordance with the details of my contract, the loud yellow Cat doesn't roll out until the ground is frozen solid. And only then because I'm no masochist. The remainder of the year it's just me and my well-worn tools, averaging four hours per plot start to finish, a few ticks longer if conditions suck.

Newsflash: there aren't a whole lot of us soil slingers left. We're a dying breed, a diminishing brotherhood of spade-wielding unicorns. It's ball-busting work and the days are long, but you won't hear me complaining. Far as I'm concerned, the good Lord gave me two strong arms, a back like a bull's, and a dedicated work ethic, and I don't waste any of that shit.

Not to mention, it's a damned fine way to keep in shape. No overpriced gym membership or in-home Bowflex needed for this boy, not at the end of my sweat-soaked workday.

And yeah, I get that my vocation's not exactly nudging the top of any Most Desired Jobs list. Suits me just dandy, though, for a variety of reasons.

One:

Being the muscle behind the shovel allows for vast, uninterrupted stretches of solitude. Eight to nine hours per day, six days a week. Oftentimes seven, when the demons drive hard. Other than a couple of other part-time laborers and the admin in the brick building at the gates, I'm the guy—tending the tombstones with a skull crammed full of Afghanistan angst and a wheelbarrow full of not-so-nice flashbacks.

Plenty of convenient spots for a bedeviled ex-infantryman to verbally vent to The Man Upstairs if he's feeling the need, dontcha know.

Then there's two, which I guess is kinda an echo of above, slightly regurgitated:

Hailing from the windswept plains of the Midwest, I've always been into open spaces and sedate silences, as opposed to noisy cities and hordes of equally noisy people. And you'd be hard-pressed to find a patch of land sportin' more silence than the lawns contained within the black iron fencing of Oaklawn Cemetery, Vermont, established circa 1822.

Well, unless you happen to be one of its 60,000-plus inhabitants, sleepin' their everlasting slumber in decaying wooden boxes.

Which brings us to reason number three:

Simple. Mud, and lots of it. Goddamn, love me the stuff. Ever since I was a gangly-limbed kid, I've found a primal satisfaction playin' in the dirt, getting assorted body parts nice and grungy. Ask my mom, and the always-filthy floors of the long-distant ancestral heap back in Bumfuck, Oklahoma, population 5,500.

GRAVEDIGGER

"Clinton Ian MacGregor! How many times must I pound it into those deaf ears of yours? Shoes off on the porch, Son!"

I bit back a grin, recalling all those messy brown footprints and unending wails from Ma. Poor lady. Never without a pine-scented sponge in her overworked hand.

Haven't exactly learned a life lesson, when it comes to that shit...

Driving my spade into dense clay and rock, I pictured the rather repulsive state of my current kitchen floor, two towns over in Bristol. Gotta say, this slobby leopard hasn't changed his spots much in thirty-odd years. I closed salt-stung eyes for a sec, concentrating on the vision behind my lids.

Yeah. Isn't that cheapo linoleum supposed to be some version of white, rather than earth-colored?

Hmm. Probably should take a day off tomorrow and spend Sunday with a mop in my mitt, as opposed to a shovel. Get my neglected man cave in some semblance of order, catch up on the laundry.

And the mountain of dishes *and* the scuzzy bathrooms *and* the overgrown front and back yards.

Likewise, trash whatever scary science experiments are currently morphing in fridge and freezer.

Yikes.

I grunted, pushing moldy takeaway containers out of my head as I smoothed soil in front of a crudely fashioned timber cross stuck in the ground. This, the temporary, hack-job grave marker spelling out in bold Sharpie caps:

Errol V. Flin
April 9, 1977 – February 13, 2021

Doing the math, I shook my head, a pang of sympathy spearing me.

Poor fucker… Saddled with an approximated name of a famous Hollywood ladies' man, and just forty-four when he exited this mortal coil.

Jesus, both of those things had to have seriously sucked. Here's hoping the guy had at least been halfway decent-looking, not weak-chinned or bucktoothed, or that handle of his would've *really* been a cosmic joke.

Wiping perspiration off my own wide, whiskery jaw, I spent an additional twenty minutes making things all nice and neat for Mr. Flin before throwing tools of the trade into the truck bed. Digging in my pocket, I pulled out a shiny dime, laying it carefully atop the mounded earth.

Dead-center (pardon the pun), right where I figured Errol's heart would be, six feet south.

This was a little OCD ritual of mine I never missed. Not ever. Old or young, rich or poor, every pile of

GRAVEDIGGER

bones I planted in Oaklawn got themselves a silver coin send-off.

Back in Kabul a lifetime ago, my best buddy Kevin K. had once told me a tale about dimes and dead people. It had been after one of our bloodier battles, a nightmare in crimson and khaki. He'd been rapping about his kid sister, and how she'd bit it in a boating accident but was always turning up as a dime when he least expected it. Kerkowalski had really believed that sentimental shit, had taken comfort that those sightings were some sort of sibling signal, a moving message from beyond.

It had been a pretty good story, if you were into that spiritual jazz.

Three days later, Kev and a couple of other unlucky fucks had been blown to bits by an IED in the desert while the rest of our battalion, including yours truly, performed maneuvers back at base.

Kevvie had been my first dime. I'd snuck one into the shoebox of whatever pieces and parts remained of him when the top brass hadn't been looking.

My eyes stung anew, not from sweat this time, and I swiped a hand over them, picturing his goofy grin. Goddamn, I sure missed that big galoot.

Jesus, MacGregor...

I turned a muscle-tight back on my masterpiece of mud and headed for the truck, laying into myself.

What the fuck you doing, idiot? Taking a stroll down Shitty Memory Lane, when there's a waaaay better lane you need to get your ass over to, stat?

Slicking more dampness off my forehead, I started the engine, heartbeat revving to match its clatter as I checked my watch.

Oh yeah, baby. It was almost eleven, and it was Saturday morning.

Time to make tracks to Perpetual Gardens, section H-3, and park this heap behind that broad oak high on the hill.

Time for Gravedigger to take himself an early lunch break.

Time to enjoy the splendiferous scenery.

My heart banged faster as I puttered down winding gravel paths, nervous as a schoolboy.

Be there, baby, be there.

If the gods were smiling and Sunshine was in her usual spot, today was gonna be viewing number six. Six, Christ, already! And let it be said, my smitten eyeballs:

Could. Not. Fucking. Wait.

I stomped on the gas, my pulse kicking up another notch at the thought of gazing upon her lovely figure, a much-needed vision after a weeklong drought.

GRAVEDIGGER

Please be there, bright angel. This addict needs his Saturday fix, bad.

To clue you in, Sunshine is the sappy name I've christened the tousle-haired, petite blond beauty who visits a pinkish granite monument etched with:

Beth Ann Kent
January 29, 1997 – June 2, 2021

Visits it every Saturday, at the exact same time. Her gorgeous bones spending an hour on-site, a solid sixty minutes between eleven and noon. Arriving solo and leaving solo, kneeling silent and still on the grass. Shoulders hunched, fair head bent. Sometimes writing down crap in a notebook pulled out of her knapsack. Pausing now and again to lean forward and trace the recently carved name with her fingertips.

Juicy, heart-shaped ass showcased to perfection in the skimpy, short sundresses she favored.

Goddamned degenerate!

I swore, raking hands through overlong hair as I scowled at my scruffly reflection in the rearview.

Mister, you are one depraved fuck. Perving on a poor, grieving girl, while hiding your mangy ass behind cover of a tree. Thinking all kinds of filthy-dirty thoughts amidst bucolic fields, a sanctified setting for prayer and peace. Lusting like a dog over an unknown female mourning the twenty-four-year-

old soul resting under that slab of stone. A soul you buried with your own grimy hands not so long ago. Fucking A, man, talk about one messed-up piece of work.

Yeah, all true, all true.

But Jesus God, that ass…

Rounding another curve, I dragged my mind out of the gutter and puzzled yet again over the identity of both deceased and mourner. Who was the taken-too-soon Beth Ann Kent to my beauteous Sunshine?

A sister? A best friend?

A lover?

That last possibility didn't sit well with me. Hey, I'm all for whatever floats your boat when it comes to sexual preferences, but not in this case.

No, please Lord, not a lover. At least in my fucked-up fantasies, let Sunshine be into dudes with dicks, not chicks with clits.

I arrowed another fast glance in the mirror. Preferably big, surly dudes with lotsa ink, heavy whiskers, and an extra-large casketful of inner demons. Dudes who spend their days lowering mahogany boxes into wormy soil, and tossing smelly, dead flowers and deflated birthday balloons into slatted trash cans.

A laugh barked out of my throat, lacking any humor.

GRAVEDIGGER

Sure, fool. Sensational Sunshine and you? Right. Dream the fuck on, space cadet.

"Morning, Gravedigger!"

A jovial greeting had my thoughts flying out the window and my neck swiveling sideways. I knew that voice, and I knew it well. Belonged to Mr. L., one of the regulars, visiting Mildred Eugenia, his long-departed spouse. (Section Y-10, plot 25.)

"Hey, Hy."

As per usual, the geezer was planted in his trusty foldaway chair—crossword in hand, watering can at feet. Hell, this guy...Oaklawn had its share of professional grave-sitters, but Hiram L. was surely king. Christ, I'd been manning the grounds for close to a decade now, and ol' Hy was faithful as they come. Rain, shine, sleet, or snow, you could count on the white head and his nylon throne to be on the scene. Talk about one devoted servant.

And, damn, the sainted Millie had bit it way the hell back in 19 and 86!

"Workin hard, Digger, or hardly working? Heh, heh, heh."

I threw the goat a thumbs-up and a mumbled reply, glad as fuck that neither he nor any of the other professional marble-gazers on-site weren't paying homage to bones buried within eyeshot of that grand old oak awaiting me.

Come on… Who wants to waste precious time scouring for another perfect vantage point from which to observe a sexy blond angel?

Not I, says the graveyard lech.

Heart pounding behind my soaked shirt and palm clammy on the wheel, I pulled in under a canopy of leaves and killed the engine. *Showtime!* I sucked in a few steadying breaths before allowing my eyes to meander a few hundred yards down the hill and to the left, midway between seven and eight o'clock.

Drawing out the delicious anticipation, jacked as a grade-schooler mooning over his first mega crush.

Is she…?

I licked hungry lips, bracing myself.

Ah, Christ, she is. She is. She fucking is.

My greedy gaze drank Sunshine in: all messy curls, honey-tanned skin, and cockjerking curves. Same as the half-dozen times previously, she was kneeling on the grass, sandaled feet tucked up under her phenomenal ass. Swallowing dryly, I stared at that plump backside, swathed in a short blue sundress with white designs stitched around the hem.

Goddamn, but I could look at this girl forever…

I propped an elbow on the opened window frame, taking a pull from my water canteen to cool my boiling blood. Hand unsteady, it occurred to me that rather than pouring the liquid down my throat, I should really be pouring it down my pants, considering the state of my dick. It was as if the fucker was straining straight to where my eyes were fixed: eager to meet and greet the amazing bounty contained within that skimpy fabric. Groaning, I ground a palm over swollen flesh, appalled by my lustful thoughts.

Really need to get out more often, Gravedigger. Ever hear of the bar scene or dating apps, you pathetic Peeping Tom?

Working on keeping the drool level to a minimum as Sunshine squirmed on her delectable rump, I tried to think of the last time I'd been with a woman, the last time I'd gotten my antisocial ass laid.

Oh, yeah... Six whole months ago, just after Christmas. Ordered by the suits to use up untouched paid vacation time, I'd flown down to Oklahoma for the holidays. Upon touchdown, my baby brother Cormac had dragged me to the one and only watering hole in town, the Hey There Haystack.

(No, I'm not making that shit up.)

Having nothing better to do, I'd gotten extraordinarily juiced, waking up in a strange bed with jeans bunched around my boots, a mouth like an ashtray, and a bottle blonde with huge knockers snoring unprettily next to me.

Uh, huh, that's what one too many Buds and a handful of on-the-house Fireball shots will do to a man's better judgement.

Thank fucking God I'd spied a tied-off condom thrown in the trash can next to Knocker's nightstand, and hadn't been moronic enough to dip my wick into anything I shouldn't have without first donning protection.

I'd stumbled out the door two-point-five seconds after I'd cracked open my lids, leaving Sleepy Unbeauty sawing logs and reeking of stale, musky perfume. The hookup had gone down as seriously seedy, drunkenly unremembered, and instantly regretted. Particularly in light of Cor's ceaseless ribbings regarding the oral skillset of Ms. Mega Tits, a subject little brother remained fascinated with right up until I'd boarded my return flight home.

"Come on, Clintie. Don't be so damn coy… Inquiring minds need to know. Major suction action, or what?"

Turned out the lady with the rack had herself quite the reputation in Bumfuck. Was it a good thing or not that, to this day, me and my johnson remain clueless as to the veracity of her oft-lauded talents? I shuddered, answering my own question.

Good thing, most definitely.

Dismissing unsavory shit, I squinted at Sunshine's profile—the lines pure and angelic, her lips full and pink and luscious, even from this distance. Damn, I could only imagine what those beauties would look like up close.

Lord, I'd fucking kill to have them wrapped around my big, stiff...

Wait. Wait, what the living *hell*—?

My filthy fantasy was interrupted by the appearance down below of a scrawny figure sidling along the path, appearing out of nowhere from behind a clump of trees and making straight for Sunshine. The guy was swathed in a dark hoodie and black jeans, his face hidden by the cowl. One helluva suspect wardrobe choice for an eighty-three-degree day in July, that was for sure.

Ah, fuck!

Instantly, years of expertly honed army training kicked in hard—my body tautening, my vision focusing.

'DANGER' flashing its urgent message in blazing neon caps.

I was already grabbing for the door handle when the deviant snuck up behind my kneeling angel, lunging forward to grab her around the waist. Swearing, I slammed out of the truck like a ballistic missile and grabbed a shovel, my six-four frame barreling down the hill at Mach-speed as he yanked Sunshine to her feet. Through the blood pounding in my ears, a sharp, startled cry pierced the silence.

"O- Oh!"

I saw red, running faster.

"LET HER GO, FUCKHEAD!"

My seldom-used voice gruffed out harsh as gravel as I roared out a warning, sending two heads whipping my way. One was concealed with a hood of scuzzy cotton, the other was fair-haired and frantic-eyed and more beautiful than I'd ever dared let myself imagine.

Fucking A. *Way* more beautiful.

Jesus God, that face… Behind burning ribs, my heart stuttered, leaping to my throat as I locked gazes with an honest-to-goodness goddess, direct from Wet Dream Casting Central. I blinked, gobsmacked. Holy hell, my bright Sunshine truly *was* an angel, a vision beyond compare.

And this big, muddy sonofabitch was about to save her sweet ass.

Shitkickers eating up the turf, I tore my eyes away from a pair of stunning, panicky brown ones and focused on the scumbag pawing at Sunshine's skirt. Baring my teeth, I hefted the spade higher.

Not your day, motherfucker. You picked the wrong boneyard to mess around in. This is Gravedigger

GRAVEDIGGER

Territory, and you're about to regret slithering your skinny carcass through those big iron gates.

I hurdled over an urn stuffed with daisies, charging toward my target like an All-Pro linebacker.

Fuck yeah, asswad.

Lemme repeat that last bit again.

Bigtime regret, you repulsive, woman-preying piece of shit.

CASEY: TWO

"No! No, please…"

Wheezing out the words, I struggled to break free of two wiry arms, one clamped around my waist, the other crushing my windpipe. Panic seized me: suffocating, paralyzing, all-encompassing.

Oh, dear God, can this actually be happening? An assault in a pretty, countryside cemetery? Not six weeks after my beloved twin, my other half, died so unexpectedly?

"Let GO!"

I thrashed harder, struggling to land a blind kick without losing my balance. Claw-like fingers dug into my hip, raising my dress as a blast of foul breath blew in my face.

"Shut it, bitch. Shut up, and I'll make it nice and quick."

Please, Sweet Jesus. Please, don't do this to—

"LET HER GO, FUCKHEAD!"

A primal roar echoed around the tombstones, drowning out melodic bird chirps and my choking, sawing gasps. It was a male voice, harsh and guttural, sounding direct from the depths of hell.

GRAVEDIGGER

"Fuck—!"

The man behind me swore, dropping his arms and shoving me away. I stumbled straight into Beth's headstone, its rough-edged border scraping my palms. Pushing curls out of my eyes, I whirled around, hands slanted in a defensive "X" over my pounding breast.

Holy shit...

A creature of mammoth proportions was plowing pell-mell down the hill toward us, a shovel raised high in two brick-sized fists. Dark, bearded, and mega muscly, he resembled a Viking overlord from that gory but man candy-heavy TV series I was addicted to, his white teeth glinting through black whiskers in a fierce snarl.

"Fuck!" My assailant cursed again, the word trailing off to a whimper.

Yeah, creepo, can't blame you there. Seeing Lord Thor appears to outweigh you by a good two-thirds of your stick-like frame.

"Goddamned piece of shit..."

Growling, the Viking drew abreast, wielding his weapon and smashing Hoodie to the ground with a single and succinct blow to the shoulder. Shock-still, I stared down at a writhing form, woozily acknowledging that sucker must have reeeeally hurt.

Is that a cracking bone noise I just heard?

The man on the grass kicked out, his voice high as a girl's as he shrieked out additional F-bombs.

"Ah, fuck! You motherfucker! My fucking shoulder!"

"Hurts, does it? Tough. Them's the breaks for attacking a lady, asshole."

Planting a mud-clumped work boot on my attacker's chest, the big guy grunted with satisfaction, slicing his eyes my way. I stared into them, their hue a most astonishing shade of silvery-pewter, framed top and bottom with spiky black lashes.

Wow, gorgeous.

Immediately following that observation, I realized I'd hit certifiable status… Admiring some unknown behemoth's eyeballs when I'd been a hair's breadth away from being raped over my dead sister's grave.

Unreal, lady!

Jerking his beard at my bargain, multi-compartmented Burberry knapsack, Thor's words were rusty and harsh, as if he rarely made use of his vocal cords.

"Got a cell in that thing?"

I nodded, starting to shake.

His shaggy head nodded back, those silver orbs sliding over me hot and fast.

GRAVEDIGGER

"Good. Grab it and call nine-one-one, pronto. Your location: Perpetual Gardens, Section H-3."

You don't say? Like I don't have that address seared in my brain, mister?

Loosening crisscrossed wrists from over my heart, I fumbled in the bag, shoving aside water tumbler, a pair of garden shears, and a recently purchased spiral notebook. This, the hefty journal with tear-dampened pages in which I compose letters to Beth and leave tucked under her flowers, after I finish clipping stray blades of grass from around her brand-spankin' new headstone.

Phone... phone... phone...

In the midst of my frenzied scavenger hunt, it dawned on me that Viking Guy was a cemetery employee—his muscly-but-lean bulk garbed in dirty khakis and a wrinkled white shirt, sporting a fancy embroidered oak leaf on its left breast pocket.

Duh, that shovel was a pretty solid clue, too.

God, how lucky am I that this sexy giant happened to be passing by on his rounds?

Inwardly acknowledging *"extreeemely lucky,"* I stabbed in three digits and instantaneously, a clipped voice droned in my ear.

"You have reached nine-one-one. Please state your location and emergency."

"Yes. I,"

Shit.

Klutzy Casey dropped the phone smack into the center of Beth's pretty bouquet.

Maybe it was those hot pewter eyes clamped on me, or maybe it was the sheer size of my rescuer. Most probably it was delayed shock setting in, given the fact that a sexual predator was twitching inches from my toes, moaning and groaning dramatically.

I seriously do *not* want to admit that it may have been thick thigh muscles straining against dun-colored cotton *or* the flagrant masculine bulge evident south of a worn leather belt that distracted me, causing my five butterfingers to slip.

Because admitting that craziness? That shit would make me practically as perverse as the lowlife rolling around at my feet!

The Viking made a "tsk-ing" sound in his throat, bending in a swift motion to snatch my cell out of mixed peonies, all the while keeping a muddy Timberline planted on black fleece. Shoving the phone to his face, he barked out an APB.

"Yeah. This is Gravedigger, over at Oaklawn Cemetery. We've got an attempted assault on a female visitor. Perpetual Gardens, Section H-3, just past the creek's waterfall on the right. Got the guy subdued and he appears unarmed, but make it snappy."

Killing the call, he held out a huge, calloused palm, my large-screen iPhone looking like a Cracker Jack toy against his skin.

"Er, th-thank you."

Stuttering, I plucked it up, sparks zapping my fingertips as our flesh connected.

"Ugnn." Grunting out a non-word, a flush darkened the cheekbones above those rough whiskers as my savior turned his attention back to the man below his boot.

Had Thor felt those sizzles as well?

I stuffed my phone away, smoothing down my dress and leaning weakly against Beth's new home, nausea cramping my tummy.

Bethie? Bethie, are you there?

Like I always did at my sister's resting place, I imagined she was watching me, with me. In tune with me, same as we'd always been with each other, since day one. Twin-like, I wondered if she'd sensed I'd been in danger, and had sent a big tank of a man rushing out of nowhere to protect—

"Hey."

Interrupting my ridiculous notion, the giant in question growled another sound, resting his shovel next to Hoodie's pale, throbbing temple. Not looking at me, he gruffed out a command, jerking his chin again.

"Listen. You go stand down on the path and wait for the heat to show. I don't want you anywhere near this twisted fu-, uh, guy. Like I said: for all we know, his ass could be packing."

The "twisted fu-" in question piped up, his denial shrill and reedy.

"No, man… I ain't armed, I swear! Please, bro, let me go. I, I made a mistake. I'm just messed in the head, off my meds. I didn't mean to scare the lady. Shit, I was only seeing if she had some cash on her."

Thor the Viking Lord laughed darkly.

"Sure you were, scumbucket. That's why you were yanking up her skirt, huh?"

My cheeks turned hot as I grabbed my bag, making a wide berth around the figure on the grass as I headed for the gravel. Reliving his clawing fingers pulling on my dress, my stomach roiled harder.

Dear Jesus. If this gravedigger hadn't shown up when he had…

Thank you, Bee. Thank you, sweet sister. It has to have been you.

GRAVEDIGGER

It took a good ten minutes for the cops to roll up. Ten molasses-long minutes, with not another soul in sight.

Well, not any living ones.

Keeping a nervous eye on the strong silhouette looming over his pleading quarry, I admonished myself for not carrying a vial of pepper spray or the like while hanging around in such a secluded setting.

Stupid girl. Do you not watch the eleven o'clock news, dumbo?

In hindsight, my bereaved butt had been vulnerable as a baby duckling's. Kneeling with head bent, immersed in a whirlpool of mournful thoughts, oblivious to my surroundings... Your picture-perfect definition of "out of it!" Although, to cut myself some slack, Hoodie's attack had been so stealth, I probably wouldn't have had time to whip out any weapon even if I'd had one.

I crouched on a crumbling curb, ruminating how totally this world really, truly sucks.

"Sucks" putting it mildly, mind you.

Yeah. As if losing your fraternal twin and best friend on the planet to a freakish, unexplained brain aneurysm isn't nightmarish enough?

As if losing your hard-won summer school teaching position because the head honchos can't wait for you to "get over it" isn't brutally unfair?

As if losing your mind over an inability to sleep or eat or pretty much function in any capacity other than zombie-mode doesn't completely bite it?

Now, we get to add who-knows-if-they'll-ever-go-away frightening flashbacks to Casey Rae Kent's already shattered mental makeup?

Beautiful. Just beautiful.

You took away half of me, God. Is that not enough? Now, I can't even visit Beth without a rapist-foiling watchdog at my side?

I flung a handful of pebbles down the path, conceding that after today, I'd be too paranoid to make the trip to Oaklawn without one—or all three—of my strapping elder brothers in tow. *Which maybe wouldn't be the worst thing...* Mike and CJ and Christopher were utterly wrecked as well. Perhaps a Kent Clan group-grieving would be more cathartic than kneeling all by my lonesome.

My mouth tightened as I hurled more stones at a distant trash can, missing by a mile.

But having company *would* slam shut the door on sisterly "alone time," a Saturday ritual that had fast become sacred ever since Bethie's poor bones had been lowered into the earth.

Getting back to that recent reflection. Yessiree, my world most certainly sucks.

Sucks. Sucks. *Sucks.*

GRAVEDIGGER

A wave of undiluted rage choked me, and I twisted around to face Hoodie, caterwauling away on the hill. Raising my voice in a howl, I screeched over rows of flower-decorated tombstones.

"YOU! YOU FRIGGING ASSHOLE! THANKS FOR SCREWING ME UP WORSE THAN I ALREADY AM! I HOPE SOMEONE CUTS OFF YOUR TINY PENIS IN JAIL TONIGHT AND SHOVES IT DOWN YOUR THROAT!"

The Viking standing guard gaped down at me, his eyes wide. Then he laughed, deep peals of masculine laughter ringing out.

"That's it, girl. You tell him. If I wasn't afraid this cocksucker would try something, I'd invite you back up here to have a whack at his other shoulder. Hell, it's only what he deserves."

We grinned at one another, our eyes locking. Then the gravedigger's mouth went flat and his gaze dropped to my lips. Nervously, I bit the bottom one, aware of the dark flush staining his cheeks as he stared.

Oh my, are those handsome eyes hot as coals.

I looked away, fiddling with the hem of my dress. In fact, everything about the man was rather hot, if I were to be honest. Granted, he was a bit on the rough side, and it appeared he'd spent the better part of the morning rolling around in a shoveled-out rectangle of mud, but come on...

Those amazing eyes? His huge, well-built bod, all sweaty and sexy and hard?

Hard, like a warrior's…

My own skin aflame, I recalled Beth's teases regarding my ill-disguised lust for the brawny marauders of the Nordic Seas, depicted so graphically in that rousing series.

"Really, Case? All those bulging muscles and untamed beards do it for you? Not me, no way. Give me a civilized Ryan Gosling or Reynolds any day of the week over those hulking cavemen. Lordy, a beast like that would crush you to ash the instant he climbed aboard. Death by hairy asphyxiation? Or worse yet, a club-sized wang jammed up your cooch? No thank you!"

Mmm…

Internal temp soaring, I revisited my first glimpse of the aptly-named Gravedigger, and how my gaze had landed without volition on the heavy bulge evident behind his zipper.

Club-sized, indeed, Sissie. Has to be. I mean, just look at the size of the guy's hands, and those big boots. Mercy, I'll bet…

My rescuer's voice bellowed down the hill, deep and harsh in the somnolent quiet.

"HEY! HEY! Hey, girl! Head's up, the coppers are here."

GRAVEDIGGER

Casey, you absolute sicko.

I shot to my feet, pressing shaky hands to scalding cheeks, scandalized to be entertaining such lurid thoughts about a big, mud-splotched stranger I'd just met. And at such a time, and in such a monstrously inappropriate setting!

All right. There was nothing to do but attribute this lunacy to yet another manifestation of crippling grief.

Yes, grief... That has to be it. Don't beat yourself up so bad, little Miss Viking Perv.

Not quite meeting the eyes of the male and female uniforms clambering out of their flashing black and white, I pointed yonder, my voice quavery.

"He... The guy's up there, on the ground. The one in the khakis standing guard came to my rescue, totally out of the blue. It was like a miracle, actually. Uncanny timing. I was really fortunate."

The bob-haired woman nodded, palm around pistol as she followed her partner up the incline. Brisk words sailed over her shoulder, snapping out rapid-fire.

"Sounds like it, miss. We've had a handful of recent rapes in this area, and with any luck, the DNA samples will match your attacker's. Please wait here until we get him cuffed and in the vehicle, and then we'll take your name and information. In addition, you and the man with the shovel will need to come to the precinct house to file your statements."

I nodded back, but she was already halfway up the slope.

Recent rapes…

Bile rising, I shuddered, flipping out over how narrowly I'd escaped becoming a statistic. This cemetery was no puny patch of land; on the contrary, the grounds were rather sprawling. It truly *was* a miracle that Mr. Gravedigger happened to be Johnny-on-the-spot at the exact time of assault.

It was almost as if, same as Beth, he's been watching over me.

"Hey. You okay?"

I blinked up into the eyes of my defender, who had somehow gotten his brawny bod down off that hill without me hearing him. Heavy-lidded and glittering under level brows, sexy silver orbs assessed me steadily, the man's hulking frame blocking the sun. *Mercy, but he is huge.* I cleared my throat, determined not to glance anywhere south of his belt buckle.

Don't you freaking dare, lady. Not again.

"Er, yes. Yes, I am, thanks to you."

Remembering my manners, I stuck out a hand, summoning a wobbly smile.

GRAVEDIGGER

"This would be a good time for a round of introductions, I think. My name's Casey. Casey Kent. And I'm truly in your debt, kind sir."

He slashed a hand, his neck reddening. "No debt necessary. Just glad as hell I was around. I'm Clint MacGregor, but everyone around these parts calls me Gravedigger."

His eyes softened, flicking back up the hill.

"Kent? That a relation of yours, under that rock?"

My chest squeezed like an accordion as I forced the words out.

"Yes. My sister. My, my twin."

"Ah, Jesus."

I sensed the Man of Few Words was perhaps going to gruff out an additional two or three more, but I was wrong. He just loomed over me, shuffling around in his dirty work boots. Searing me top to tail with a pair of hot, slitted eyes.

Very hot eyes.

It's true that in the months before Beth passed, I hadn't done much interfacing with guys, other than hanging with my trio of ridiculously protective big brothers and stepping out on the occasional, go-nowhere date.

(This due mainly to an intensive teacher-training schedule, combined with successful blocking machinations by aforementioned ridiculously protective big brothers.)

Add to that my all-girl high school with its utter lack of opportunity. Followed by four years attending a rinky-dink community college so lacking in menfolk resembling studly network Vikings, it was laughable. Concluding with the current and woefully slim pickings scattered around town, sprawled on assorted bar stools and staring at sports screens.

Talk about your custom-made chastity belt. Small wonder this chick's so clueless when it comes to the opposite sex.

Clueless? You betcha. We're talking virgin unicorn at age twenty-four here, my friends. Pathetic, I know. Sheez, even my twin had lost it a few years back to some smooth-talking Ryan Reynolds look-alike!

Nonetheless, the way those hungry eyes were gobbling me up? Naïve or not, I was willing to wager I wasn't the only one in this land of the unliving feeling the attraction.

Floating on a faint breeze, I swear I heard Beth's teasing voice murmur in my ear.

"Go for it. Go for it, Case."

Skin burning, I cleared my throat again, peeking past a tatted arm to observe the "Best way to stuff a rape suspect with a compromised shoulder into the rear seat of a cop car." (Findings: firmly but gently, taking care with the cuffs.)

"Come on. *Go* for it, Sunny."

Beth repeated herself, using that dumb family nickname, and even though I recognized I had to be batshit-crazy, I mentally answered her back.

All right, bossy boots. If you insist. Here goes... My first social overture since I discovered your body on the stone pavers seven agonizing weeks ago.

I flicked my eyes back to Clint MacGregor's bulging biceps, addressing inked, sun-bronzed contours heavy on the vein-showcasing side.

Yum.

"Uh. I haven't really been doing anything, uh, pretty much nothing at all, not since my sister passed. But, uh, if you're up for it, maybe I could repay you with a drink after we go and give our statements? Er, if you don't drink, just a coffee, or a Coke?"

The cops had the doors shut on Hoodie and were headed our way, so I blabbed faster.

"Um, only if you want to, of course. Only if you have no prior commitments. Because the truth is, somehow, I can't bear the thought of going right home afterward. Not after such a close call."

My cheeks had to be absolute crimson as I plodded on, twisting my skirt.

"Sad to say, I still abide at the old homestead while I'm saving up for a place, and my mom and dad… They're going to be so upset when they hear. Like I said, though, only if you—"

Two voices mingled in the warm summer air, layering over each other. One was no-nonsense and capable, the other husky-deep and excitingly fervent.

"Okay, miss. First off, may I have your full name?"

"Damn *straight,* girl, do I want to."

DIGGER: THREE

"Let's grab this last booth, 'kay?"

Making for a murky corner, Sunshine plopped down on a wooden bench and I followed suit, mute as a bag of rocks as I maneuvered my ass onto the plank opposite. An awkward silence commenced—her fiddling with the stir stick thingie stuck in her drink, me twisting my longneck brew and struggling to keep the eyefucking to a minimum.

But Christ *Jesus*, that shit was not easy.

Peeking out from under long-ass lashes, my stuff-of-wet-dreams companion started the conversational ball rolling, the girl no doubt realizing I sucked at small talk.

"Hey, good call, this place. Nice and dark and seedy, the perfect setting to get one's day drink on. I can't say I've ever stepped foot in here before, although I've driven past it probably two zillion times."

Shocker, babe. A rare gem like you gracing Mitch 'Moonlighter' Tirone's hole-in-the-wall? Fucking A, the regulars at the wood almost crashed off their ratty stools when your fine ass sauntered in.

My neck heated up as I second-guessed my suggestion to hit Mooney's.

"Uh. We can go somewhere else if you'd rather, no sweat. My buddy Sledgehammer is tight with the dude behind the bar, and drags me in from time to time. I know it's kinda crappy, but I figured—"

Sunshine interrupted, talking over me.

"No way. This is fine, really, old-school badass." She paused, crinkling her nose. "Sledgehammer, huh? Interesting name."

I rubbed my ear. "Yeah, that's not his real handle. He's, uh, a contractor, a refurbisher of old houses."

"Cool." Nodding, she paused for a sec, twirling her glass.

"So. Er, that didn't go too bad at the station, right? Those cops were pretty decent, I thought. And you have to admit, we were in and out without undue hassle."

In and out.

I bit the inside of my cheek, watching plush pink lips form words I wished pertained to a different subject entirely. An image of a buck-naked Sunshine spreadeagled underneath me blazed in my brain—vivid and raunchy and hot as fuck.

God, she'd be so wet, so tight. And I'd be so damned hard, same as I am now. Propped on my palms as I rail into her juicy cunt like a piledriver. Banging my bright angel so deep, I hit the back of her spine.

GRAVEDIGGER

Swallowing her sweet screams with my hungry mouth...

Shifting uncomfortably, I flushed anew, ashamed by filthy-as-my-boots fantasies.

Head out of gutter, you dick-thinking cretin.

"Er, yeah." I cleared a clogged throat, picking at my label as I mumbled an affirmation. "Not bad at all. And from what they told us, sounds like they might've gotten their guy. If the DNA sticks, with any luck that piece of trash will be goin' away for a good, long while."

Sunshine blew out a breath, nodding. "We can only hope. Officer Fletcher hinted if that most recent girl positively IDs him, it should be enough evidence to—"

She shook her curls mid-sentence, clamming up.

"No. No, I don't want to talk about that sicko anymore... I'm still feeling his disgusting hands on me. I've yet to face my parents, relive it all over again. And once my brothers get wind, holy crap! I was thinking of taking the easy way out and not telling anyone, but you don't know my mom. One look at my face, and I don't stand a chance of subterfuge. It was the same with... with Beth. She always knew when I was holding something back."

Big brown eyes welled up as Sunshine gulped her Stoli Orange and soda. I remained silent, longing to squeeze her in a bear hug, to cover that lovely, sad face with a thousand kisses. Naturally, I did neither, taking a pull from my Bud as I discreetly adjusted under the table.

Setting down her glass, the beauty repeated crap she'd spewed at the station.

"Anyway, Clint. Once again, I have to say: I still cannot *believe* how you happened to be around the instant I was grabbed. You must admit, in a place as big as Oaklawn, the odds are astounding."

My neck turned hotter as I cut evasive eyes sideways, studying the paneled wall.

You'd believe it well enough if I told you I timed my Saturday lunch breaks to the minute, baby.

Voice rusty, I spoke to a gawdawful painting of a garish sunset hanging off-kilter in a dime store frame.

Jesus, how hideous. I've thought it before, and I'm thinking it again: *The Tirones have them some seriously sucky taste.*

"Yeah, astounding, I'll give ya that. Pretty freaky."

Another protracted silence. When I couldn't take a lopsided neon-orange sun and amateurishly rendered cotton ball clouds any longer, I glanced back across the table.

GRAVEDIGGER

Sunshine had her head tipped, cockteasing lips pursed.

"So. How in the world did you end up as a gravedigger, Clint MacGregor?"

I swallowed a silent groan.

Fuck me... If I had a dollar for everyone who'd asked that question over the past dozen years, I'd be Croesus. Most people, I brushed off with a vague non-answer. With Sunshine, especially on account of her poor sister, I dredged out the condensed version.

"I'm from a tiny, podunk pin-dot in central Oklahoma. Hit the road right after school, joined the service. Ended up in Afghanistan, saw some pretty heavy action."

Kev's grinning, freckly face swam before me, and my chest tightened.

"My, uh, one of my best buddies in our outfit is from this town, and after he, er, after I got out, I settled here. Lots of nice trees and nature, a total one-eighty from the dust I was used to. There was a job posting that one of my, uh, one of my counselors found for me, a posting that'd been up for a while, and I grabbed it. It beat staring at the four walls all day, reliving a tankerload of bad shit. Thought I'd last a couple of months max, but it suited me, and there ya have it."

My bright angel smiled; teeth white, lips rosy. I fixated on the tiny gap separating the front two, yearning to explore the sexy imperfection with my tongue before I stuck it halfway down her throat.

Messy curls cocked again. "Does your friend still live here, Clint?"

The bands around my chest tautened, suffocating me.

"Uh, yeah. Yeah, he does."

Address: Veterans Field, Section N-4. Whatever blasted-to-bits parts remain, planted six feet under the clay with a small Stars and Stripes for company. A flag that yours truly replaces every three months, so the cloth never gets tattered.

Sunshine smiled wider, reaching for her drink.

"Oh, that's nice. You guys still hang together?"

I remembered the first stop on my rounds this morning, and yesterday morning, and the morning before that. My reply husked out a hoarse grunt, the words strangling in my throat.

"Yeah. All the time."

Wincing, Sunshine paused with glass halfway to lips, looking concerned.

"Ouch, your voice. All that hollering you did earlier, charging down that hill… You sound really scratchy, Clint. Better stop and get some lozenges to suck on before you get home."

GRAVEDIGGER

Say wha? Suck?

Once again, a pair of porn star lips was shaping a word that wasn't helping matters any below the belt. *Christ, lady, have mercy!* Trying not to moan out loud, I choked down a cooling slug of hops, shrugging.

"I'll be okay."

Mumbling the dismissal and pushing Kevvie out of my mind, I fantasized about something else I'd much rather be sucking on than a nasty, menthol-flavored pellet.

Or, to be more specific, fantasized about two something elses.

Do not look at her tits, tool. Do not. Do not. Do not.

Being a huge pig-beast when it came to this woman, I did look, and none too subtly. Thankfully, Sunshine didn't catch my despicable lack of restraint, seeing her nose was buried in clear liquor.

Goddamn my life, such firm little tatas. So lush and round, the absolute perfect fit for my greedy, itchy hands.

Beneath half-mast lids, my eyes burned, honing in on two sweet mounds as I silently posed the $64,000 question that had been dogging me for hours.

Is she wearing a bra under that thin dress? Or are those gorgeous tits free and unfett—

"Boy, I hope you're not coming down with a summer bug, Clint. First your throat, now your face is all flushed. I will say it's pretty warm in here, though. Shall I run to the bar and grab us two more libations and some waters, and ask that bartender to crank up the A/C a notch?"

Busted!

I scrubbed a hand over my mouth, regressing to a fifth-grader who just got caught crushing on the prettiest girl in the classroom. Sliding sideways, I lumbered to mud-caked boots, skin sizzling.

"No, I'll go. You sprang for the first round, against my wishes."

In addition, I don't want your ass anywhere near that hound dog Moonlighter, considering he's likely still rolling his tongue up off the floor.

Slicking back clumps of hair, I jerked my chin at Sunshine's almost-empty glass.

"Same poison?"

She threw me a thumbs-up, angling on her bench seat and leaning against the wall.

"Yeah. And ask the man in the apron for a bunch of extra orange slices. I haven't eaten all day, and at least I'll get a few nutrients sucking on something besides copious mouthfuls of grain alcohol."

Ah, Christ, there was that word again.

GRAVEDIGGER

Sucksucksucksucksucksucksuck.

My cock jerked in my pants as I processed Sunshine's request and the sexy way her full, wet lips were curving up.

Jesus, girl… Are you that unaware of the shit you are saying?

I half-turned, terrified she'd see the thick bulge riding down my leg.

"Uh, sure. Extra oranges. You, you want a bag of chips, or something?"

Fucking idiot. You couldn't think of a better place to bring this stunner than a murky hellhole with no menus and super-scary wall decor? It's going on three o'clock; she must be starving.

Arrowing a fast glance south, I swallowed a sigh.

Oh, right. Maybe because you look like a filthy derelict in sweat-stained rags? Not exactly dressed for that fancy bistro the next block over, are ya, Prince Charming? Hey, at least your nasty ass picked the joint with the dimmest lighting.

Sunshine shook her head, dismissing the offer. "No chips, I can hold out. But maybe a few lemon slices to go with the oranges. I like sucking on those babies, too. Nice and tart going down. Yum, yum."

I blinked at the scuzzy floor, wondering why The Big Guy in the Sky was messing with me so badly.

Then, I fled.

Two hours later, we were still planted in our back-corner booth. The tabletop was littered with four empty Bud bottles, three drained rocks glasses, five decimated bags of kettle chips, and a whole orchard full of sucked-off citrus slices.

The brews had rendered me subtlety snockered.

The grease had taken the edge off.

The sucking shit Sunshine had been tormenting me with for one hundred and twenty prickteasing minutes had me ready to blow in my boxers.

"Mmm, yes. Nice and tart. You want to try one, Clint? Full of vitamin C!"

Thank fuck the mothers were all history, and that Sunshine's new and fawning fan behind the bar had run clean out of pulpy orange and yellow garnishes.

Thank fuck also that Casey Kent "despised limes with a passion."

Because, I swear to Christ... I don't know if Sunshine was truly clueless as to what the sight of a beautiful woman sucking off lucky little wheels of fruit does to a man, or if the petite demoness was well aware of her powers and intent on bringing a bewitched fool to his knees.

Fuck, yeah, this fool would like to be on his knees. Right now, with my head up under that skimpy cotton dress.

"My brave Gravedigger…"

Elbows on table, Sunshine rested chin in palms, grinning over at me. A trifecta of Stoli and sodas in, she was feeling no pain, adorably tipsy. On account of her size, significantly more oiled than I was. Not wasted or anything, let's just say mighty relaxed.

And miiiiighty talkative.

During the past two hours, I'd learned a whole lot about my bright, broken angel. Gotten the lowdown on Casey's family: her parents, her brothers, her late sister.

"She was so awesome, Clint. You would've hands-down have loved her."

Sitting silent, I'd heard about the freaky way Beth had bit it, and how it was Sunshine who'd discovered the poor girl's body, face-planted on their parents' back patio.

"I'll never forget it, not ever. Even if I live to be a hundred and ten."

Nodding mutely, I'd caught how she still bunked with the folks but was squirreling away for her own place—a spot in some new condo complex she'd planned on going halves in with her twin.

"I have almost enough saved for a sweet corner unit. Mom and Dad offered to help, but I want it to be all me."

Draining the brews, I'd been regaled with the details of her getting canned from her summer school teaching gig mere days after she'd landed the position.

"Can you seriously believe it? Such an absolute lack of compassion, so soon after the funeral?"

Chest tight, I'd been privy to the crushing weight of her vast and overwhelming grief.

"It hurts. Oh God, Clint, it hurts so much. So terribly, so overwhelmingly *much*."

Yep. That part, most of all.

Fucking shit had gutted me.

Let it all out, beautiful. After Kevvie K. and the troops? Trust me, sugar, this soldier can relate.

Tucked in our undisturbed booth, it's like the floodgates had opened, and every awful thing that'd happened, every black and terrible emotion Sunshine had experienced since June the second came pouring out.

GRAVEDIGGER

That was cool; my buddies back in the trenches always said I was a good listener. And Sunshine was so sweet, so sorrowful, so in need of a sympathetic ear. And, fuck, I'm not going to lie… Any excuse to linger in this almost-deserted dive and gaze upon such perfection while the woman unloaded wasn't exactly a hardship.

I stared across the table, watching plush lips disgorge slightly slurred, cathartic words. Captivated by a pointy pink tongue, slicking against a sexy tooth-gap.

Hardship? Holy Jesus, not even remotely.

"Bethie told me to go for it, you know."

I rubbed my beard, mesmerized by the way Sunshine's eyes glowed beneath their curly lashes.

So fucking alluring.

Struggling to concentrate, I mumbled a need for clarification. "Uh, pardon?"

Those lustrous peepers latched onto my hand as I stroked my whiskers.

"Beth, my sister. I heard her voice, clear as day, just before the cops took our names. I swear to you, Clint; it's true. She told me to ask you out for a drink, to follow my attraction."

My blood surged, thick and hot in my veins.

"Attraction?"

Sunshine giggled, playing with that damned stir stick, twirling it between her fingers.

Goddamn. I wanna be a stir stick, so fucking bad.

"Yeah, Gravedigger, attraction. The first non-crappy emotion I've felt since Beth passed. It hit me as soon as I saw you barreling down that hill. Hair flying, shovel held high."

Her lashes flicked against flushed cheeks as Sunshine bit her lip.

"Your big, muscly body, the expression on your face… You looked like a Viking, Clint."

Huh?

I sat mute, unable to drum up a single blessed syllable in reply.

Other than a fervent and unspoken rejoinder: *Attraction? Tell me about it. Christ, the things I want to do to you, girl, I can't even see straight.*

Keeping that shit to myself, I balled my fists into rocks so I didn't reach out and grab.

Or, in Viking-speak, plunder what I needed to make mine.

Sunshine's teeth with their enticing gap released her lip and her tongue reappeared, tracing plump curves. I stifled a groan, licking my own starving lips as she tacked on a tipsy addendum.

GRAVEDIGGER

"FYI, I'm really into Vikings. The look of them, I mean. Big and rangy and wild, covered with lots of wicked tats."

Those long-ass lashes rose, and Sunshine was eyeing my forearms, both of them heavy on the ink.

"Bethie used to tease me about it. Sissy was into preppy kinds of guys, but not me, no way. Me, I favor a more rugged type of man."

A tiny finger reached across the table and stroked my bunched wrist.

"A man like you, Gravedigger."

I honestly don't know what would have happened next. Probably, being incapable of forming a coherent sentence and about to be zipper-tatted by my straining, swollen dick, I would've stuck Sunshine in one Uber and me in another. Would have left both our cars in the lot until morning, seeing we were each legally over the limit. Would have regrettably called it a night.

But then the little witch stroked that finger up my arm and rose to her feet, circling the booth and scooching in next to me, and any further details regarding modes of transport flew right out my lust-addled skull.

I swallowed hard, every corpuscle I possessed attuned to the magnificence planted six scant inches away.

Her curls at my shoulder. The light, honeyish fragrance coming off her skin. Her tight bod, encased in that sundress that was lacking (I was almost ninety-nine-point-nine percent certain by now) a brassiere beneath it.

What about her panties? Lacy thong or satin bikinis?

Sunshine edged closer, thigh pressing against mine. Humming, she tipped up her chin, her angel face nothing less than a dream.

"Clint?"

I grunted around the rock stuck in my throat, staring down at half-parted lips.

"Yeah?"

"What would you say if I phoned my parents and told them I was staying at my friend Laura Lynn Swanson's house tonight? Told them I was ready to rejoin the land of the living, that I wanted to kibbitz and crash with a compassionate gal-pal?"

I didn't know where she was going with this, and seriously, having her so damned close, I could barely fucking think.

"Uh, well, I—"

Sunshine interrupted, her voice a whisper.

"Except, I wouldn't be crashing at Laura Lynn's. No, I'd be angling for an invite from the big, brawny

GRAVEDIGGER

Viking Lord who saved a damsel in distress this afternoon."

She licked those shiny lips again, her eyes locked on mine, drowsy and seductive.

"What do you think, Gravedigger? Feel like hosting a houseguest? We could order a pizza and talk some more."

Another slow tongue swipe.

"Or, not talk."

My dick jerked, the bastard harder than a length of steel tubing.

Holy fuck. Is this wet dream saying what I think she's saying?

Shifting slightly, Sunshine placed her palm on my thigh, where it burned through wrinkled cloth, surely leaving a brand.

"Also. Got any eggs in your refrigerator? I'm known to whip up a mean cheese omelet for breakfast."

I drowned in deep chocolatey pools, my heart slamming in my chest, my cock about to bust my zipper. Then I bent my head, and did what I'd been dying to do for weeks, for days, for hours.

And motherfuck me… Was our first kiss in that dark corner booth better than all my wildest, dirtiest fantasies starring Sunshine put together?

Hell, yeah. *Waaaay* the fuck better.

Way hotter. Way longer.

Way deeper, way wetter, way more desperate.

Christ, you should have seen the envious-as-shit look Tirone leveled at me when we stumbled out of his dive, mouths and bods fused. Swear to God, from outta the corner of my eye, I saw the prick adjust his junk.

And if you think *that* kiss was something? Fucker was positively G-rated compared to its follow-ups in the Uber's back seat during our steamy, twenty-five-minute ride to my man cave.

Ask mister googly-eyed driver, and my tented, pre-cum spotted fly.

Sunshine's fingers traced damp cloth and a bulging zip, and I moaned under her soft digits like an untried kid.

Jesus. One more flick of those fingers, and a stain stick's gonna be needed, for sure. A situation most fucking embarrassing.

Listen: in spite of my current six-month drought, I'm no hit-it-and-quit-it schoolboy. *Usually,* I have a reserve of control as high as Everest. *Usually,* I can put it on ice when need be. *Usually,* there's no fear of me blowing the wad in my skivvies simply from sucking face with a chick.

GRAVEDIGGER

But this was no ordinary chick.

This was *Sunshine*.

And the way my angel was kissing me back, moaning into my mouth, digging her little fingers in my hair and my cheeks and my shoulders?

Her citrus-tart tongue, her sweet, panting breaths?

That naughty hand on my dampening fly?

"Oooh, Clint… So big and hard and hot."

"Fuck, baby. Fuck!"

Shit, another minute more? Another thirty seconds of Sunshine and me plastered together in that sweaty back seat, going fuck-all crazy on each other?

No chance in hell would me and the beast below my belt have made it unscathed.

Thank the Good Lord Jesus for that last green light!

CASEY: FOUR

Clint mumbled to his fingerprint-smudged refrigerator, two tense-looking shoulders twitching.

"You, uh, want anything to drink? Your choices are beer, beer, or beer. Sorry, I don't have any wine or mixers or anything."

I hovered like a spare part in his messy kitchen archway, fiddling with the straps of my knapsack.

"No, er, I've had enough hard stuff, thanks. Just a water would be great."

The King of the Un-Castle grunted, stomping over to a cupboard. His voice was hoarse as he fumbled for glasses somebody with a fair-to-middling immune system could actually drink from.

"Right. Don't have any fancy bottled stuff, either. Hope you're cool with tap."

I nodded, belatedly realizing the man wasn't looking at me. Clearing my throat, I squeaked out a reply.

"Tap's fine. In fact, I eschew plastic bottles. Mama Earth and all, you know?"

Mama Earth? Eschew? Ugh. Dork much, Kent?

GRAVEDIGGER

Gravedigger was currently addressing an unshiny water faucet. "Yeah, I hear you. Hang on while I get it cold."

Lowering my butt to a wooden chair and grabbing one of the dozens of sports mags littering the table, I pretended to soak up accolades about some college football phenom while Clint stood silently at the sink, running water for so long it was a miracle the pipes didn't dry up.

Okaaaay. This is getting reeeally awkward...

I flipped a page, humming under my breath. Wishing I was brave enough to cross the room, yank off that tap, and pull those delicious, whisker-framed lips back down to mine. Reacquaint myself with the incredibly talented, exceedingly greedy mouth I'd so savored during the last panty-soaking half hour. But, intensely intimidated by the taciturn giant looming ten feet away and experiencing a rapidly diminishing vodka buzz, I stayed put, moving on to peruse PGA standings.

Fascinating stuff. My, was that Rickie Fowler gifted with the clubs!

The print turned blurry, and I snuck a glance sideways, ten shades of confused.

All right... How the heck had the program nosedived from passionate make-out session to stilted guest and host in the space of three minutes? Once Mister Man and I stumbled out of that steamed-up back seat and into this slobby batch pad, we've morphed into a pair of robotic strangers.

Any Joe Blow peeking through the window never would guess a crowbar would've been necessary to pry us apart mere minutes ago.

As I bit kiss-swollen lips, my cheeks heated.

Shit. Maybe I'd pushed it too much at the end, putting my palm on his—

"Here ya go."

Interrupting my inner babble, Clint slammed a pilsner glass sloshing with Vermont's finest in front of me.

"Should be cold enough. I, uh, I don't have any cube trays full. Wait, lemme move some of this crap out of your way."

I gave another nervous nod, forcing down a sip and hoping Gravedigger was a better dishwasher than he was housekeeper. As I swallowed, I couldn't help but notice what was front and center in front of my face.

Seriously, I doubt any woman with a working pulse could.

Namely, the big guy's crotch, right the frig *there* as his large, calloused hands scooped up magazines, piles of papers and bills, and a slew of abandoned coffee mugs.

GRAVEDIGGER

Face flaming, I blinked, noting an El Grande-sized bulge and a golf ball-sized splotch staining the fabric to one side of a straining zipper.

Wait. Is that...

My significantly saturated bikini briefs instantly saturated some more.

Holy crap, it is. An honest-to-goodness wet spot. Oh, good God, how hot is that?

Before I could click off any more mental snapshots for future fantasy sessions, my broody host was across the room again, dumping cups in the sink and flinging mags into a recycle bin. I perved on his fine buns, excitement prickling me.

He'd gotten that worked up from our kisses. Just like I had.

Just like I still am.

Avoiding my eyes, Mr. Erection Most Mighty raked fingers through his hair, blowing out a breath. I sat silent, watching his wide chest expand and contract as he gruffed out a curt newsflash.

"Listen, uh... I really need a shower, need to wash the grime off. You wanna order that pie? I'm not picky; get whatever you want. Buncha menus on the counter behind you."

He paused, the bronzed skin on his neck reddening.

"There's another bath down the hall, past the den. It, uh, it might be a little, er, untidy, but it should be stocked. Feel free to have a look around, too, if you can handle it." A rough laugh. "Lord knows the place could use a cleaning crew; I'm not around much. Uh, okay. I'll be, like, fifteen minutes..."

Trailing off, Clint threw me a fast look, silver eyes incendiary as they shot up and down. Then he bolted out the room, leaving clumps of dried mud on the already filthy linoleum.

Mercy. Didn't anyone ever tell the man dirty treads come off at the door?

I sat there a minute, wondering if it would be presumptuous of me to wipe up some of the worst spots or deal with the dishes heaped in the sink. Concluding that it probably was, and that the soaked state of my undergarments was far more pressing, I rose, heading down the hall in search of the facilities.

Passing a shambolic living room, a dining room with table legs that appeared in danger of collapsing under mountains of unfolded laundry, and a trashed den that screamed MAN CAVE in *Flintstone*-sized letters, I eventually hit pay dirt. Flicking on the bathroom light, I wrinkled my nose.

"*Untidy?*" Sheez, talk about an understatement!

Reluctant to linger in the slovenly space any longer than necessary, I swiftly took care of business,

GRAVEDIGGER

washed my hands and splashed my face, and sopped up what Clint's amazing kisses had wrought.

Or, tried to sop up. Realizing the effort was futile, I stepped out of pretty periwinkle lace and wrapped the undies in a wad of tissue, stuffing them in my bag. Immediately, I felt more comfortable, and a lot less damp. Smoothing skirt over thighs, I contemplated rifling through those piles in the dining room and borrowing a pair of Tommy Johns.

I snorted, picturing my puny frame swimming in oversized boxers. No way, they'd drop straight off my hips to the unvacuumed rug.

It'll have to be commando, my girl. Just watch the way you sit.

Backtracking, I squinted for a comfy chair on which to alight, but every cushion I spied was already occupied by sheaves of newspapers, discarded food wrappers, or soiled dishes. Man cave, indeed. Reentering the kitchen, I plopped down in my previous seat, taking another sip of piss-warm water. Bored with golf, I attempted to get up to speed on the latest NASCAR news, but I shoved the magazine aside after three sentences, a boatload of second thoughts swamping me.

Those doubts soon swelled to a tidal wave, swirling and spinning, dragging me under

What the hell am I doing here? Waiting around for a big, sexy stranger in his messy-ass house, clueless

and confused? Regretting the bold overture I'd made in the bar, guilt assailing me that I'd experienced such exciting kisses, such overwhelming passion, while Beth lay stone-cold dead in the clay?

I stumbled to my feet, feeling sick.

Have to leave. Have to go home, barricade myself in my bedroom, get back to grieving my sister. I have no right to be lusting over a hunky, taciturn Viking. Have no right to hope that when Gravedigger returns all spic-n-span, we can take up where we'd left off in that rideshare. Where we left off, and where we can get started on a lot more fun stuff.

As I scanned cluttered counters for pen and paper, the guilt ramped up, digging in deep.

That's right. Scribble down some excuse, grab your things, and scram, lady. How can you even consider indulging in such wicked decadence, when—

A breath brushed my ear, sending shivers up my skin.

"Case. Case, wait…"

Phantom Beth interrupted, murmuring. Paralyzed in place, I gripped the back of the chair, her semi-bossy tones faint yet unmistakable.

"Case, no. Don't you dare leave. Stay, Sunny, stay. You know you want to. And it's what I want for you, too."

GRAVEDIGGER

My eyes welled up and I chewed my lip, not sure if this was Stoli Orange aftereffects, or if I was legitimately losing it.

Lord, her voice sounds so real…

I shuddered, jerking forward and draining the rest of my water in a gulp. Vodka vapors or not, I had to be losing it, for sure.

Still…

My fingers shook, and I raked them through my hair. Mental condition notwithstanding, did I *really* want to exit Chez MacGregor to go lock myself in my room? Curl up in a ball, and weep until the wee hours? Upset my parents after I'd dreamt up that bogus yarn about staying at Laura Lynn's place for the night, splashing out for an extended Sunday brunch tomorrow?

Mom had sounded so relieved I was finally making an effort…

Beth piped up again, decidedly approving.

"That's the spirit, Little Miss Sunshine!"

The tears in my eyes spilled over and I scrubbed them away, her corny nickname lacerating like a blade.

Sounds so freaking real…

I whirled around, fumbling for a handful of takeout menus. Clutching them in trembling fingers, I headed for the living room, the least repulsive digs I'd encountered. As I hit the linty carpet, I flicked half-believing eyes skyward, silently conversing with my twin.

All right, Bethie… As per usual, you're getting the last word. I'll find some not-so-slobby surface to perch on, order up some calories, and hope the man of the house is in a more convivial mood when he climbs out of that shower.

Shower…

A devil on my shoulder had me glancing down the hallway—the door at the end of it slightly ajar.

Shower…

Unbidden, a vision of Clint twisting and turning under a soapy spray flashed in my brain.

Huge. Wet. Muscly. Naked.

Yuh-um.

I licked kiss-puffed lips, a deliciously forbidden idea taking hold.

Oh my God, do I dare?

The short answer? Yes, I did indeed dare.

Not allowing myself to dwell on the depths of my depravity, I tossed leaflets aside and smoothed my panty-less skirt, creeping down the corridor on stealth feet.

GRAVEDIGGER

It hadn't even been ten minutes... Maybe if I was lucky, I could get a super-quick peek through that open door and spy my hunky host shouldering into a clean shirt.

Or, better yet, reaching for his pants.

Lord, I was so bad. Beth had always labeled me a naughty little voyeur.

Peeping out the window at that buff lawn dude buzzing the neighbor's hedges.

Timing the comings and goings of Ms. Gleason's hot biker boyfriend across the street, until they split and he and his souped-up Fat Boy hit the road.

Drooling over a vat of popcorn at all those brawny, bearded Vikings...

My heartbeat kicked up, pounding out of control.

Clint MacGregor was brawny and bearded. And I'll bet he really looked like something, all wet and flushed and slick.

I was at the door. With a trembling pinkie, I eased the wood an inch or so wider, squinting through the opening. Dang. Nothing to see but more mini mountains of clothes on the floor, and a corner of a big bed that looked as if a monster bomb had exploded on it.

Maybe he was still in the shower. He *had* been pretty grubby.

Squeeeeeak... I pushed the door open a scad more, a cloud of steam and the sound of running water emerging from a narrower open archway opposite.

Casey Rae Kent, turn tail this instant.

Ignoring my screaming conscience, I slithered through the door sideways. Skin burning and heart slamming, I held my breath, tiptoeing into the Viking's lair and straight toward those thick billows.

Just one lightning-fast peek. Just one teensy-tiny gander. Then it was back to those greasy menus before anyone was the wiser.

A deep, protracted groan rent the air. "Unhhhhhh…"

My ears pricked, hot blood burning the tips.

"Ughhh…"

Convinced that the horned demon on my shoulder was making certain I'd have a special, reserved spot in his fiery domain, I slunk forward, drawn by another masculine moan.

"Aw, *fuuuuuck…*"

A third grunt, guttural and hoarse.

Stop. Turn back. Get the hell out of here immediately and go dial up your damn sausage and mushroom pie, you world-class perv.

Deaf to the voice of decency shrieking in my skull, I crept still closer. Truthfully, a round of dough oozing

GRAVEDIGGER

with cheese was the *last* thing on my mind. Hey, can I help it if I wasn't hungry? Must have been all those chips I scarfed down earlier with the orange slices.

"Sunshinnnnnneee..."

I froze, the hair on the back of my neck standing on end.

"Sunshine?" Did I just hear "Sunshine?" My goofy familial nickname, whispered not in my deceased sister's teasing tones, but growled in a real-live, flesh and blood, manly cadence?

Okay. The jury was in. This world-class perv honestly *has* lost her marbles.

Forcing myself to move, positive I could not have heard right, I drifted to the bath's threshold, panting shallowly as I peeked around the jamb.

Oh. My. Freaking. God.

Clint stood wide-legged in a spacious and soap-scummed shower, his handsome head tipped back under the spray, his saturated beard pointed toward the ceiling.

And that wasn't the only thing pointed toward the ceiling, believe you me.

I goggled, peering through the mist at his naked cock: huge, thick, and angry-looking, all lurid with distended veins as he manhandled it in his big fist, opposite arm braced against the tile. Hot moisture bloomed between my thighs as his hand pumped up and down, fast as a piston.

"Beautiful Sunshine. Sexy girl…"

Jesus, Mary, and Joseph! Clint *had* said my name: the jokey moniker my family had saddled me with in reference to my blond curls. And he was *still* saying it—groaning out the syllables as he jacked himself, eyelids screwed shut.

"Sunshine. Baaaaaby…"

Helpless to look away, I watched that fist fly, the beast jerking beneath its grasp red and raw and jumbo-sized. Gravedigger bit his lip, face flushed and jaw rigid as he slurred out hoarse sounds and half words. All the while getting himself off like a wildman before my incredulous eyes.

Getting me off.

I moaned under my breath, sneaking a hand under my dress. Shaky fingers brushed against my slit, coming away wet, and I whimpered again. This time, a fraction louder.

A dark head whipped around and pewter eyes shot open, pinning me where I stood. Clint and I stared at each other through damp fog, his cock in his fist, the burn on his cheekbones deepening to brick. Yanking my hand free, I crossed boneless legs, squeezing them tight—the throb and clench of my pussy forcing out a third mewling sound.

GRAVEDIGGER

Yes, you guessed it: still louder.

Sweet Mother Above, Kent... Shut the crap up!

Clearing my throat, I wiped betraying moisture on my skirt, hyperaware of those narrowed eyes latched to my glistening fingers.

My own face surely crimson, instead of heading for the hills and letting the man finish up, I gasped out a string of nonsensical noise to the masturbatory Viking towering behind a panel of scuzzy glass.

"Oh! Oh, I'm so sorry! I... thought you were out of the shower, and I heard a... I heard a noise. I, er, I thought that you called me. Anyhow, super quick..."

I grabbed a rumpled towel hanging off a hook, scrubbing sticky fingers as I squeaked out a question, the only thing I could think of to save my soul.

"Um. On the pizza. You prefer sausage, or pepperoni?"

As if drawn to a lodestone, the instant that idiocy stuttered from my lips, my gaze dropped to the extra-large "sausage" gripped in Clint's fist, its size undiminished.

Undiminished? *If anything, that salami looks even huger.*

Not waiting to hear The Hung One's topping request, I tore my eyes away from tumescent flesh with a mighty effort, stumbling out of the bathroom. As I tripped over piles of flung-off graveyard shirts and khakis, Beth sounded off again, her intonation clear as crystal.

"Case, Case, Case… You are a real piece of work. Didn't I always say all that peeping would land you in hot water someday?"

I pressed palms to cheeks, half-giggling to the phantom voice in my head.

Hot water?

Too true, sweet sister.

Too freaking true.

DIGGER: FIVE

Teeth gritted, I examined the flushed reflection glaring back at me, positive this was one of the absolute worst moments of my life. And trust me, there's been a lot of them.

Jesus God, MacGregor.

Fumbling fingers did up my belt buckle, taking their sweet-ass time.

Yeah, sorta had to go slow, didn't I? Seeing my damned dick was still hard as silicon carbide, my caught-in-the-act face remained red as the side of a fire truck, and I had less than negative zero idea what I was going to say to Casey Ray Kent when I walked out that door.

If the wide-eyed lady was still on the premises and hadn't headed for the hills to scrub out her eyeballs with bleach, that is.

What to say? What the Christ to say?

Okay, let's see. Best excuse to roll with when you're discovered beatin' the meat…

Guess I could try for a casual, "no-big-deal, every-dude-does-it," strategy:

Sorry about that, babe. No biggie, other than the size of the pipe you saw strangled in my fist. What say we forget all about it, and order up that pizza? I, for one, am starving. And, in answer to that last question, pepperoni. Double the serving and a tad on the charred side, if that's cool with you.

Fuck, idiot, no!

All right. How about a hangdog-shameful, heavy-on-the-justifications approach?

God, I really apologize, Casey. I have no excuse for what you saw, other than my ass being buried under a mud pile of stress as of late. Chalk it up to too much work, not enough sleep, and the never-ending PTSD noise upstairs. See, it's been a while since I've made an appointment with my shrink, and—

No, no, no, jackass!

Well, hell... Don't they always say you can't go wrong with the simple, unvarnished truth?

Baby, I'm gonna lay it on the line. I've been jacking my junk for six solid weeks now, to your image and to yours only. Haven't been this riled up in all my days, but ever since I first saw your smokin' little bod kneeling at that headstone, I've been—

Motherfuck me, no freaking way!

I spun away from the mirror, slicking back damp hair and trying to ignore the dull, throbbing bulge behind my zip. Praying that Sunshine didn't get a load of it

GRAVEDIGGER

either, and brand me more of a sicko than she already must. Yanking aside my tee, I shot a fast glance down.

Shit, still chubby as fuck. Well, what did I expect after that extended make-out session in the Uber, and just getting thwarted with the self-love jazz? Damn, if only I'd been able to rub out a quick one, take the edge off the overwhelming hunger, maybe things wouldn't be so bad.

Wincing, I adjusted, jostling my spunk-laden balls.

Guess it would be fairly obvious if I tied a sweatshirt around my waist, huh?

Yeah, guess it would, Skippy.

Acknowledging the prepster look was so not me, I grabbed a *Sports Illustrated* from the crap on the nightstand, hovering it in front of my crotch as I exited the bedroom. Real unobvious. Still, it was better than morphing into a yachty dweeb direct from Martha's Vineyard.

"<Ahem>"

As I passed the living room en route to kitchen, I was startled by a nervous throat-clearing.

I spun sideways, clocking Sunshine curled up in Kev's beat recliner—the oversized, beige-hued throne his mom had gifted me years ago, which just this morning had been piled high with a shit-ton of half-read newspapers. Blinking, I spied that stack neatly folded and set on the carpet, right beside a pair of spectacular, sun-kissed legs.

Sunshine spoke to her twisted-together fingers, not meeting my eyes.

"Hey. I uh, I ordered from Vinny's Express. Out of all your menus, they seem to have the best Yelp reviews. I got us jalapeno poppers and a medium New York Style. Cheese, mushrooms, pepperoni *and* sausage, since I, er, wasn't, er, sure which… meat you preferred."

My skin turned hotter as I replayed Miss Surprise Visitor's unanswered query back in my bathroom.

Cool. Hope you requested those pork products well-done.

And did you really have to whisper "meat" in that sexy-ass voice, baby?

Smiling tightly, I nodded, me and big boy taking cover behind my ugly plaid sofa.

"Good call. Their sauce is the bomb."

Struggling not to drool at those bare legs, or any other part of Sunshine's anatomy that would result in additional chaos below my belt, I threw the mag on a table, sucking in a deep breath.

Okay, MacGregor, go. Your interrupted whack fest that the lady witnessed must be addressed, no matter how hideous. To ignore the elephant, or should I say

GRAVEDIGGER

the erection in the room, is not an option. Be a man, own it, and come up with something.

Anything.

I smoothed a palm over my still-wet beard, the words husking out of my throat stilted and gruff. As lame as it was, I'd decided to go with rationalization number two, figuring the hangdog approach squeaked out ahead of the alternative options by a pube hair.

"Uh. Casey. That shit you saw. I'm really sorry. I have no excuse, other than lately, I've been mega stress—"

"Wait."

Sunshine interrupted, uncoiling herself from grungy upholstery and rising. She walked up to me, curls on level with my sternum. Tipping her head back, she looked me full-on, her cheeks flushed pink.

"You don't need to apologize, Clint, I do. I'm the one who invaded your privacy, walked in on you."

My own cheekbones burned as I slashed my hand.

"No. No, what you saw was—"

The beauty cut me off again, biting a plump lip.

"Besides, I thought what you were doing was hot. Really hot."

Those rosy cheeks turned from pink to red. Peeking through her lashes, Sunshine's eyes glowed as she repeated herself, putting emphasis on the first word.

"*Really* hot."

I swallowed hard, my prick jerking like a snake in my jeans.

Jesus.

Gulping again, I tried to think of something to say, but it appeared that all the gray matter between my ears had decided to take an extended holiday to parts unknown.

"Uh…"

Sunshine took a step closer, her juicy tits inches from my chest. Whispering, she laid a palm over my banging heart, fingers stroking.

"Your big hand on yourself, Clint… I can't stop seeing it. I, I'd like to see it again. Or, maybe… Maybe my hand this time."

Behind an about-to-burst zip, my dick lurched harder, pressing painfully against interlocking metal teeth.

Holy fuck. Did I just hear right?

Before I could ascertain whether I was back in bed tripping out on some wild fantasy, Sunshine licked her porntastic lips and placed a second palm on my pecs. Ten tiny fingertips burned holes in my shirt as those downcast lashes flickered.

"Er. If that's taking it too fast, maybe we could just kiss some mo—"

I crushed her words with my mouth, bracketing her face between my palms. Hunching low, I gobbled up sweet sugar, my head spinning, my body shaking. Every nerve I possessed zinging with incredulous, scalding excitement.

Fuck me running... Sunshine thought my one-man show had been hot. The woman is turned-on. She wants to kiss me, wants to put her hand on my cock.

Licking deep, I groaned, that last part flashing on and off in my skull like high-voltage neon.

HAND ON COCK. HAND ON COCK. HAND ON COCK.

She said it. She did. This dream girl wants to put her pretty hand on my big, greedy dick. Wants to—

"Cliiiint…"

Interrupting my inner monologue, Sunshine moaned my name, her honeyed tongue busy. Through slitted eyelids, I drank her in—beautiful eyes fluttering a lash-breadth away, lovely face hectically flushed.

Christ, so goddamned gorgeous. So fuck-all sweet.

"Yeah, baby. God, yes. Open for me."

Maddened, I gripped her jaw harder, aware that my beard was roughing up baby-soft skin but unable to help myself. Help myself, shit…! I ate my angel like a starved man, intoxicated by her taste, her breaths, the sexy sounds she was making.

"Ah, fuck, girl."

I spun her around, crowding her against the back of the couch. Widening my stance, I kicked her legs into a splayed "V," grinding her squirming bod to mine. She felt like fucking heaven: curvy, warm, luscious. Perky tits seared twin brands on my chest and I lowered a shaky hand to her butt, palming it through thin fabric, dragging her still closer. Sunshine gasped, her hot mound pressed flush against the bulge in my jeans.

Tight little pussy. Firm, sweet ass…

My head swam, the buzzing inside of it loud as a beehive.

Fucking hell, is she wearing any panties?

Fingers twitching, I smoothed them over one taut rump cheek, not encountering any lines. I groaned into her mouth, croaking out a need-to-know question.

"Baby. Jesus. Are you bare under this little dress?"

Messy curls bobbed as Sunshine whispered against my lips.

GRAVEDIGGER

"I... I took them off in your bathroom. They were all wet from the ride here."

"Aw, fuck!"

Okay, it was official. After that cockjerking newsflash? Yeah, I was a fucking dead man.

I bent the goddess backward, crouching low, covering her petite frame with my bulk like a cape. My other hand slid south and joined its mate, both palms cupping what surely had to be the finest tush on the planet. That thin material did jack shit to disguise the bounty it was covering and I growled deep, clumsy fingers grabbing handfuls of cotton and pulling up.

Sunshine wriggled in my arms, squashing closer, which to my mind signaled a solid green light: no amber or red in sight.

Yessssss!

Half a nanosecond later, her skirt was shoved to her waist, and there was nothing between my shaking fingers and smooth expanses of fragrant, golden skin.

"Ah, sweet baby..."

Delirious, I bent for another kiss, licking wildly as I caressed silky globes, one stray finger brushing over the cleft bisecting them.

God*damn,* fucking hot.

We kissed for ages against my butt-ugly couch—our mouths frantic, the sounds splitting the silence wet and lewd and erotic as living hell.

"Mmm, Clint. Oooh, yes. Oooh, your hands…"

Stuttering, Sunshine panted against my mouth, her neck lolling like a flower stem. I thought about moving one hand back north to support her head, but there was no way, not with all the spectacular flesh filling my palms. Instead, I stroked and squeezed and petted, running increasingly emboldened caresses over her ass, her flanks, the backs of her creamy, lithe thighs.

Naturally, it didn't take this boy long to head for The Promised Land. Especially how my angel was carrying on—squirming around like she was, making all those breathless noises, driving me fucking insane.

Grinding my dick against her once, twice, thrice, I drew back, heart crashing behind my ribs. I looked down between us as my hands moved to the front of her hips, unsteady fingers stretching out to frame her sweet, waxed slit like the masterpiece that it was.

Oh, holy fuck.

Oh. Holy. Fuck.

People, I kid you not: I almost blew in my trou at that first sight of Sunshine's phenomenal pussy. Christ, what a sight… All bare and pink and shiny with dew,

GRAVEDIGGER

the contrast between its puffy glory and my rough, calloused fingertips off-the-charts exciting.

"God, baby. So fucking beautiful, you are…"

I slurred out half-formed fragments of garbled praise, the words thick and impeded as I stroked a single digit sideways. Flicking it against that drenched mound, I groaned, my eyes shooting from Sunshine's dripping cunt to her lovely, flushed face.

"Oooh, Clint…"

Her eyelids drooped, lashes fluttering as my forefinger explored further.

Slowly, carefully…

Ah, Jesus. Her slit was sweetly pulsing, silky cream soaking my skin. Abundant juices slicking my knuckle, I felt sure my head was going to fly off my shoulders. And that the other head south of my belt was gonna blow like a geyser real fucking soon, with or without the lady's assistance.

"So wet, baby. Goddamn, so crazy wet for me."

Chocolatey eyes glittered through those heavy lashes as Sunshine bit her lip, nodding and gasping.

"Yes. Oh, yes, do that some more…"

Breathing hard, I added a second finger, gauging how snug she was, how tantalizingly tiny. My teeth gouged a hole in my own lower lip as my prick battered against denim, bigger and hungrier than it had ever been in its thirty-three-year-old existence.

Way bigger and way hungrier, no question. Making zero allowances for Sunshine's dainty size, trying to punch its way through tough cloth to get to where it needed to be. It jerked again, swelling like a zeppelin, a rude and unruly beast.

Yeah. Where it needed to be:

Right. The. Hell. NOW.

My teeth clamped down harder, the taste of blood acrid on my tongue.

Not yet. Not yet, you greedy fucker.

I slicked sweat off my forehead with the wrist not in play, cautiously corkscrewing my digits deeper. Encountering more cream and listening to more breathy sighs, it took every molecule of self-control I possessed not to topple us both backward over scratchy plaid fabric and start fucking Sunshine in two.

"Mmm, Clint. Feels so good. So *gooood.*"

More perspiration coated me, gathering under my pits and in the small of my back as I continued to finger Nirvana. *God, this girl...* I shifted on my shitkickers, pressing the heel of my palm against a sopped slit, my moan long and low and agonized.

"Beautiful Sunshine…"

GRAVEDIGGER

Before I could suck in another lungful, the wet dream in my arms pushed me back, panting hard, her hand to chest.

"Wait. Wait, what… Did you just say 'Sunshine'?"

Neck hot as a forge, cock a spike in my jeans, I stared into saucer-wide eyes, silently cursing my runaway yap.

Busted again, you moony moron.

"Um, huh? Er, I'm not sure…"

"You did! You just called me 'Sunshine.'"

My angel looked away, her cheeks rose-red as she stiltedly addressed my left shoulder.

"I, I thought I heard you say it before. In, the, in the shower. While you were, uh."

My skin cranked to broiling.

Yeah, while I was "uh."

Face flaming to match my neck, Sunshine peeped back up at me, biting the lips I'd been so thoroughly ravishing.

"This is seriously bizarre, Clint. Twenty minutes ago, I thought sure I was hearing things. But now… Lord, I can't believe it. Am I going crazy here? How could you know 'Sunshine' is my family nickname? Everyone in the clan calls me that, on account of my hair."

She crinkled her nose, pulling on a curl.

"When I was younger, this mop was even lighter—practically white—and my brothers would tease me endlessly with that dumb name. My dad, too, and all my uncles. Bethie was the worst, she would chant…"

Sunshine trailed off without finishing, a shadow darkening her irises.

Ah, Christ, her sister. Goddamn, I can't stand this shit. Can't stand to see this beauty looking so sad, so anguished.

So fucking lost.

I swallowed, watching kiss-puffed lips droop and quiver.

Make her feel better, A-hole. Say fuckin' something. Explain yourself.

Internally freaking that some mysterious force had led me to style Sunshine with her childhood handle while I perved on her from under cover of a big oak tree, I cleared my throat, stroking her cheek.

"That *is* really nuts, baby. Kinda impossible to explain. But, Jesus, I didn't mean to spook you. I don't know how I came up with the thing or how come I said it, except for the fact I think your folks hit the nail on the head. That name is perfect. Hell, you *do* look like sunshine, Casey."

GRAVEDIGGER

I gruffed out an addendum around the rock wedged in my larynx, holding her eyes.

"Like a glowing ray of light, almost too pretty to look at for long. I thought it the second I saw you, baby. And I'm still thinking it, now."

Sunshine gulped, blinking flyswatter lashes.

Sensing she needed more, I gave it to her, forcing more words out. Not a bunch of pap, but *real* words, words I fuckin' meant. Which wasn't exactly a piece of cake for a solitary, messed-up slob of a gravedigger like me.

"If you want, I can stick to calling you by your legit name from here on in. But it won't be easy. Because, like I said, 'Sunshine' is what you look like to me, baby. Even if I call you 'Casey' out loud, you gotta know I'm gonna be thinking that other name in my head."

A tremulous smile tipped her lips in the right direction as Sunshine reached out, latching ten fingers onto my tensed-up biceps. She pulled me to her, pressing us both back against the sofa. Her voice sank to a whisper as she slid her hands up to my neck, short nails scratching, sending shivers down my spine.

"No, not 'Casey.' I like 'Sunshine' better. Especially how you say it, Clint."

Pink mouth curling, her gaze slanted to the hallway.

"And *where* you say it, too."

Fuck. Me.

I'll say it again in that steamy shower, baby, over and over and over. Soon, after we christen this ugly couch. But this time around, your fine ass will be under the spray with me.

I was lowering my head to connect with those sweet lips and take up where we'd left off when, out of the corner of my eye, I spied a baseball-capped dork squinting through the screen window, brandishing a flat white box.

"VINNY'S EXPRESS. CASH ONLY!"

Ah, Christ.

Fuck. *Me.*

⚰ ⚰ ⚰

"Mmm. This is pretty good, huh? The pepperoni's really tasty, although I do prefer mine a bit less burnt."

You call this flabby shit burnt?

GRAVEDIGGER

I nodded across the coffee table, pretending to agree when I really wished the fuckers were three shades crispier.

Sorry, baby. Too bad you didn't stick around my bath while you were talkin' toppings.

Sunshine gestured to the opened pizza box and the container of peppers sitting next to it, frowning as she picked up her beer.

"Jeez, I'm a whole two slices ahead of you, Gravedigger. A guy your size… You've barely touched the pie, and none of these yummy poppers. Don't you know it's not polite to fast in front of a gluttonous female?"

I forced myself to choke down a bite, chewing methodically before mumbling out an excuse. "Er, sorry. Guess I'm not as hungry as I thought I was."

Sure you are, hoss. You're real hungry, fucking starving. Just not for triangles of dough with undercooked discs of meat baked on top. Nor for deep-fried, nasty-looking green things.

Swallowing some Bud, Sunshine dunked one of those nasty-looking green things into a pool of ranch dressing, shrugging.

"Well, all the more for me. And don't think I'm not good for at least two more. You're looking at a professional pizza hound, mister, tops in her class. On my best days, I can polish off a twelve-inch singlehandedly, and that's no lie. Shoot, Beth calls me—"

This time, I didn't hesitate when those sexy lips turned down and Sunshine clammed up.

Leaning forward in my chair, I laid a hand over hers, clearing my throat.

"You don't have to quit talking when you're thinking about your sister, baby. I know it's gotta hurt like hell, but I'm a good listener. I, I lost people close to me, too. My counselor back in the day always said it's better to try to let it out than to keep all that crap bottled up."

I sat back, shoving fingers through my hair as Kev's face, along with a bunch of other dead soldier's mugs, blurred before me. Curtly, I tacked on an addendum.

"Not that I necessarily succeeded in following the quack's advice."

Sunshine took another sip, her big eyes moist. "Yeah, I know. My mom wants me to go talk to a grief guru, the five-star-rated lady she's seeing or somebody else, but I'm not there yet. Maybe someday soon…"

She blew out a sigh, setting down her plate.

"You know what? Suddenly, I'm not so hungry anymore, either."

GRAVEDIGGER

Stretching her legs sideways, Sunshine shifted on the sofa, linking fingers behind curls. This series of actions caused her gorgeous gams to be shown to full advantage, her little dress to ride up sleek, bare thighs, and her tight, braless tits to strain against thin fabric.

Motherfuck me. Like a kid in a candy store, I didn't know where to look first.

Tipping her head, she pursed suds-shiny lips, eyes gleaming.

"All this grease, and the beer… Not to mention what happened earlier. I have to say, I'm feeling sort of knackered, Clint."

She slithered down into the cushions, patting orange and gold plaid.

"This beast's nice and deep, practically as wide as a bed. You feel like taking a short snooze next to me, recharge our batteries? When we wake up, maybe we can watch a classic SNL or something."

I sat there twitching, starting to sweat.

Fully horizontal, Sunshine smiled across the table, her drowsy eyes seductive as a siren's.

"Come on, you. Indulge me. Let's see if big, bad Gravedigger's a snorer."

CASEY: SIX

Gazing across the table into a pair of wide, wary eyes, I patted the cushion again, scarcely believing this brazen creature lolling on hideously patterned upholstery was me.

Blame it on the Buds, lady.

No… Easy as that excuse was, I swiftly dismissed it. ABV was not the culprit here. That longneck bottle was still three-quarters full, and my earlier buzz from the bar was but a mellow warmth in my veins, rendering me heavy-limbed and sleepy.

Well, heavy-limbed, sleepy, and high-grade horny. And yes, I was acting completely out of character, but too frigging bad.

Bethie's teasing tones had told me to go for it again while I'd been munching on that last popper, and go for it, I intended. I was here, I was alive, and I was in the presence of possibly the finest hunk I'd ever clamped virgin eyes upon, even counting the televised parade of half-naked beefcake battling and pillaging distant enemy shores.

Plenty of time to get back to the grieving when I rejoined the real world and this atypical interlude was history.

GRAVEDIGGER

Right?

Right. Silently agreeing with myself, I ventured a flirty question, my fingers lightly patting.

"Aren't *you* tired, Clint, after coming to my rescue so forcefully?"

pat pat pat

I pushed a curl out of my face and smiled wider at my host, showing the tip of my tongue.

Gravedigger blinked, hot eyes latching onto my lips as he scrubbed a hand over his mouth, shifting in his burnt-orange, old lady-style chair.

Gad, every stick of furniture in this joint is uglier than the last. Had the man's bedroom suite been as horrendous as his living room appointments? After that headlong master bath exit, I must admit I hadn't gotten a good look.

My pulse sped up, pounding fast.

At least, not yet...

"Uh, I guess I wouldn't say no to a couple of winks. Lemme get rid of this chow first."

Voice hoarse, Clint stood up, fumbling with the hem of his T-shirt. Not that it did any good disguising the mighty bulge riding down one thick thigh.

No siree. It surely did not.

An exciting flush of feminine power suffused me, tingling in my veins and other more interesting places. Trying not to gawk at that virile display, I rolled onto a hip, scratchy material abrading my bare legs.

"Okay. Could you grab me a glass of water? I can't finish my beer, sorry I wasted it. I shouldn't have said yes to one, not after those Stolis earlier."

I leveled this request to the hard-on hovering inches from my nose as rough hands swept up pizza box and plates.

"Yeah, sure. I barely touched my brew, either."

He shot a glance down, eyes burning as they swept the length of my supine figure, lingering on mouth and breasts.

Beth murmured in my ear, egging me on.

"Case… Case… He wants you. You know he does."

Even as I conceded the voice in my head was all kinds of messed and not possibly real, I stroked a hand down the side of my leg, eyelids at half-mast.

"Hurry back now, before I fall asleep."

The box in Gravedigger's grasp jerked, and he nodded, biting his lip. Above his beard, twin cheekbones flushed, a hard band of color painting the sun-burnished skin.

GRAVEDIGGER

"Right, I, er, I have to use the john, first." His neck reddened to compliment his cheeks. "Uh, you?"

I shook my head. "Nope, I'm good."

As soon as his yummy buns disappeared, I scrabbled in my bag for some mints, sucking on wintergreen as I rearranged lumpy pillows under my head and smoothed down my dress. Or, should I say, smoothed *up* my dress, leaving more thigh exposed. My pantyless loins quivered as I lay wondering what the next hours would bring before I was back home with the folks, finished slurping down made-up mimosas with Laura Lynn Swanson.

Would the Man of the Mansion and I remain here on this upholstered behemoth, or head to more comfy quarters?

Would the program stick to sucking face, or proceed to second base and beyond?

Was I seriously contemplating handing over my V-card to a virtual stranger, albeit a super-smokin' Viking who saved me from a sexual attack?

Was I out of my everluving gourd?

A few minutes passed before the thud of boots came clomping back down the hall. During this brief intermission, I waffled between leaping up and getting my commando ass out of Dodge, or whipping off my dress and giving Clint MacGregor the surprise of his life. In the end, I did neither—remaining recumbent in the same position my marble-mouthed host had left me in, heart kicking behind my bodice like a wild thing.

"Still awake, huh?" Gravedigger's question grated out low and rough.

I peeked up beneath lowered lashes, simulating a dainty yawn.

"Barely."

Yeah, barely awake, right.

My throat dried as I drank in six-foot-something of hard muscle and brawn, towering over me in disreputable threads.

Raggedy T-shirt, hugging a wide chest and veiny, chiseled, biceps…

Worn, faded jeans, hugging…

Yowza.

I forced my eyes above that scarred leather belt, meeting Clint's fixed stare. Maybe it was my imagination, but he also appeared to be having trouble keeping his eyes north.

"Sunshine, uh. If you're too shot, I can head to the den and watch the tube, go through my mail. Let you crash for a few hours in peace, get some—"

The newly discovered demoness in me stretched out a hand, pulling on his thick wrist.

GRAVEDIGGER

"No. After what happened in Oaklawn, I want my knight in unshiny armor right here next to me."

I yanked hard, sending two hundred-some pounds toppling onto the cushions. Shimmying back, I made more room as Clint aligned his bulky bod with mine.

"There. Isn't this nice?"

Thick-lashed eyes blinked, pewter irises inches from my own. Grunting, my reluctant sofa mate stuffed a pillow behind his head, clearing a roughened throat.

"Uh, yeah. Nice."

Clint's reply was hoarse, his chest moving with fast breaths. Sliding a hand between us, I placed my palm on a pounding pec, thrilled when the thrum beneath my skin accelerated. Striving for a light tone, I smiled into his rigid face, the lines of it rather desperate.

"Boy, this couch is sure deep. Able to accommodate your mighty frame and another passenger, besides. What, did you have this boat custom-built?"

Gravedigger barked out a laugh, staring at my mouth.

"How'd ya guess? Was it the gorgeous fabric? Try a second-hand rummage shop, baby. And even though they threw in that ugly orange chair, I'm convinced to this day I was majorly ripped off."

I laughed in tandem, and then we both stopped, a thick silence filling the room.

Clearing his throat again, Clint's hooded eyes flicked down. "You want a blanket or anything for your nap? To, uh, to cover your legs, if the A/C gets too chilly?"

Blanket? Are you kidding me, mister? There's enough heat coming off your hunky hide to start this plaid monstrosity on fire.

"No, thanks. I've got you to keep me toasty."

Boldly, I eased my uppermost leg across a thick, jean-encased one, rubbing toes to and fro over a tense calf. Another delicious frisson of femininity seized me as Gravedigger groaned, squeezing his eyelids shut.

"Sunshinnnne…"

"Mmm, hmm?"

I moved my foot higher, watching his face flush above heavy whiskers.

"You gonna settle down? 'Cause, Christ, baby… That shit you're doing…"

I eased my other leg into play, sandwiching a twitching denim tree trunk.

Parroting his words, my reply was low and teasing. "The shit I'm doing…?"

Silver eyes snapped back open, dark and turbulent, lit with banked flames. Clint growled through his teeth, his jaw barely moving.

GRAVEDIGGER

"Yeah, baby. The shit you're doing. It's driving me fucking insane. If you want that catnap, you'd best get real still, real quick."

My bare toes moved higher, exploring a kneecap. Licking my lips, I whispered a provocative query, feeling all kinds of wicked.

"What if I want a kiss first?"

"Fuck—!"

Clint mashed his mouth to mine, gripping the back of my head. I sighed, sinking back into the cushions as his fingers dug deep in my curls, angling my face to his satisfaction. He moaned, bringing his other hand up to cup my cheek. Then he rolled closer and proceeded to kiss the living tar out of me.

I purred, secretly triumphant, twining tight arms around his neck.

"Oooh, Clint..."

"Yeah, babe, that's it. Open nice and wide for me. Ah, Jesus, fucking delicious."

Delicious? The man should talk. He tasted masculine and minty, a slight tang of hops mingling with fresh toothpaste. My pussy clenched as I realized he'd taken time to brush, perhaps hoping for the sexy scenario that was unfolding right now. Panting, I did as requested, savoring his velvety tongue and all its myriad talents.

Boy, for a taciturn soil slinger self-proclaimed not to get out much, Le MacGregor sure knows how to make out.

"Sweet fuckin' mouth. Never had it so goddamned sweet. Gets me harder than fuck."

And how to get a girl mega riled with the dirty talk.

I threaded fingers into thick, shaggy hair, raking Clint's scalp with my nails. He seemed to thoroughly enjoy that, growling as he pushed my head deeper into the pillows. Moving one hand to my neck, he encircled it, his fingers hot and restless.

"Christ, babe… Jesus, you make me fucking nuts." He shifted, mumbling the words against my lips. I wriggled in return, trying to get closer, half-trapped beneath one heavy leg. My gyrations set him off and he groaned again, wedging that limb between mine.

"Aw, fuck. Feel that snug little snatch…"

He ground his pelvis against mine, kissing me madly, the bulge behind his fly impossible to ignore.

So exciting, what I did to this brute of a Viking…

Gasping against ravaging lips, I tipped my hips up, rubbing shamelessly against a long length of steely flesh. Back and forth, up and down, sliding my cotton-covered slit against rough denim, the friction divine, intensely erotic.

GRAVEDIGGER

But it wasn't enough. I wanted more, wanted our layers of clothing to melt off our bodies. Wanted the big, hard cock I'd glimpsed so excitingly under that spray of water sliding against my naked pussy.

Sliding, then slowly, deeply, penetrating…

I bucked again, picturing it, the salacious vision turning me on like crazy.

"Oh! Mmm, Clint…"

"You feel me, baby? Feel what you fucking do to me?"

Half-laughing, half-groaning, Clint drew back, his mouth full and reddened. He bit down on his lip, chest heaving as he spoke to the ceiling.

"Goddamn, I need a shower, arctic temp."

I tried to pull him back down but he resisted, swatting my hands and stumbling off the sofa.

"No, baby…"

Blowing out a shuddering breath, he raked hands through hair, looking everywhere except at me.

"This shit is moving way too fast, babe. Fuck, we've only just met, and in a pretty freaky way, too. You escaped a close call today, Sunshine, and I'm not gonna take advantage of the situation or the alcohol swimmin' around in your veins."

"But, Clint…"

I pouted, protesting.

"I'm not drunk, or barely buzzed anymore. Seriously, I know what I'm doing. Come back here, and let's—"

He sucked in a lungful, molten eyes at last connecting.

"No, angel. We're not gonna take it any further, not today. Here's the plan: I'm gonna go in the other room and wait for my dick to go down, and you're gonna stay here and take your nap. After that, we can watch the tube like you said, or shoot the bull and finish off the leftover pie. What we're *not* gonna do is any more fooling around."

I struggled to sit up, smoothing my skirt, the moisture between my thighs causing them to stick together like paste.

"But, Clint…"

My repeated plea was ignored as he presented me with his broad back, clenching and unclenching white-knuckled fists.

"Sleep tight, baby. After what you went through this afternoon, hell, after what you've been going through for weeks now, I'd say you damn well need it."

"But, *Cliiiiint*…"

It was useless. He was already stomping down the hallway, headed for another slobby room. I flopped down in the cushions, half-waiting for Beth to chime back in on the situation.

Okay, Sis. Now what?

When all that hit my ears was some ballgame clicked to a barely discernable volume, I sighed, reaching for the ugly afghan at my feet.

Crap, only me. Rescued from the clutches of rape by a veritable Viking, only to find out that instead of possessing the marauding spirit of his kin, the man turns out to be a sensitive softie. Just my frigging luck!

I drew the blanket up, inhaling a faint, woodsy scent on its fibers.

Mmm, smells so good...

Yawning, I closed my eyes, a heavy lassitude sinking deep. Frustrated? That I was, most assuredly, but maybe my gentle giant was right. Maybe I *could* benefit from a few z's. Fragments of the past few hours flashed on my lids like an over-the-top soap episode—both chilling and thrilling, surreal to the point of absurdity.

The terror at Oaklawn. That grill session with the cops. Those potent vodkas and sodas. Clint and me in that corner booth, in our ride's back seat, on this couch. Me, goggling at the man's private parts from outside his shower.

My skin heated up a degree. Mercy, that segment alone would drive the ratings through the roof!

I added the *pièce de résistance,* the jewel in the crown:

My deceased twin's voice in my ear, prodding me to get it on with a hot gravedigger.

Jaw cracking in another mammoth yawn, I snuggled into scratchy secondhand upholstery, resigned to snoozing solo.

Well, hell, Sissie…

You can't say Miss Clueless Virgin didn't try.

DIGGER: SEVEN

Creeping down the unlit hall and holding my breath, I peeked over the edge of the sofa at Sunshine: a tousle-headed lump under a butt-fugly blanket. Her thick lashes lying on flushed cheeks, she resembled some angelic fairy princess. A sexy, sleeping beauty this frustrated non-prince wanted to wake with a motherload of kisses so damned much, it was painful.

Reeeeal painful.

Behind a taut fly, my cock twitched, two squashed balls heavy and achy.

I watched a dainty snuffle blow out her parted lips, my sleep-deprived eyes tracing their plump curves. Jesus, the girl was dead to the world.

Me and my fucking bright ideas.

Turning away, I made for the kitchen, easing open the fridge to snag a brew and a piece of leftover pizza. Yech. I ranked cold pie on par with a trip to the dentist, but no way was I going to risk waking my guest with the ding of the micro. Quiet as a rat, I headed back to the den, doing a double-take when I passed the wall clock.

Christ on the cross, really? Small wonder my gut was grumbling. Going on two a.m., and I hadn't put anything in the fucker since I'd choked down that partial slice ages ago, while pint-sized Sunshine demolished prodigious portions.

Sunshine…

Plopping ass onto leather and fumbling for the remote, I scrolled through muted, late-night crap, mentally berating myself.

You could be on that sofa with her right now, fool. She fucking invited you, didn't she? Instead of jackin' off in here all by your lonesome, you could be out there with a slumbering goddess, all nice and cozy under Grandma MacGregor's homemade afghan. The lady of your dreams could be wrapped around you, tight as ivy. Your hands buried in those messy curls, caressing her bootylicious rump. You could be kissing, touching. Might've maybe moved the party to your big king bed by now…

I groaned, chomping off a rubbery triangle of dough and washing it down with a swig of Bud.

Fucking moron.

Even as I thought it, I retracted, cutting myself some slack. No. Agonizing as it was for my dick and his swollen sidekicks, I'd done the right thing in leaving Sunshine alone. Hell, what kind of a guy takes advantage of a girl who's had the kind of day she's had? And not only day, but month-plus, ever since her sister died.

GRAVEDIGGER

Not this guy, thickheaded as I could be.

Shoving congealed cheese and a barely touched bottle aside, I slumped in the cushions, eyelids heavy.

Goddamn, I was shot. Casey Kent wasn't the only one around here who'd had herself an eventful twelve hours. It's not every day this boy stymies a would-be rapist, lays the details out at a cop station, and ties one on with a smokin' sexpot at a dumpy gin mill, watching his drinking companion make love to little wedges of fruit.

I bit back another moan, recalling Sunshine's wet, red lips sucking on bright orange rinds.

So fuckin' hot.

Thinking I should've grabbed a couple of toothpicks to keep my eyeballs open, I flicked to a twenty-four-hour car auction, struggling to stay awake. Irritating doubts plagued me, piling one on top of another, making my head hurt.

Maybe I should rouse Sunshine, get her to eat some more.

Maybe it isn't wise letting her sleep so long on that rock-hard beast, curled in a ball.

Maybe I should relocate her, suggest she grab a hot shower. Offer her the comfort of my bed.

I stroked a palm over my prick; the vision of her naked, curvy bod undulating under steamy waterdrops or swirling in my sheets turning me titanium-solid.

Maybe I should go stick this stiff fucker in the basement deep freeze with all those other cuts of oversized meat.

Gritting clamped teeth, I squeezed the head hard and let go, forcing my hands flat either side of my thighs.

Not going there again, ace. I stifled a humorless laugh, bleary eyes following a vintage Thunderbird glide by on the screen. Yeah, wouldn't that be just fabulous… Sunshine walking in here, clocking her host choking' the chicken again?

Jesus, the lady would run screaming out into the night!

A sweet '69 'Vette was next on the belt, and I squinted at its fine lines, struggling to stay awake. But it was no use: Morpheus was pulling me under. I let my head loll backward, sinking ass lower and closing weighted-down lids.

Just a few winks. Just a short siesta until my angel stirs. Then I'll make her a nice bacon and egg breakfast and hopefully when she finishes, she'll be ready to…

Ready to…

Rrrrea…

GRAVEDIGGER

Delectable odors tickled my nose and I shifted on cold cowhide, rubbing my eyes.

What tha'?

I was twisted in the sectional's corner like a pretzel, bod jammed in a highly painful position, my clothes and work boots suffocating. On the tube, the cars were still rollin'—the never-ending parade currently showcasing a big black Lincoln. I blinked at sweet whitewalls, running my fingers through what felt like a porcupine's worst nightmare.

Muzzy with sleep, my slow-moving brain was piecing together a whole clusterfuck of confusing shit when a perky voice chimed from the doorway. I eased my sore neck around, blinking.

"Good moooorning, sleepyhead."

Sunshine!

Gone was the confusion. Every mindboggling moment from the day prior hit me like a cartoon sledgehammer as I drank her in, my heart slamming.

Oaklawn. Sunshine. Cops. Sunshine. Bar. Sunshine. Uber. Sunshine. Sofa. Sunshine.

Holy hell, we'd had us quite the Saturday. And that last sofa part? Most definitely the best part.

My bright angel was leaning against the jamb, little blue dress switched out for my one of my plain gray tees. The cotton swamped her from collarbone to kneecaps, worn fabric caressing delicious curves. Her curls were all sexy and tousled, falling in her face, and those sensational golden legs were seriously sick.

Moreover, it was fuck-all obvious that, same as last night, the lady wasn't rocking any undergarments.

At. All.

"Uh. Morning."

I croaked out a delayed response, struggling to a sitting position and grabbing a pillow. This, I threw over my lap, seeing as the sight of a lingerie-less Sunshine swaddled in my Hanes had me springing wood so mighty, it was a miracle my dick didn't crack in half.

"Waal, you sure needed your z's, mister. Same as me. I figured I was out for a good ten, eleven hours. I woke up around three and used the bathroom, inhaled about twenty glasses of water. Boy, those poppers must've been loaded with sodium!"

Plush lips curved up as Sunshine grinned over at me.

"That didn't stop me from polishing off the rest of the suckers straight from the fridge, and the remainder of the slices at your kitchen table. Mmm, I adore ice-cold pizza!"

Straight up? Lemme guess… You like sittin' in a dentist's chair and getting your teeth drilled, too. Well, they do say opposites attract, don't they?

My gorgeous guest continued, pushing a curl aside. "I was worried I might wake you, but you were out big-time. And FYI: in case you were wondering, I bring unto you glad tidings. No, Mr. M., you do not snore."

I rubbed my beard, skin prickling as I pictured Sunshine watching me saw logs.

"Er, good to know, I guess."

She shifted, sticking a hand on one killer hip.

"I held out as long as I could, reading enough sports articles to last me a lifetime, until I couldn't stomach any more baseball stats. And speaking of stomachs, it's been five hours since my last pig-out. I figured it was time to treat the King of the Castle to one of Casey Rae Kent's famous bacon and cheese omelets. Lucky for you all the necessary ingredients were in-house. Shame you don't have any potatoes, though, because my hash browns are equally stellar."

Shit. I loved me some crispy spuds doused in puddles of ketchup.

Sunshine waggled the fingers on her other hand at me. "Come on, big guy. Up and at 'em. The eggs are in the oven on 'warm,' the table's set, and the bread is in your crumb-filled toaster, waiting to be slathered with gobs of butter."

My gut gurgled, the scent of salty pig making my mouth water. Not nearly as much as the sight of Sunshine's tits against my tee made my mouth water, but hell, it seemed like a lifetime since I'd enjoyed a homecooked meal. I pushed down on the pillow camouflaging my wood, voice all casual.

"Wow, sounds great. You didn't have to, but thanks a lot. I'll be right in." My neck turned hot as I cleared my throat. "Just, uh, gotta use the john first."

Sunshine blushed, her eyes flicking to my cushion-covered crotch.

"Oh, right. Okay, me and my magnificent repast will be awaiting you."

It ain't the meal that's magnificent, darlin'.

I waited until her phenomenal tush cleared the doorway before I stood up—my bones stiff, my cock a bowling pin in my jeans. Bumping into walls, I headed down the hall, wincing with each step.

Ouch. Ouch. Ouch.

Once in my bathroom, I took a whiz and washed my hands, groaning when I got a load of my reflection. Damn, I looked like a frigging caveman: all shaggy-haired, bleary-eyed, and rough-bearded. Wishing I had a few dozen hours to work on getting more

GRAVEDIGGER

presentable, I blew out a sigh before splashing my face and grabbing the toothpaste.

Lastly, I took a few moments to wrap my prick in an icy washcloth until the fucker went down, sort of.

Resigned that I'd done the best I could in that department and not a fan of cold eggs any more than I was of frigid pizza, I threw on a fresh tee, leaving it hanging loose over my semi-bulge as I made tracks toward the delicious food smells.

"All set. I'm here…"

The words died in my throat as I stared into the room, my mouth hanging open.

Wait. What *was* this place? And who made off with my scuzzy kitchen?

"Coffee?"

Holding out a steaming mug, Sunshine stood in the middle of the bright, un-filthy floor, her smile as white as the scrubbed linoleum under her painted toes.

Fucking A, there isn't a muddy footprint in sight!

I grabbed the proffered java like a dummy, taking a slurp and swiveling my head, more bizarre sights smacking me in the kisser.

Whoa. The counters were all cleaned off and orderly, the stainless sink gleaming and bereft of its sky-high stack of crusty dishes. My fridge was no longer a mass of smudgy fingerprints, and the oven? Goddamn… My seldom-used but much-abused Maytag had morphed from a greasy white box into a thing of beauty—its burners free of baked-on grit and its glass door unsplotched and sparkling.

I blinked over at the table, swiping a hand over gobsmacked eyes.

Oh, yeah. That thing *was* made out of maple. Birdseye, and decent quality. Been awhile, but I remembered now.

Jaw slack, I studied its "long time, no see" honey-hued surface, freakishly free of newspapers and mags, pens and papers, cups and dishes. In their place were two perfectly arranged place settings, fancy cloth napkins I vaguely recalled receiving one Christmas from Ma, and a pair of matching wine goblets filled with OJ.

Fuck my life… Do I even possess matching wine goblets, or did Sunshine sneak into one of my neighbors' cribs and make off with their stemware?

I blinked again, my eyes alighting on a green glass vase sitting in the middle of the table, stuffed with wild flowers.

Okay. No goddamn *way* do I own a—

"I hope you don't mind me straightening up some? Truthfully, untidiness makes me sort of nuts. I did most of it while you were zoning, finished setting the

GRAVEDIGGER

table just now. I found the vase stuffed way back in a cupboard, and picked the flowers from the lot across the street."

Staring at the pretty stems, I struggled to think of something to say.

Sunshine continued. "Um. I realize it might not be cool, but all those dirty dishes, and the mud..."

An apologetic note tinged her words and I spun around, my chest burning when I saw how my angel was twisting her little hands.

She thinks I'm pissed?

Slamming down my mug, I grabbed her wrists. "Baby, no. This is amazing. Jesus, I'm just freaking flabbergasted. This kitchen hasn't looked so good since I hauled in the moving boxes twelve years ago."

I shook my head, running a palm up her arm, the skin under my callouses smooth as a baby's.

"But it's too much. After what you've been through, you should be taking it easy, not cleaning up a big slob's mess. And making me breakfast... Shit, babe, *I* should be treating *you* to a nice brunch, letting you—"

Sunshine stretched up and placed two soft fingers over my mouth, shutting me up mid-sentence.

"Stop. Didn't I promise you yesterday a Kent omelet in return for a crash pad? I told you I didn't want to go home and face my parents, not after what happened. As for the merry maid routine, well, just consider it a perk for getting saddled with a semi-OCD houseguest."

She smiled at me, and I grinned back, the expression on her lively, lovely face making me happy. I couldn't detect any traces of the sorrow I'd grown accustomed to seeing shading her big brown eyes, and damn if I didn't want those beautiful peepers to stay that way.

Plenty of time later for her to unload some more, if she needs to.

The grub staying warm in my unrecognizable oven smelled outstanding, and I was fuckin' starved, but a desire more urgent than breaking bread seized me. Well, what did I expect? Having this unreal creature so close, my hands on her silky flesh…

I tipped Sunshine's chin up, staring at her lips and licking my own.

"Baby. Before we eat, can I have a good morning kiss?"

Long lashes flickered, and golden cheeks turned rosy.

"Um, well, the bacon…"

GRAVEDIGGER

Widening my stance, I pulled her between my legs, moving one hand to her spine and pressing her close. My reply was thick as I hunched low, hungry lips seeking.

"The bacon can wait. I fucking can't."

"Clint..."

She moaned against my mouth, sagging in my arms. I groaned in return, my tongue licking deep, tasting toothpaste and orange juice and sweet, sweet sunshine.

Fucking delicious.

"Wider, baby. Open up for me." Heart banging, I walked Sunshine backward, pinning her shoulders against the fridge. Sparkling stainless was swiftly smudged as I ran my fingers through her hair, caressed her curves, grabbed her cotton-covered butt with a growl.

"Do you have any tiny idea what the sight of you in my shirt does to me, girl?"

My ten greedy digits smoothed over soft cloth, savoring taut ass cheeks, grinding her pelvis against my "I'm-back-with-a-vengeance" hard-on. I moaned again, circling, thrusting, bucking.

"Oh, *Clint*..."

"Yeah. Yeah, baby..."

I bit down lightly on Sunshine's busy tongue, plastering her against me, dizzy as a drunkard. She smelled amazing and tasted even better—her lips wet and luscious, her fingers bracketing my face, burrowing into my beard. That shit made me crazy, and I swore, dragging my mouth away to suckle her honey-scented neck.

"Ah, Jesus, babe. Your breakfast… We better stop."

Sunshine pulled my mouth back to hers, and she whispered against my lips, her breath sweet as flowers.

"Not yet…"

My cock lurched hard and I stumbled sideways, spinning us against a counter. I plucked my angel up, setting her on a surface that had recently been buried under all kinds of crap, but that now boasted uncluttered orderliness and the most fantabulous ass in existence.

Easing her legs wide, I wedged my bulk between them, my kisses turning wilder. The thought of what lay between those mouthwatering thighs maddened me, as did the feel of two juicy tits smashed up against my chest.

Holy fuck, one thin tee between me and Nirvana. And speaking of tees…

"Clint… Take off your shirt. I want to see you."

GRAVEDIGGER

Sunshine slurred her request against my cheek, tongue flicking my whiskers, fingers fiddling with my collar. I shot still harder as her words sank in.

Sure, baby. Whatever you say. Whatever your sexy little heart desires.

Leaning back, I fumbled with uncooperative cotton, the loss of her lips cruel. My iron-hard dick screaming to lose its own strangling entrapments, I flung the cloth to the floor, watching chocolatey eyes go wide.

"Oooh, Clint. You're so big…"

Big everywhere, darlin', you can count on it.

"So built…"

Humming, Sunshine stretched out a hand and placed it on my heaving chest, where it sizzled like a brand:

PROPERTY OF CASEY RAE KENT

Fucking fine with that shit. Stick one on my ass while you're at it.

Her fingers sketched circles over one pec and ran through the sparse fuzz, a questing thumb flicking over my nip.

Fuck!

Beneath her teasing touch, my heart slammed, sweat stinging my brow. Swallowing dryly, I grunted out a few garbled sounds, fists bunched at my sides.

"Baby. Baby, the food…"

The demoness purred in her throat, pulling lightly on my chest hair.

"It can wait. I want to hear about all these wicked tats, the stories behind them."

Her fingers moved to my left bicep, and the trio of numbers stamped in a five-pointed star. "First, this one."

Voice hoarse, I croaked out that it signified my regiment back in Afghanistan.

Sunshine scrunched up a sympathetic face, but thankfully she didn't press.

"And this arrow?" Dainty digits outlined a zigzag shape, and I cleared my throat, longing to grab those fingers and shove them down my Levi's.

"That's, uh, that's for my gramps. It's actually a flint arrowhead, copied from an actual fossil. That was the old man's nickname—'Flint'—because everybody always said he was tough as the stuff."

Her dark eyes softened, stunning and lustrous.

"Oh, how sweet. Is your grandpa still alive?"

I shook my head, trying to smile over the ongoing agony in my nuts.

GRAVEDIGGER

"Naw, he passed a few years back. Lived to the ripe ol' age of eighty-eight and died in his sleep, and that's all anybody can hope for, right?"

"Right."

Sunshine's reply was terse. Clocking a familiar shadow darkening her irises, I could've kicked my backside with a steel toe boot, if I was flexible enough.

Fucking lamebrain. Her sister was what, twenty-four? Think much, you insensitive tool?

I had half a dozen more markings on that arm, and plenty of ink on the other, but Sunshine's fingertips had stilled. Additionally, I really wasn't into pointing out Kevvie's name twined around the *Star Trek* symbol tatted on my left pec—the dork's lifelong, nerdy obsession.

My heart clenched beneath that galactic design, not a new thing.

Nope, I sure wasn't into it. Nor was I keen to discuss any of my other buds who'd bit it overseas and whose initials were likewise hidden in appropriate symbols of shit they'd dug before the unlucky fucks had been shipped back to their hometowns in army-reg body bags.

Or, in the case of Kevin Kerkowalski, dinky army-reg body boxes.

Yeah, definitely not into a round of brotherly Show and Tell. Fuck, who wants to see a grown man get all teary-eyed before breakfast?

Shoving Trekkie Man from my mind and getting back to my asinine faux pas, I grabbed Sunshine's hand, squeezing it as I gruffed out an apology.

"Jesus, baby, that was a real dumb thing to say. Christ, I'm such a fucking—"

Sunshine shook her head, interrupting. "Don't apologize, Clint; it's okay. I realize I have to come to terms with Beth. It won't be easy, but I don't expect—nor do I want—to spend the rest of my life coddled in reams of cotton wool. Yesterday's events helped me to see that more clearly, weird as that seems."

She swallowed, addressing Kev's tat.

"I heard her voice again in my head while I was scrubbing your floor. She told me that she was happy I was here, and not back home in bed coiled up like a zombie."

Chocolate-colored eyes flicked back to mine, the shadows lifting and a mischievous glint taking their place.

"And, if I'm not mistaken, I believe Sis decreed this kitchen the slobbiest one she's ever seen."

I let loose a laugh, the tension easing. Well, except for the tension in my trou. But that, I was determined

GRAVEDIGGER

to ignore for the time being, seeing how hard Sunshine had worked to clean up my crib and cook me a meal. Hopefully, the fucker would go down once the bacon came out. Highly unlikely, but at least I'd be sitting and it wouldn't be all out in the open and shit.

Bending to snag my tee, I hauled it over my head, trying to modify my breathing as I raked tangled hair back.

"Babe…"

I ran a finger over a pair of puffy pink lips, jerking my head toward the oven. "How about I dish up now, and we dig into your world-famous omelet? If those eggs taste even half as fantastic as they smell, I just might hafta chain you to those resurrected burners."

Sunshine snorted, nipping my finger.

"Good luck with that, big guy. And one warning: absolutely *no* ketchup on my culinary creation, or You. Are. A. Dead. Man."

I groaned under my breath.

Ah, hell. First the flabby pepperoni, now the no ketchup?

Shit, it's true.

Opposites really *do* attract.

CASEY: EIGHT

"Well? Are you surviving without the Heinz?"

Clint rolled his eyes, feigning ecstasy as he speared another forkful of omelet.

"Are you fucking kidding me, lady? These are seriously the best damn eggs I've ever had in my life. Forget teaching little rug rats how to use computers... You need to open a diner, stat."

I laughed, taking a sip of juice. "Thanks, but no thanks. What's piled on your plate, the hash browns you're missing out on, and Sloppy Joes out of a box total the extent of my culinary prowess. Trust me: I'm far more skilled in front of a Mac than a Maytag."

My smile faded as I set down the goblet.

"Although, maybe I *should* start leaving my calling card in the local greasy spoons. Or hire myself out for dishwasher detail. Or start an illustrious new career scrubbing out motel toilets. Seeing I got the axe on that sweet job I worked like a dog to hook."

"Hey..." Clint frowned, looking fierce. "Screw that, baby, and those jerks who canned you. Something else will come along. Something even better, I don't doubt it for a second. You've got the credentials, and you said the school promised you kickass referrals. Hell, it's not your fault that your sister di—"

"That my sister died at the start of the course?" I completed his sentence, throat tightening but voice amazingly steady.

"No, *shit,* I…"

Flushing, Gravedigger began to backtrack, but I cut him off, shaking my head.

"Don't, Clint. Don't. I told you; I'm okay. Granted, I haven't been, not at all, but something about you lets me discuss Beth without mutating into a sobbing, red-nosed basket case. I can't explain it… It must be the bizarre way I keep hearing her in my head: telling me to stick around a heroic digger of graves and his messy batch pad."

I grinned, trying to make light of it, but actually, what I said was true. I *did* feel better talking about my twin with Clint. For the first time since June the second, I was somewhere else besides hiding at home or kneeling in front of a pink tombstone. Doing something different besides bawling on my bed or writing Beth notes and sticking them in her weekly bouquet. Communicating with a real, live person separate from my intimate circle of grieving relations.

Flicking a glance across the table, I met a pair of hot pewter eyes, locked onto me like lasers.

Communicating? I'll say. And I'm not merely referring to word of mouth.

"There's more bacon. Why don't you finish it up?"

Voice squeaky, I flapped one a hand toward the oven while making a production of buttering a slice of toast with the other. This despite the fact I didn't want the thing, as it was rye with seeds, and I absolutely loathed rye with seeds. Same as I detested ketchup on eggs, or burnt meat products ruining a perfectly good pizza.

Hmm... I pulled a piece of crust off, stealthily checking for stray flecks of caraway before popping it in my mouth. This might only be our second meal together (not counting all those chips at Mooney's yesterday), but I was getting a solid feeling Master M. and I didn't share the same taste buds.

I mean, take those peppers. What self-respecting day drinker doesn't adore a greasy fried jalapeno or twelve to soak up the booze? *Insane!*

"Okay. More bacon, if you insist."

Clint drained his coffee, scraping back his chair and rising.

"Got a kink…" Six-foot and change performed a slow, sinuous stretch and I goggled—his bod lean and mean and packed with acres of sinewy, hard-cut muscles, flexing and popping all over the gosh darn place. Drool, drool, drool. Quickly, I stuffed a napkin

GRAVEDIGGER

against my mouth to prevent rivulets of saliva from saturating a loaner tee.

Concluding his little show, instead of heading straight for the stove, Gravedigger circled the table, looming behind my left shoulder. My nose twitched, inhaling the subtle, manly scent emanating from his skin. Pine, leather, soap… intoxicating.

A thick finger coiled around one of my curls, painting the ends against my cheek.

"You want any, baby, or should I eat it all up?"

Oh God, he makes that sound so sexy. Sexy, as in he isn't talking about cured strips of blubber at all, but something else entirely.

The squeak factor in my voice ramped up as I shifted in my seat.

"No, er, I'm good."

Clint didn't move, just hummed deep in his throat as he kept playing with that stray lock. Heat came off of him in delicious-smelling waves as he pulled lightly, his thumb tracing my earlobe, niggling a tiny garnet stud.

"Your hair's so soft and pretty, Sunshine."

I squeezed quivering thighs together, my reply a set of gasps.

"Um, thanks."

Jeez, what the hey is wrong with me? I'm acting like a spaced-out schoolgirl. What happened to the bold bitch who inspected intricate swirls of ink not twenty minutes ago? Who commanded this hulking warlord to strip off his shirt so she could get an up-close-and-personal tour of major man can?

"And your skin… Like a fucking baby's."

He slid his thumb over, tracing the underside of my jaw. Staring straight ahead, I tried to silence a whimper, the feel of his calloused fingers wildly exciting. But I refused to turn, to stand, take the reins.

Reins? No way. This chick's already been shot down twice!

She sure as heck has. Last night, on the Plaid Beast. A short while ago, my butt planted on yonder cleared-off counter. Both times, Clint calling a halt to the proceedings, acting the gentleman. Therefore, even though I was horned-up as a cloistered nun, I wasn't going to be the one who begged for more kisses this time around.

I bit my lip as that rough thumb continued to stroke, my achy nipples peaking.

More kisses, more caresses, more diabolical pussy play, or any other items featured on the MacGregor Seduction Menu before Mr. Self-Control pulls the plug again.

"Beautiful girl…"

GRAVEDIGGER

A hot palm landed on my opposite shoulder, brushing over the collarbone exposed by a drooping neckline. Meanwhile, Clint continued to tease my ear and cheek with his other hand, a lock of hair still within his grasp. I stifled another moan, shivering, my bare pussy pulsing.

Gad, does the man know how to use his hands. Thick, rough fingers. Soft, seductive touches…

"Startin' to rethink things, babe…"

Hinging at the knees, Gravedigger bent to growl in my ear, and I gulped, staring down at scraps of eggs and globules of melted cheddar.

"Y… yes?"

Not answering, he moved his right digits down past the edge of cotton, sticking them in my (his) shirt and stroking the upper slope of my breasts. A few inches south of four fingertips, my nipples stiffened further, blatantly jutting against soft cotton.

Oh, Lord. Headlight City. There is no way the devil can't see the havoc he is wreaking.

Eager, untried unicorn… I panted, acknowledging my response to this man's touch as both insanely arousing and massively mortifying. All the signs were there, ganging up in an unholy union, making it impossible to suck in a steady breath.

The way my heart was galloping, thundering in my ears.

How lewd those betraying points looked, sticking straight out like bullets.

How wet my panty-less pussy was becoming, slick juice moistening tight-clenched folds.

The big demon moved closer, and Clint's thighs straddled either side of my chair as he husked out a delayed response.

"Yeah, I changed my mind. I don't think I need any more bacon. Cravin' something sweeter, with a dash of hot salt."

His head descended, beard nuzzling the crook of my neck. He mumbled as he nipped a tendon, his lips soft and hot.

"You got to see me with my shirt off, angel. Can I ask you to repeat the favor?"

Thick fingers curled around a sagging collar, stilling, burning against my skin like bars of heated lead.

"Huh? Will you show me your gorgeous tits, baby? Let me love on these sweet, stiff nipples that are making my mouth water?"

Licking my skin with the flat of his tongue, Clint crowded closer, his belt buckle clanking against the back of the chair.

"Making my fat dick hard as fucking granite?"

I whimpered, his dirty talk causing more cream to dampen my thighs. I'm not certain if I managed to

GRAVEDIGGER

pant out a "yessssss," or if I just nodded dumbly, but two seconds later, my borrowed tent was decorating the just-scrubbed floor and I was hauled to my feet.

"Fuuuuuuuck…"

Gravedigger hissed out the word, his eyes burning over my exposed chest. Kicking the chair aside, he shoved me against the table, hunching low.

"Jesus, Sunshine. Jesus…"

I must admit I was surprised he kissed me first, as opposed to going straight for the girls. Not that I was any sort of an expert on the subject, but come on, men and breasts! But kiss me, my hungry Viking did, and quite thoroughly, indeed.

"Fucking hot little mouth…"

Snatching me close, Clint speared curls with one hand and pressed a palm to my spine with the other, plastering us together. He tasted as divine as he smelled: coffee and mint mixed with a piney, masculine finish.

"Mmm. Mmm, Clint…"

We made out for long, delicious minutes, swiftly reaching and surpassing our prebreakfast passion pinnacle. Head lolling, I was moaning into his mouth when Gravedigger took a last dirty lick and pulled back, clutching me by the shoulders.

"Christ, baby. Fuckin' look at you."

Voice slurry, his fingers dug into my traps as he stared down, silver irises eclipsed by black.

"Beautiful angel. Such sweet, sweet tits…"

He swallowed hard, those orbs positively molten as they dipped south. A heartbeat later, Clint's mouth was all over my breasts. And not only his mouth. His tongue, his palms, and his ten big fingers, too.

"Oh… Ohhhh!"

I cried out, the suction of warm lips and the burr of a beard sending me into paroxysms. Clint half-laughed, half-groaned, drawing a nipple into the hot cavern of his mouth.

"Ah, fucking delicious, baby. Fuckin' unreal. Never gonna get enough of these beauties."

He bent me backward over the table, sending dishes and flatware skittering. Dimly, I heard a glass overturn, but I could give two figs. Not in light of what the man was doing to me and my ecstatic breasts, I couldn't.

A puddle of OJ on the table? Hell, a herd of mud-covered pachyderms could wander in and roll all over the clean floor, and I wouldn't budge an inch away from the wicked, whisker-framed lips that were suckling left, then right, then left again—rocketing me into a sensual, sybaritic stratosphere I'd never imagined existed.

"Cliiiiiiinnnnt…"

GRAVEDIGGER

My fingers scrabbled in shaggy hair, pulling him closer. Gravedigger laughed, his mouth wild and his query thick.

"Feel good, baby? You like it? Like my mouth all over these sweet, sugary tits? Wait until I get it on your tight little pussy. Fuck me, I'll never come up for air."

Oh my God, this filthy-talking man, so freaking hot. Never would I have thought yesterday, holed up in that dark dive where he scarcely grunted two words, that Clint MacGregor would turn out to be such a—

CRASH!

What the?

"Whoa! Whoa-ho, Digger, you dark horse! Shudda told me you was entertainin'… I would've moved our date back an hour."

A booming masculine voice sounded in my ears, fast on the tail of the porch door bashing open and hitting the wall.

"FUCK!"

Clint roared the curse, stumbling back and releasing me. I bounced against the table, not understanding, my boobs wet and throbbing and stubble-scratched, my eyes unfocused and dreamy.

Dreamy that is, until they lit on a short, rotund stranger garbed in mom jeans, a "Life Is Brewtiful"

T-shirt a size too small, and a pair of army camouflage Crocs boasting fake gems decorating their rubber holes.

We blinked at each other, the man's mouth hanging open, his eyeballs glomming to my tits like Super Glue.

"GET THE GODDAMNED FUCK OUTTA HERE, LEON!"

Gravedigger bellowed again, blocking me with his bulk as his boot swept the floor for my missing shirt.

Brewtiful grinned, showing a mouthful of big chompers as he hoisted two hands, backing toward the door.

"Okay, man, okay. I'll go wait outside 'til you get your woman dressed. Guess you forgot about helping me with my sump pump, huh? I'd make it another day, but the thing is really shot, and I'm afraid with the shitty forecast—"

"GET OUUUUUUT!"

"All right, Digger, all right!" A pudgy denim butt scampered out the doorway, and I gasped, fighting my way into the tee Clint was hauling over my head, his hands rough and shaking.

"Ow."

I winced, my curls catching.

GRAVEDIGGER

My careless valet paid me no mind, yanking cotton down to my knees—the friction of the cloth against my distended, ravaged nipples eliciting another yelp as my head popped free.

"Owww!"

Stormy eyes pinned me as Gravedigger ground his jaw and slicked back his hair, hissing unfinished sentences heavy on the cussing through nonmoving lips.

"Godfuckingdammit. Can't believe I fucking forgot. Jesus, fuck. Asshole barges right in like he fucking owns the joint…"

I cupped starfish palms over my aching flesh, struggling to catch up with the program while trying not to freak over the fact that some leering redneck with gawdawful taste in threads had just eyefucked my bazoombas.

On cue, Brewtiful's voice came sailing through the doorway, imparting a need-to-know newsflash.

"Truck's a'runnin', Digger. Should I turn it off, or how long you gonna be? Also, I brought along a few growlers, nice 'n' cold. Never too early to start on a Sunday, hey?"

Clint gnashed tight teeth, his face flushed and fierce. I sensed he was attempting to control his temper, but he wasn't succeeding so well. Truthfully, he looked almost as lethal as he had yesterday afternoon, barreling down a grassy hill with spade in fist.

And anyhow, what was *he* so doggone bent about? *I'm* the one whose mammaries were just in another guy's slack-jawed sights!

"Go on down the hall, babe, while I get rid of this clown."

Upon issuing this directive, Clint stomped to the door, sticking his head out.

"We'll have to do it another day, Leon. Today's not gonna work."

I was righting an upended goblet and mopping up a puddle of OJ when Mr. Fashion Plate came charging back into the kitchen on his rubber soles, looking deranged.

"ANOTHER DAY? No way, man! My sump's toast, and they're calling for heavy rains tomorrow and Tuesday. Shit, Digger, you promised!"

Brewtiful side-eyed me and my swollen tits, smiling ingratiatingly.

"You don't mind if I borrow your squeeze for a couple hours, do ya, girlie? I'll have his big hide back before ya know it."

I blinked at him, clutching a juice-wet napkin to my chest.

"Uh…"

GRAVEDIGGER

Clint made a snarling sound akin to a leashed Mastiff, grabbing my wrist and pulling.

"Sunshine. Get your behind in the other room, now."

"Sunshine? That your name, little lady? Purdy. Suits you real well."

The butterball grinned at me and I found myself grinning back, loathe to be a bitch. For one thing, it really wasn't my nature, and for another, the way I figured it, the man had already checked out the merchandise, so what was the point in getting all hot and bothered?

Hey, it was my own fault I hadn't relatched the lock after picking those darn flowers!

Twisting out of Gravedigger's grasp, I adjusted the cloth concealing my nips and smiled wider.

"Thanks, but it's just a nickname. My real name is Casey Rae, Leon, and it's nice to meet you."

I paused, sensing behind me a powder keg of rage about to blow. But too bad. I wasn't about to let this poor man's basement flood, not when my talented Viking had so kindly offered assistance.

Clearing my throat, I continued.

"And no, I don't mind if you borrow Clint. In fact, let me throw on my clothes and I'll go with you guys. I have no set plans for the rest of the day, so if you don't mind teaching a tagalong a thing or two about plumbing, I'm game."

"Sunshinnnnne…"

I ignored the protracted hiss at my shoulder, throwing a wink over at Brewtiful.

"Is there a growler in your truck for me, Leon? I'll trade you one for some tasty leftover bacon and a slice of rye toast."

DIGGER: NINE

"You've got just that one today in Immaculate Grace, Gravedigger. After that, don't forget to tidy up the twin Lawrence obelisks on the hill behind the creek. The relations are breathing down our necks in light of their generous donation last Christmas. Finish up with that gate repair in section W—the mess those punks left us with."

I nodded at Albert the Suit as he zapped the locks on his Benz and hoofed it toward the admin building, an oversized umbrella shielding his bald dome.

My own hair sopped, I gruffed out the assent.

"Right."

I eyed his retreating back with disdain.

Jesus, what a job that bootlicker has… Spending his days pimping out available plots six feet under, or the drawers for up grabs in Oaklawn's fancy mausoleum. Sucking up to dead folk's relatives whenever a few weeds spring up or if a bouquet of rotting stems isn't disposed of quick enough.

I turned to my ride, shuddering.

Kissing all that ass? No fucking thank you. This boy would rather just play in the mud all by his lonesome.

Grabbing my water canteen and a couple of foil-wrapped PBJ's from the passenger seat, I squinted up at charcoal-colored clouds, groaning.

Although, gotta say… Dry mud versus mucky mud is definitely preferable.

The sky opened up, and I made fast tracks for the cemetery's garage and my work wheels, resigned my day was gonna suck big-time. Once inside, I shook off and skirted the big Cat and a couple of smaller earthmovers, passing the well-stocked wall of boneyard necessities I'd meticulously organized over the past twelve years. Throwing my lunch in the truck, I checked its back bed to make sure I had everything I needed.

Ah, shit.

The compartment was a wreck—piled with mud-encrusted shovels, filthy tarps, and other nasty tools of the trade. After what had happened the day before last with Sunshine and that sick fuck jumpin' out of the bushes, I hadn't had time to tidy up before heading to the copper station. And that, I didn't like one fucking bit.

Offloading an armful of grubby spades, I walked them to my cleaning station, leaning them against the tile where I'd wash 'em up later with the rest of my crap. Grabbing a set of fresh ones, I grunted out a half-laugh.

GRAVEDIGGER

Man, I'll bet my bright angel with her "semi-OCD" would be surprised by how neat and orderly this slob's work domain was, as opposed to the mighty clusterfuck of his crib. Damn, the woman wouldn't believe it! I paused, licking hungry-but-not-for-food lips.

Well, maybe Casey Rae Kent could see Gravedigger's Digs for herself.

Maybe this coming Saturday.

Instantly, I retracted, scoffing out loud.

Yeah, moron, right. I'm sure Sunshine would be all for cutting short her grieving session at her sister's stone to check out your impressive pegboard and awe-inspiring collection of chisels.

Fucking asshat.

I flung the crap into the truck's bed, hauling my bulk behind the wheel with a sigh.

Okay. Heigh-ho, it's off to work I go. Here's hoping Leon the Weatherman was wrong, and that today and tomorrow wouldn't turn out to be quite as sodden as the worrywart had predicted. Pulling out into a mini monsoon, I rechecked the sky through fast-moving wipers, not optimistic.

Who was I kidding? That beer swiller was almost never off-target when it came to Mother Nature. Hell, Walker watched The Weather Channel more than our last president tweeted!

I gritted my teeth, pissed-off all over again as I remembered yesterday.

Well, not *all* of yesterday. Not the part before breakfast, when Sunshine and I had made out like mad against the fridge. Not the part when I'd moved things to the counter, planting her tight ass on freshly scrubbed Formica to feast on her sweet lips. Not the part when she'd asked to see my chest, stroking her fingers all over my ink.

And *especially* not the part after we ate, the part when I'd gotten the beauteous Ms. Kent topless. The part where my tongue and my teeth and my fingers had been all over her incredible tits.

My dick twitched under regulation khakis, he and my blue balls continuing to give me grief for allowing a Croc-shod neighbor to cockblock them. *Sorry, boys.* But, Jesus, what was I supposed to have done? I hadn't exactly been firing on all cylinders after the clod had barged through the back door, effectively ruining what had been gearing up to be Clint MacGregor's most sensational day on Earth.

Sunshine's question before she'd exited the room to shimmy back into her sexy blue sundress haunted me still.

"Is there a growler in your truck for me, Leon?"

"Sure, thing, little lady!"

GRAVEDIGGER

Jesus, the guy was clueless, the worst friend ever. What sort of an idiot rolls with *that*? Especially when it's obvious as fuck what your dimwitted carcass just walked in on?

I mean, naked tits, *hellooooo*? Talk about your dictionary definition of "anti-wingman."

Damn the man and his busted sump pump and his cooler of inferior brews...

Curses on Sunshine for her sweet, agreeable ways, and her just-discovered fondness for cheap hops and barbecued pork rinds...

I still could hear her now, her voice all growler-mellow, her fingers all junk-snack stained, as we clattered up to the Walker shack in his piece-of-shit ride.

"Thanks for the growler, Leon. Never drank from one of these big boys before... I'm going to post a pic on Insta! I'll just chill on this glider and finish it up while you boys take care of biz. If it gets to be lunchtime and you're still at it, I'll fix some grilled cheeses or whatever else I can burn in your kitchen. Sound good?"

Grinding down a gravel path, I shifted the truck's gears, jamming steel toe to gas.

Lunchtime, baby? How about lunchtime, dinnertime, and well past nine o'clock until Leon Walker's smelly basement was back in order? By that time, you'd been long gone—headed back home after dishing up three lukewarm mugs of outdated ramen noodles.

To her credit, Sunshine had stuck around until almost two. Which, in hindsight, considering the circumstances and Leon's lack of reading material, was pretty amazing. But eventually she'd bailed, making her announcement to a pair of grease-slicked plumbers.

"Wow, I had no idea how involved replacing a sump was. It's a good thing the Kent Clan boasts a passel of menfolk who hate to pay professionals. Guess I'll leave you to it, and get out of your hair. My mom just checked in anyhow, wondering why my Sunday brunch with Laura Lynn is lasting four-plus hours."

Fuck, had I wanted to howl!

Arriving at my dig site, I killed the engine, unhappy eyes tracking heavy trails of water running down the windshield.

Yippee, *this* was gonna be fun.

I stayed in my seat another few ticks, tormenting myself further by recalling Leon's running commentary as the two of us watched an Uber whisk my beautiful Sunshine away.

"Hot damn, man! Where the *hell* did you find a looker like her? Shit, Digger, I've known you how long? In all that time, I've never seen you tight with a chick, least not in broad daylight. And you've been

GRAVEDIGGER

on a dry spell worse than me; don't try an' deny it. Last summer you hooked up with that babe from Mooney's, but that was like maybe three times, max. And that was the *last* time I've seen you with a broad. Hell, hoss... I was beginning to think maybe you started playin' for the other team. You could've knocked me sideways when I walked in your place and saw you all over those sweet little titt—"

"Yeah, you can stop talking now."

I'd cut the lunkhead off before I punched him in the face, turning to stomp back into his flea-bitten house.

"Come on, get it in gear, fool. I wanna make it home before fucking midnight."

I have to say Leon took the hint, sticking to sump-ish subjects and not bringing up Sunshine anymore. Good thing for him and his jaw. We'd worked straight through dinner on that motherhumping pump—mostly silent, and mostly on account of me and my foul, cockblocked mood.

Every crank of the wrench had been like a corkscrew to my gut.

Goddamn. Sunshine's tits had been in my hands. Under my greedy tongue.

Her lips had been so luscious, her needy moans so delicious.

In less than two minutes, I'd have had her laid out on my table, sexy thighs spread.

"How about a beer break, Digger?"

"NO!"

Yep, I'd been a major prick, but it's only what the putz deserved. You wouldn't catch *me* pulling such a bonehead move, regardless if someone had promised me their services for the day. Furthermore, contrary to his claims, Walker knew detail zero about my sex life, which is exactly the way I wanted it.

Hell, I'd been with at *least* three chicks since that girl from the bar.

Four, if you count Vacuum Mouth in Oklahoma, my unremembered and much-regretted holiday hookup. Shit… Just because Leon rocked plastic clogs and Farmer Brown jeans and never got his pudgy ass laid, didn't mean the rest of his brethren couldn't score.

Sunshine's tits had been in my hands…

I swore, shouldering into hooded raingear and slamming out of the truck. The deluge was heavier now, sluicing down in thick sheets. Grabbing shovels out of the bed, I squinted over at the section of grass marked with a red flag, groaning.

Four beastly hours of digging in this gooey soup. Four hours, *minimum.*

Briefly, I hesitated, picturing the machines back in the garage, and how fuck-all easier they could make my day. How thrilled the suits would be if Gravedigger joined the current century and got his

GRAVEDIGGER

holes dug more expeditiously. How I could sit my kiester up on that big Cat, crank a few controls, and let steel teeth do the work. But just as quickly, I dismissed the temptation, zipping up.

No way, not until the ground was frozen solid. Same as last year and the year before and the year before that, I'll do my digging by hand. It was my thing. It was my therapy. And those stuffy farts behind their desks can't do jack shit about it, because I had me a Distinguished Service Cross, a stipulation in my contract, and a whole nogginful of post-battle PTSD demons they know better than to mess with.

"Uhhh!"

I jabbed the spade into uncooperative earth, flinging the first shovelful over my shoulder.

Yeah, Albert... My rules, my domain. Them's the way the tombstones tumble.

Five-plus soggy hours later, I dragged the last plywood plank over the yawning rectangle I'd fashioned, cursing as I almost wiped out on boot-sucking mud. Despite the protective gear, I was drenched and soil-splattered and, if possible, stewing in an even shittier mood than the one I'd been in last night when I took my leave of Leon.

I glared at sodden strips of wood, sending a message to whomever I'd soon be lowering into that gaping hole.

Hope you appreciate honest-to-goodness manual labor, friend, because this boy just busted a nut.

Sloshing back to the truck, I peeled off filthy gloves and lost the coat, throwing them in the back and my ass in the front. After slicking back saturated hunks of hair, I sucked down half the contents of my canteen before fumbling for the sandwiches. Fucking A, I was starved.

Long time since those flavorless noodles Sunshine whipped up yesterday at noon.

Sunshine…

Munching on dry rye slopped with peanut butter and jam, I tasted not it, but velvety, honey-scented skin.

God, had she been sweet. Her plump, warm tits. Those fat, juicy-red nipples.

My dick throbbed dully and I swore, catching sight of myself in the mirror.

Christ, I looked like a piece of work, like a goddamned beast. It was a fuckin' miracle someone as beautiful, as utterly exquisite as Casey Kent had

GRAVEDIGGER

allowed me to lay so much as a fingertip on her, let alone all ten of the grubby fuckers.

Not to mention my ravenous mouth.

Choking down a crust with another glug of water, I scrubbed a hand over my beard, enraged that I'd been so out of it when me and my abused prick had stumbled out of our jack-off-to-Sunshine bed this morning that I'd forgotten to grab my cell off the nightstand.

Although, what was the big deal? It's not as if I dared to imagine I'd actually receive a call from a certain blond angel I'd exchanged numbers with, but still...

I barked out a laugh to scraps of bread, neck hot.

Oh yeah, Gravedigger. Too bad about the phone. The lady's left like twenty messages in a row, dying to hear your dulcet tones in her ear. Get fucking real, loser.

Wiping dirty hands on dirtier pants, I started the engine, heading for Mister and Missus Bigwig up on their hill. An evil smile twisted my mouth. Shit, all that water and ball-busting work... I needed to take a leak, bad. That pair of pretentious obelisks were nice and tall, the perfect camouflage for relieving a full bladder.

Not that I'd ever piss *directly* on somebody's stone; I wasn't that crass. Come on. I'm motherfucking caretaker of this damn boneyard!

Beast-mode cranked, I puttered down winding paths, passing the crème de la crème of Oaklawn—the centuries-old individual mausoleums bisected by the creek. Twenty-some limestone edifices housing the richest of the rich, holding pride of place in the most coveted real estate on the spread. As always, I appreciated their solemn beauty, each blockish shrine unique and elaborately fashioned. Impressive tributes to a bygone era when grand ships sailed and rail travel was king and folks appreciated the finer details of artisan-crafted architecture.

Something caught my eye as I passed the VanEvery crypt, one of the grandest of the lot. I blinked through heavy raindrops, squinting at what looked like a faint light flickering through the iron grills on the doors. I blinked again, shaking my head.

Weird. *What the fuck?* Couldn't be the sun's reflection because the cunt was MIA today. It almost looked like a lit candle in there…

I shook my head again, turning down the next lane.

You're fucking seeing things, dude. Should've gotten more shut-eye last night, instead of twisting in the sheets with prick in fist.

A few minutes later, I was back in my clammy jacket, yanking out dandelions some snobs had complained about. This, after I'd relieved myself behind Ma and Pa's matching tombs, taking care not to splash.

GRAVEDIGGER

By now, my mood had morphed from foul to abysmal—boots soaked, hair and beard dripping. I half-contemplated heading back to the garage to tinker with my tools under cover of a roof, but what the hell… I was already drenched. And if I did blow off shit today, then I'd be that much behind tomorrow. Christ, I had a pair of back-to-back digs starting at seven-thirty, and according to Leon's crystal ball, Tuesday's forecast was gonna be equally sucky.

I stuffed yellow weeds into a bucket, slipping on the wet grass. Fuck. Might as well ungrin and bear it.

As I finished up, I fantasized about Sunshine, and if and when I was going to see her again. The way I figured it, my odds were forty-sixty.

Pro: Crazy as the circumstances of our getting together look on paper, there was no denying the wicked chemistry. Shit, right from the get-go, right from minute one. Our first kiss at Mooney's. Then that Uber ride, all the hot action at my place. The way my angel had kissed me back, let me touch her, all over. Saturday night, Sunday morning. The sweet way she'd petted me in return…

Pro: I'd rallied to her rescue, taken down that deviant scumbag, and Sunshine couldn't quit thanking me for it. True, little did she know I'd been spying on her from above, but, nonetheless, I'd come out hero man. And that shit goes a long way when your ass saves a lady from getting raped, or worse.

Pro: Sunshine seemed pretty comfortable with me. Unloading all kinds of angst in that dark booth, inviting herself to crash at my crib, yakking over pizza. Advocating for a cozy catnap on my big, scratchy couch.

A suggestion this most gigantic idiot in the history of idiots had shot down.

Arghhhh.

Bucket full, I stomped back to my wheels and tossed it into the bed, still not believing what a dunderhead I'd been. What an absolute and utter imbecile, leaving Sunshine lying horizontal with pouting lips and shoved-up skirt while I went and hid in the den like a tool, determined not to take advantage.

Fuckin' Sir Lancelot with a go-nowhere cockstand, that's me.

Flinging my saturated carcass in the front seat, I got back to my odds list. Okay, those aforementioned points had been the forty portion of the equation. The sixty chunk?

I grunted, staring down at my grubby knuckles.

That would be the con. A big honkin' mother of a con, fairly fucking simple to figure out. To wit: the man who wanted to get with a glorious bright angel was a goddamn *gravedigger.* An oaf of a soil slinger boasting not only an unsavory vocation, but also a

GRAVEDIGGER

sloppy crash pad, piss-poor social skills, and a tankerload of front-line poison polluting his brain.

Wow, MacGregor, some package deal.

Still, there *were* those pluses. A guy never got anywhere in this life without trying, right? And Jesus, with Casey Rae Kent, I wanted to try. Wanted it like I've never wanted anything before in my life. Wanted her like I've never wanted any other woman, not even close.

When I get home, I'll call her. Keep it light, casual. Ask Sunshine about her day, ask if she started looking for a new job, as she'd mentioned she might. Hint that I'd like to see her again, big-time see her again, but no pressure, only if she was up to—

BEEP! BEEPBEEP! BEEEEEEP!

Huh?

I dug head outta ass, peering through fogged-up glass. A snazzy VW SUV pulled up alongside me, wipers flappin' like mad.

Fuck. Don't tell me it was The Snobs, ready to ream me over the rails for pissing on their parents.

As I worked on drumming up an excuse, the driver's window rolled down and Sunshine's gorgeous face appeared, her gapped teeth flashing in a saucy smile.

"Hey, you. I borrowed my dad's car, because would you believe I never picked mine up from Mooney's lot yet? I thought I'd track you down here, and may I say it took a while. You feel like meeting me at 'our booth' for one after you're done? Only one, though, because my brother CJ is bringing Dad to get *his* car, I'm hopping into *my* car, and then we're all going to Rocky's Roadhouse for burgers. It's going to be my first meal out since Beth. And this I owe to you, Mr. M., after taking the plunge with pizza and poppers."

I opened my mouth, but nothing came out.

Sunshine wrinkled her nose, eyeing me up and down.

"Boy, Gravedigger, you look *reeeeally* dirty. Not that I can blame you, with this rain. All right, I'm going to visit my, uh, my sister, and then I have to hit the drugstore and the bank. Afterwards, I'll head to Mooney's in hopes that handsome bartender has replenished his supply of orange slices. I should be there just in time for happy hour, around five-ish, if you can swing it."

She tapped her wheel as I sat there trying not to dwell on the unhappy fact that she'd just called 'Lighter Tirone handsome.

Does she think that big prick looks like a Viking, too?

"You're welcome to join us for burgers, BTW. No pressure on either offer, of course. If you have other plans, no biggie. I just thought, after yesterday…"

I was out of my truck before Sunshine could finish, taking two big squishy steps to her window. Not

GRAVEDIGGER

allowing myself to chicken out, I hunched, tilting her chin with one filthy finger.

"I'll be there, baby."

Shoving through her window, I crushed my lips to hers, feasting on her sweet sugar. My head spun as my tongue speared deep, exploring delicious nooks and crannies. Sunshine made a hot little noise in her throat, cupping my beard and kissing me back, rain streaming down our cheeks. The kiss went on and on until I was drowning in driving raindrops and my heart was pounding and my straining cock could pass for one of the chisels in my toolbox. With a mammoth effort, I broke away, gasping.

"God*damn,* girl…"

Sunshine sat back, fumbling for a towel on the seat beside her. Wiping her mouth, she blew out a breath, panting hard.

"Whew. Whoa. Wow. Well, er, okay. I'll… I'll see you in a while."

She flicked me a shaky salute, rolling up wet glass and driving off. I stood under the teeming skies with chest heaving and dick throbbing, licking honey off my lips. Then I grinned, tipping my face up to the deluge.

More orange-slice-sucking in that crappy back-corner booth?

Right on!

CASEY: TEN

Four lemons rinds decorated the tabletop, and I got started on a fifth, trying to keep my eyes off the door. Trying to play it cool. Ruffling rain-damp hair, I checked my watch for the hundredth time.

5:22. Same as it had been ten seconds ago, dork.

Determined not to look again, I shoved hands under knees and glanced around the murky room, noting that there were about as many clients enjoying Mooney's gloomy environs as there had been on Saturday. In other words, less than a handful.

How the heck does this joint stay in business? Must draw in a massive late-night crowd.

Far across the room, I locked eyes with "Call me Moonlighter, gorgeous," and threw him a smile. The bartender returned it widely, his gaze skittering down to my chest and sticking there. My skin turned hot and I glanced away, studying the awful artwork at my shoulder.

Don't encourage the man, Kent. Somehow, I have a feeling my Viking wouldn't like those flirty eyes on me, not one bit.

My cell dinged and I grabbed for it, heart thumping. But no: it wasn't Clint stiffing, but my brother,

GRAVEDIGGER

returning my just-sent text. This would be the fabrication informing CJ I was running late with my errands, and could he and Dad push back half an hour? Swiftly, I perused his response, blowing out a relieved breath.

"Bettr 4 me. CU 630"

I pushed the phone aside and bit my lip, thinking I should have asked for an hour. A perfectly believable request, as my so-called "errands" were the first I'd attended to since June the second, not having left the homestead in all that time.

Except to drive straight to Oaklawn Cemetery and back, every Saturday afternoon.

Sipping my drink, I pictured Beth's pretty pink headstone, and how different it had looked today, darkened with rain. Huddled beneath an umbrella, I'd realized that this afternoon was the first time I'd visited her in crappy weather, the first time I'd been unable to kneel on the grass. My chest ached, dull knives burning. Sunny summer would soon segue into chilly fall, and then into cold, harsh winter. First, there would be all kinds of dead leaves piled up around her, and then a heavy blanket of snow.

Pretty tough to kneel in the white stuff, lady.

CRASH

The door banged open with a bell clang and my attention shot to the big man shouldering through it, slicking back fingerfuls of hair. *Clint!* I pushed aside morbid notions, sitting up straighter. Narrowed eyes sliced over to me curled in my back booth, and a crooked smile tipped stern lips as Gravedigger strode over on colossal legs. Trying not to make it obvious, I gobbled him up, inwardly declaring his massive and muscly bod hot as hellfire.

Lord a'mighty, those rangy shoulders and inked, muscular guns. His thick, sexy thighs…

Muddy boots halted inches from the table, and Clint gazed down into my eyes, his own glittering with hidden messages. They flicked to my lips, then south to my breasts, pewter darkening to ebony. Unlike Mitch the Moonlighter's bold glances, which had done zilch for me, this man's searing stare turned me to a mass of unset Jell-O.

"Sorry I'm late. With the rain, took a little longer to clean up than usual." He cleared his throat, a flush tinging burnished cheekbones. "Well, tried to clean up."

Stroking a hand over broad pecs encased in an unsoiled tee, he scowled at his filthy khakis and boots.

"Had an extra shirt to throw on, but no jeans. I can run to the Men's and try to wash—"

"No…" I interrupted, reaching out to tap a tough wrist.

GRAVEDIGGER

"You're fine. This place isn't exactly the Taj Mahal and neither is Rocky's, if you're thinking of joining. Come on, have a seat and take a load off."

I struggled to keep the stammering to a minimum, as I nodded across the table.

"I, um, I got you a Bud, same as last time. Unless you're in the mood for something else?"

"Yeah. Yeah, actually, I am."

Clint's reply was hoarse as he continued to loom, his big crotch in my face. *Right* in my face. I mutilated a discarded lemon rind, my skin prickling.

"Oh, sorry. I shouldn't have presumed. Tell me what you want, and I'll run to the bar and grab it."

Two hundred-plus pounds of sexy male brawn crashed onto the bench seat beside me, a steaming-hot thigh pressing against mine. Tipping up my chin with two fingers, Clint held my eyes, licking his lips.

"Not talkin' about booze. Talkin' about you, Sunshine. You're what I'm in the mood for. Can I have a hello kiss?"

Holy Kamoley.

I managed a nod, my heart walloping as his bearded face came closer, filling my vision. Watching that unsmiling mouth growl out exciting words, I squeezed my legs together, dying for that tough, masculine kisser to connect.

"Damn, baby... I can't wait to taste you." Gravedigger swallowed hard, his Adam's apple jerking in a strong brown throat. Licking whisker-framed lips again, he ground out a question, fingers twitching on my chin.

"How much time until your old man shows up, babe? How much time do I have to eat up your sweet sugar?"

Trembling, I whispered the answer, anticipation choking me.

"I, uh, six-thirty. I pushed them back half an hour."

Clint sucked in a deep breath, shutting his eyes for a sec. "Not long enough, but it'll have to do." He snapped opened his lids, cheeks flushing as he slashed a hand at our drinks.

"Babe. I'm afraid as fuck to kiss you here. We put on enough of a show for that dog behind the bar the other day. How about we go sit in my truck 'til your folks get here? Listen to some tunes, have us some privacy?"

I chewed my lip, reading the unspoken agenda burning in those sexy silvers loud and clear.

You mean, go make out like mad in your front seat? Yes, please!

"Okay." I cleared my throat. "But, but, what about your beer?"

GRAVEDIGGER

He jackknifed up, dragging me out of the booth, five fingers tight around my wrist.

"Fuck the beer. That's not what I'm thirsty for."

I grabbed my knapsack, stumbling in Gravedigger's wake as he made fast tracks to the door. Passing Moonlighterwhatsis, I babbled in the guy's face, arrowing a thumb backward.

"Hey, can you hold our table? We'll be back shortly. We, uh, we need to go run a quick errand."

"Sure." A sly grin curled his lips as assessing eyes tracked my unsubtle companion.

"Errand, huh? Looks pretty... urgent."

Detecting the, "Nice try, but you can't bullshit me," note in his voice but not caring, I flew out the door behind Clint as he hauled me through sideways-falling raindrops. Reaching his big Silverado parked alongside my cute, abandoned Kia, he practically flung me into the passenger's seat before circling the hood in yardstick-wide strides to slam in behind the wheel. Three heartbeats later, the A/C was humming, his mouth was on mine, and two wet hands were in my hair, buried deep.

"Fuck, baby..."

"Oooh, Clint..."

He tasted heavenly and I opened wide, his kiss both wildly erotic and strangely comforting. Comforting in a surreal way, as if I belonged in this man's strong, enveloping arms. As if I was exactly where I needed to be. Of course, the way Gravedigger was going to town, "strangely comforting" soon switched fully over to "wildly erotic," and I twined my arms around his neck, moaning against hungry lips.

"Yes, Clint, *yes…*"

"All day, baby. All goddamned day, this is all I've fuckin' thought about."

Clint's confession was harsh as he mumbled against the corner of my mouth, slid his lips to my cheek. Whiskers rough against my skin, his fingers dug into my scalp as he angled my head, pushing me back against cool leather.

"Sweet, sweet sugar…"

Lowering one hand, he stroked my neck, repeating himself, his fingers shaking.

"All goddamned day. All last night." His mouth crushed mine, a velvet-rough tongue licking deep.

Delicious.

"Mmm, more, Clint. More…"

My needy request set him off and he cursed, crowding up against me.

"Fuck yeah, baby. Yeah, I'll give you more."

GRAVEDIGGER

We made out for long minutes, the rain beating against the windshield competing with feminine moans and masculine groans. In between frantic kisses, Gravedigger growled out graphic half-sentences, every slurry syllable sending shivers over my skin.

"You have any idea how much I wanted to kill Walker for showing up yesterday?" His tongue traced my teeth and caressed the bow of my upper lip. "Destroying what was gonna be the best damned day of my life?"

I moaned against his mouth, my hands dropping to clutch two boulder-like biceps.

"Me too. I... I wanted to stay. Wanted to keep on doing what we were doing."

Wanted you to continue to ravish my boobs. Wanted you to take me to your bed, and move on to other needy body parts. Wanted to lose my cherry to a wild, ravaging Viking Lord in his messy, ugly-furniture-stuffed house.

Framing my face between cupping palms, Clint drew back to shudder in a breath. We stared at each another, both of us gasping like we'd run a 5K. Underneath my baby doll frock, nipples peaked and pussy tingled, causing more goosebumps to spring up. Gravedigger groaned, his sharp eyes missing nothing.

"Ah, Jesus. These gorgeous nipples..."

He licked parted lips, staring at my chest. "I can fucking see them, girl, poking against that pretty fabric." His eyes cut to mine, molten and fierce.

"You want my mouth on them again, baby? Want my tongue and teeth all over your sweet, tight tits? My lips sucking you up?"

I nodded, mute. Turned-on like crazy by the look in his eyes. By his fabulously filthy kisses. And by his even filthier talk.

Pulling in another lungful, Clint traced a finger over my clavicle, breathing hoarsely.

"You look so beautiful, angel, in this sexy little dress. Hot as fuck." That thick finger slid to my ear, playing with a curl. "You always wear sexy little dresses, baby?"

My voice was unsteady as I nodded again, excruciatingly aware of my braless, diamond-tipped breasts flaunting themselves shamefully.

Remember us, mister? We want your talented mouth back, on the double.

"I, um, mostly. In the summer, at least. I, er, find them more, more comfortable than shorts."

Gravedigger growled his approval. "Yeah. And I fucking love it. Sensational bare legs, your golden skin. I've never seen you in anything different, babe, not in all these weeks."

GRAVEDIGGER

A buzzing noise started in my head, and I blinked, drawing back.

"What? 'All these weeks?' What... What do you mean, 'all these weeks?'"

Clint turned red above his beard, and below it, too, his neck burning to match his face.

"Uh,"

His jaw rolled as he gritted out words to the soaked windshield, avoiding my eyes.

"I might have seen you a time or two, before we met."

My heart pounded sluggish and thick, no mistaking the locale to which he was referring. How could there be a mistake, when the only place I'd set foot since Beth's funeral and reception was the silent, gated community where her fancy cream casket was buried?

"Oaklawn? You saw me at *Oaklawn*?"

Guilty-looking eyes shifted to mine as Gravedigger jerked his head.

"Yeah. I saw you on my rounds. Visiting your, uh, your sister." He bit his lip, the flush on his skin deepening. "Not that I knew it was your sister. I'd just see you every Saturday, kneeling in your pretty dresses, looking so beautiful and sad."

I blinked at him and he plowed on, his voice turning huskier.

"Looking like an angel. Looking like Sunshine."

Pressing fingers to temples, I whispered, the words squeezing from my throat.

"So, it wasn't a miracle at all the other day. How you 'just happened' to be there to come to my rescue. It wasn't a sign from Beth, at all. You were already there, watching me."

My voice turned higher, shriller.

"Just like that sicko from the bushes. You were watching me, *spying* on me!"

"No, Sunshine. No, it wasn't like th—"

"Sunshine!" In a screech, I interrupted, parroting his syllables. Shaking, I slapped away the hand that was reaching for me, fumbling for the door handle and hissing between my teeth.

"Don't call me that! Not ever! That's my family's name for me and you're not allowed to use it! You, you *Peeping Tom*!"

"Baby, wait."

That big hand landed on my shoulder and I whirled on him, throwing it off.

"Don't!"

GRAVEDIGGER

As I wrenched the door open, heavy showers pelted me, stinging my legs as I clambered out backward and dropped to the ground.

"I can't talk to you, Clint. This shit is seriously creeping me out. What kind of a man spies on people at a freakin *cemetery*? Cemeteries are supposed to be private places, sacred places. Not places where weirdos perv on mourners from some secret hidey-hole, or jump out from behind a tree to attack them!"

Sticking him in the same category as the degenerate who'd assaulted me, I laughed insanely as rain doused my shoulders. Pinning his tensed-up frame with daggers from narrowed eyes, I spat out an addendum, laying emphasis on the last word.

"You of all people should know that, *Gravedigger*."

"Angel, wait! Wait, let me explain…"

Untensing himself, Clint made moves to exit the vehicle, and I shrieked anew, presenting him my palm.

"No! Don't you dare get out of that truck." I slashed my other hand behind me, pointing. "Here's what's going to happen. *I'm* going back into that dive and wait for my father and brother. *You're* going to drive your creepy ass away. And lose my number, Clint MacGregor. I don't ever want to see you again."

"Sunshine, no—"

Freaking to the max, I gripped wet curls, apoplectic.

"I said, don't you EVER call me that name again!"

I grabbed my Burberry and slammed the door shut on Clint's miserable-looking face, dashing through soaking pellets to the bar's entrance. The man in charge of the bottles looked up as I burst through the door, his handsome brows rising when he saw I was solo. Stomping over, I pulled out a stool, plopping down with stinging eyes and a forced smile.

"You can forget about saving that booth; I prefer it here. Can I get another Bacardi and Diet, with extra, extra lemons and oranges?"

Moonlighter of Mooney's Place smiled a slow, wide smile, his baby blues heating up.

"Sure. Sure, beautiful. Extra fruit, no problem."

Checking me out more closely, his face softened as he reached across the wood and patted my hand.

"I'll give you all the oranges you need, darlin'. You running short, you just let 'Lighter know."

I threw him a watery smile, leaning elbows on his well-scrubbed bar. A vision flashed in my mind of my idiotic self, wringing out a filthy sponge yesterday at the crack of dawn.

This joint may be a hole-in-the-wall, but Mr. Moonlighter keeps his counters a hell of a lot cleaner than that big, slobby Peeping Tom does.

GRAVEDIGGER

Watching capable hands fix my drink, I strove for social butterfly-friendly, wiping my dripping face with a bar nap.

"Relation?" I gestured at a grainy photo over the register, noting the similarity around the nose and chin. "Is that your dad, perchance?"

The bartender grinned proudly, setting a tall glass simply *loaded* with citrus in front of me.

"Yup, that's the old man, Mooney himself. This is his place. I help him out when I'm not sweatin' in my other gig, rehabbin' houses. Hence, my name. Put in a few afternoons here and there, but mostly nights. I figure, let Daddy-O kick back in his twilight years, not that his ass isn't still fulla piss 'n' vinegar. Actually, you may get to meet him shortly... He's comin' by to drop off his latest masterpiece."

He waved an arm in a broad, sweeping gesture.

"All the paintings you see, those are Pop's. Every one an original. They're for sale, if you spy anything you like. We haven't had a chance to stick price tags on 'em all yet, but feel free to make an offer."

I dredged up an impressed expression, recalling the hideously rendered sunset hanging over that back-corner booth.

"Wow."

Luckily, just then my phone buzzed, so I didn't have to maintain the frozen smile any longer. Holding up a finger, I scrabbled in my bag, my mouth tightening when I checked the screen.

Lord Thor.

Yes, supremely cringeworthy, I know, I know.

Like an infatuated schoolgirl, I'd assigned the uber-sappy handle to Clint's number last night while I lay fantasizing in bed, along with a close-up pic I'd snapped of his sexy, slumbering face the night previous as he snoozed in his dirty den. Eyes smarting, I deleted both contact and photo with a jab, stuffing my cell away.

Plastering on a new and improved phony smile, I flashed my Chiclets over at Moonlighter, formulating a spur-of-the-moment Plan B, starring Bartender Guy in a leading role.

Why not? The man was pretty dang hot, even though it was obvious he was a player with a capital 'P,' likely turning it on for anyone possessing a semi-decent pair of breasts. Better to engage in a bit of harmless flirting than to dissolve into a flood of angry tears all over his dad's rickety barstool.

"Hey. I have half an hour to burn before my own dad shows to take me out for a Rocky Rodeo Burger. How about I buy you a shot, and you can regale me with the history of this fine family establishment?"

Moonlighter grinned, grabbing a bottle of Seagrams.

"I won't say no, hotstuff."

GRAVEDIGGER

He poured and we clinked, and I chugged down a big gulp of brown liquor.

Chhhaaaa-aaaahhh!

It tasted harsh yet marvelous, and I immediately decided a single round wasn't going to cut it. Not after what I'd just found out in that parking lot, it wasn't. I downed the remainder with a shudder, grinning into a pair of sky-blue eyes.

"Another?"

Hey, I can always leave my car in the lot again and collect it tomorrow.

This time, I'll ask Christopher to help me out. Brother number three can never say no to me.

Fishing around in my cocktail, I pulled out a plump orange wedge, sucking on the goodness as I leaned palm on chin.

"So, Mitch Moonlighter. Start talking."

DIGGER: ELEVEN

I planted a shiny dime on a crumbly mound of mud, stepping back and wiping my hands.

Godspeed partner, whoever the fuck you are.

Unlike ol' Errol V. Flin, this stiff wasn't sporting any temporary nametag until their personalized hunk o' granite arrived, so I had clue zero as to whose recently departed bones I was sweatin' over. For all I knew, they could belong to some unlucky bastard from Mooney's Place I'd crushed at the pool tables.

Too bad I couldn't give half a rat's ass.

Heading back to the truck, I flung spade in bed, leaning against sun-hot metal to squint at my watch.

Goddamn. Not even one yet, and I'm soaked to the skin. And I still have another hole to dig, a mother of a monument to set, and a shitload of shovels to clean before I get to go home and stare at my fucking four walls for twelve hours.

I rubbed itchy eyes, my heavy workload and the emptiness of the night bedeviling me.

Up for debate which scenario sucks worse.

Mood blacker than tar, I jabbed key in ignition and hung half out the window, guzzling from my canteen

GRAVEDIGGER

as I waited for the lame A/C to kick in. Once it wasn't ten thousand degrees in the interior anymore, I took a time-wasting detour on the way to my next dig—the path below Sunshine's sister's plot.

Go ahead, say it. Yeah, I'm that much of a pathetic, glutton-for-punishment loser.

As I drove slowly past, my eyes locked on a distinctive pink stone and I blinked at the gorgeous, tousle-haired angel shimmering in the sun. I blinked again and the mirage was gone, replaced by green grass and empty air. Cursing, I ground the gears, enraged that I kept traveling this road, praying that I'd see Sunshine for real. A fantasy as foolish as it was painful.

It's been two weeks-plus, fuckhead. Not only has the beauty skipped back-to-back Saturday visits, she hasn't returned a single one of your calls or texts. Time to acknowledge those sexsational sessions with Casey Rae Kent are now consigned to both memory and jack-off banks, never to be repeated except in your pining, Peeping Tom peabrain.

Speaking of texts, my cell pinged on the seat beside me and I grabbed the thing, rapidly reading a missive from Albert the Suit.

"Reminder: you agreed to work overtime tonight. Lawns need to be mowed around the private mausoleums for the cameras in the morning. METICULOUSLY mowed."

I scowled, flinging the phone away. Shit on a stick, I *had* forgotten. Some stuffy ceremony was taking place at one of those mini mansions tomorrow, a hundredth anniversary of some muckety-muck's demise.

Great, lovely. Now I wouldn't get home to stare at my fucking four walls until well after dark. Only to shove some tasteless frozen dinner in my yap, toss and turn in my lonely bed, and wake up tomorrow to get covered in mud and sweat and dead lily petals all over again.

Good times, good times.

The remainder of the summer yawned before me, Sunshine-less and terrible. And after Labor Day, things would get even worse, with warm days giving way to nippy frosts and eventually to ball-shriveling deep freezes. Shivering despite the broiling temps, I groaned at a mental snapshot of my numb ass planted up in the big Cat's cage, its steel claw battling snowy, rock-hard ground.

Christ bless it. Old Man Winter would've been *so* much more bearable with a honey-sweet goddess heating up my sheets…

For the thousandth time since I'd blurted it out, I cursed my big mouth for spouting to Sunshine my admiration for her sexy sundresses. Jesus, if I'd kept those spying-from-behind-a-tree compliments to myself, the two of us would still be together.

GRAVEDIGGER

Would still be talking. Still be learning one another.

Still be touching, teasing, kissing.

Would have graduated to hot and nasty fucking, all over my big, rumpled bed.

My gut twisted as I rubbed tired eyes, picturing once again a pair of chocolate-brown ones widening as Sunshine absorbed my confession.

"I've never seen you in anything different, babe, not in all these weeks."

Goddamned idiot! Yeah, if only I'd kept my fat trap shut, my bright angel never would've freaked. I'd still be the Viking hero crashing down the hill to rescue her from the clutches of some twisted perv.

Now, in Sunshine's mind, *I* was the twisted perv.

Hideous words reverberated in my head, her parting shot quavery but firm, impossible to misinterpret.

"Lose my number, Clint MacGregor. I don't ever want to see you again!"

Fucking hell, that had been awful.

Naturally, my immediate and burning inclination had been to book into the bar after her and plead my case. But being a huge and mud-stained chicken, I'd settled on half a dozen calls, leaving bumbling voice messages and hastily misspelled texts, begging for forgiveness. Not one of which had been answered, as noted. Not those, nor any of the scores of others I'd left like a pining fool in the days and weeks since.

Innards clenching anew, I winced as I recalled my last attempt this past Saturday, three endless nights ago.

Saturday, two weeks to the day since I'd sprawled on my sofa with Sunshine's silky curves wrapped in my arms.

Saturday, the night I'd gotten so shitfaced at my kitchen table that I'd left a long, rambling message at one-thirty in the morning. The ignominious details of my blottoed monologue mostly, but not completely, lost to the vapors of Master Jack Daniels.

Regrettably, I remembered enough.

"Baby, I missh you. I need to exshplain, need you back. Need your schweet lips on mine, your schweet tits in my hands."

I moaned out loud, my neck turning as hot as the sun in the sky.

Crackerjack wordsmith, Gravedigger. Big fucking surprise the woman hasn't returned your calls.

"Excuse me! Excuse me, sir!"

A shrill voice had me crashing back to Planet Earth and I peered out the window, startled.

The fuck?

GRAVEDIGGER

A middle-aged female sat astride a dorky cruising bicycle on the side of the path, her cheeks red from exertion. Hands strangling rubber grips, she peered over her shoulder and then back at me, breathing hard.

"You work here, right?"

Negative, lady. I'm just driving around in this regulation rig wearing a shirt sporting the same oaky logo it does for the fuckin' fun of it.

"That's right." I attempted a polite smile, figuring she needed directions.

"Well, you should know there's a suspicious-looking guy creeping around. I saw him earlier on my ride and again just now, over by those thick bushes."

She jabbed a finger over at a clump of evergreens skirting the creek, and even from a couple of yards away, I could see that her hand was shaking.

"He's wearing black jeans and a hoodie, and like I said, he looks really…"

Releasing the handles, she curled her fingers into air quotes.

"…really 'off.' Gave me the willies, the spooky way he looked at me. And those heavy, dark clothes… Who dresses like that in this heat? I was thinking of riding over to the office when I saw your truck."

Hoodie?

A chill slithered up my spine, mingling with rivulets of perspiration. Just like that, I was transported back two weeks—my spade raised high, my boot planted on a supine, concave chest.

Working on keeping my voice steady, I nodded again.

"Thanks, I'll check it out right away. Ten to one it's some homeless dude, but you should probably head on out of here, just to be safe."

Red Cheeks jerked her sun-visored head in agreement. "Exactly what I plan on doing. The one day my husband decides to tinker with the clothes dryer instead of biking with me!" She stomped down on the pedals, putting her mom bike in motion as she muttered to herself.

"What a world. Can't even enjoy a peaceful cemetery anymore…"

She took off in one direction and I in the other, semi-losing it as I hit the gas.

Can't possibly be the same asshole…

Even as my eyes scanned dense foliage, a voice in my head derided me.

Why the fuck can't it? You don't know jack shit about what happened to that twist who attacked Sunshine. For all you know, the fuzz couldn't match his DNA to anything and had to let the scumbag walk.

GRAVEDIGGER

The thought of him springing out on another unsuspecting victim had me homicidal, my military-trained instincts slavering for retribution. This time, retribution on my terms, without a pair of uniforms in attendance.

I'd been too easy on the psycho, waiting for those cops to show. After what he almost did to my angel...

Vision hawk-like, I wove up and down gravel paths, pushing the truck to the max, all the while conceding I was on a fool's errand. Jesus, this jalopy wasn't exactly quiet... If that asshole was indeed lurking around, he'd hear me in heartbeat and hide his weaselly carcass. And fuck, I could be ten sections over if the sicko decided he wanted come out and play.

After about fifteen minutes, I gave up, considering calling in Bike Mama's report to the coppers. At the very least, I should clue in Albert and crew. Maybe it wouldn't be a bad idea to stick some sort of a subtle warning at the main gates to let—

"YO! Yo, man, watch it!"

Out of nowhere, a well-built, yellow-haired jogger rounded the bend right in front of my rig's bumper, causing me to smash on the brakes.

Shit!

We stared at each other through the windshield, both of us wide-eyed. Christ, that'd been close. Bikers, walkers, joggers… Nothing new in Oaklawn, but not thick on the ground, either. Whenever I did encounter a person with a pulse in the wild, their alive-and-not-dead presence tended to throw me. Especially when I almost turned some dude's ass into roadkill!

I tossed him an apologetic look, leaning out the window.

"Sorry 'bout that. Guess I was going a little fast."

"Nah, it's cool. My fault… I shouldn't have been in the middle of the path." The guy slashed his hand, running in place. Something about him looked vaguely familiar, and I wondered if maybe he frequented Tirone's dive.

Swiveling his head, he squinted left and right. "Didn't even plan on going for a run, but I'm meeting my sis, and she's running late from a job interview. Thought I'd blow off some steam while I waited. But this place is pretty big, and I'm all turned around. Which way to Perpetual Gardens, bro?"

My heart beat faster as I studied the lines of his face.

Don't even fucking tell me.

I pointed off in the distance, making my voice all casual.

"Way over the other side of the creek and up the hill. Just came from there myself, but I can drop you if you want, seeing you're outta juice."

GRAVEDIGGER

Jerking my chin at the empty Propel bottle dangling from his fingers, I gestured to the seat beside me, even though it was against cemetery protocol to go around offering visitors buggy rides.

"If you don't mind sittin' shotgun with a ripe gravedigger, that is."

Jogger Guy hesitated, checking his watch. "Well, er, okay. Yeah, sure. It *is* hot as hell, and Case should be here any minute."

Case. Casey. Christ, I was right. This fucker is one of Sunshine's damn brothers!

Mr. Fitness hopped in, slamming the door.

I shifted the gears, flicking my eyes to a tall row of cypresses. Still on the hunt for a scumbag. Trying to focus on what that bike rider had told me, and not on who was meeting my passenger in front of a carved pink marker. Clearing a jammed throat, I kept my expression bland and my tone nonchalant.

"Uh. You didn't happen to see a dude dressed all in black while you were running, did ya? A skinny guy in jeans and a hoodie?"

The man next to me stiffened, and a water bottle crunched.

"Guy in a hoodie? Are you serious?"

Willing me to glance his way, he frowned, the expression on his mug morphing to murderous.

Knew that look... Pretty much identical to the one my rearview had reflected back at me the past quarter-hour.

"Jesus! My kid sister was attacked in this cemetery a few weeks ago by a fucker matching that same description. You're not telling me he's still on the loose? What the hell kind of a place do you people run here?"

I rounded a curve, my jaw tight. I have to say I took offense at that jab, particularly in light of how I'd spared his sweet sibling. Speaking through set teeth, I addressed the bug-flecked windshield.

"We've never had any trouble of that kind before, and I've been the main man here for a decade-plus. Punks climbing the fences after hours, minor vandalism to stones and shit, weed parties, that's the extent of it. Nothing like what happened to Sun... Uh, nothing like what happened to your sister, not ever."

Brother Kent grabbed my arm, staring in my face.

"It was you, wasn't it? You're the guy with the shovel, the guy Case said came to her rescue."

Mutely, I gave a curt nod, not bothering to deny it. Christ, what would be the point? All the man had to do was describe to Sunshine the bearded, muddy slob he hitched a ride with, and the jig would be up.

GRAVEDIGGER

Please, God, don't let her have spilled about my Saturday spying sessions, because Brother K. here looks like he can throw a pretty mean right hook.

"Well, hell!"

Releasing my arm, he slapped my shoulder, blowing out a breath.

"Shit, I owe you a massive 'thank you,' man. Hell, my whole family does! When we heard what almost happened, when Sunny told us how some big mother came charging down the hill, knocking down the trash who attacked her—!"

My neck turned hot as I shifted in my seat.

Okay. Appears he doesn't know about the other part, thank fuck.

I mumbled out a mouthful, shrugging. "It was nothing. Just glad I was around."

Kent turned up the friendly as he slapped my soiled shoulder again.

"Jesus, so the hell am I! By the way, the name's Christopher, man. Chris. Chris Kent. I'm Casey's brother, youngest of her three watchdogs."

I could tell he was waiting on my moniker, so I gruffed it out as we rattled across the creek's rickety wooden bridge.

"I'm Clint. But everybody calls me Gravedigger."

That got him going, and he laughed out loud.

"No shit? *Gravedigger?* As in, that's what you do around here? You mean the old-school way, with your bare hands? Damn, that's badass, man."

Even though I had eyes on the gravel, I sensed his gaze boring into me, and my skin ratcheted up a degree.

Yup, that's exactly what I do. Feast your eyes on big, muddy, hairy, and sweaty, my friend. Quite the Prince Charming, no? Would you ever in a million years believe that your goddess of a sister allowed me to put these filthy paws all over her luscious, golden skin?

"Yo, man, you okay? All of a sudden, you're red as a beet, brah. Hot as hell, I know, and with all the digging you do… Looks like you're headed for a wicked sunburn. I'm feeling it myself, just from a ten-minute run. Listen, I've got some sunblock in my glove if you're planning on being out in this heat the rest of the aftern—"

"I'll be fine." I cut him off, feeling like a schoolboy caught doing something dirty.

Fuck me. If the guy only knew.

"Suit yourself. Anyway, getting back to the dude in the hood…"

GRAVEDIGGER

Chris broached the subject half my mind was still fixated on, the half that wasn't obsessing about getting my eyeballs on Sunshine again.

I semi-listened, the noise in my head drowning out his words.

Had that lady on the bike been right? Was that sick fuck roaming around here again?

The entire time I'd been driving, I'd been searching the grounds for a scrawny figure in black, my senses as attuned as they'd been back in bloody, war-torn Kabul. But I'd seen jack squat... Just a desert of tombstones, trees, and acres of grass, with no skulking predator in sight.

Maybe Ms. Two Wheels had been seeing things.

"...Thinking we should report it to the police. It's too much of a coincidence, and seeing they had to let the guy you tackled go free..."

My lungs seized as Kent's last words sunk in.

Go free?

Motherfuck me... So, the cops *had* let that twist walk! Recalling a pair of shifty eyes glaring up from where I'd had that sicko pinned to the ground, I gritted out a barrage of questions, voice harsh.

"They did? When was this? The asshole wasn't charged?"

Big brother started to answer, but before he got a word out, a familiar tangerine-colored Kia drew abreast of the truck and Sunshine's face filled my vision. Rocking a prim blouse instead of trademark strappy sundress, she gawped through her window at me. Then, past my shoulder. And her plush pink lips formed a shocked "O."

A tick or two of silence descended as my blood pounded thick in my veins.

Holy hell, is my angel something. So bright, so beautiful. And Jesus Christ, I've missed her so damned—

Before I could complete the thought, those big peepers flashed back to me, narrowing to slits of chocolate between their thick lashes. Cheeks flushed, Sunshine tensed her jaw, addressing her brother while butchering me with drilling death lasers.

"Christopher? What on Earth are you doing in this… In this *peeping pervert's* truck?"

Ah, fuck.

"Peeping pervert." Okay, that sounded bad. *Reeeeal* bad.

The man riding shotgun sucked in a breath, and I saw, out the corner of my eye, Brother Kent's fists bunch as he barked out an incredulous and outraged reply.

GRAVEDIGGER

"Wha... Cassie, what? *What* the hell did you just say?"

Ah, shit.

I braced myself, watching one of those curled fists twitch.

Get ready for it.

Mean right hook coming straight atcha, Digger.

CASEY: TWELVE

"So. Come on, girl. Let's hear it. You've been here five days already and we know diddly-squat 'bout 'cha. Condensed version of Casey Rae Kent, computer wunderkind: GO!"

I glanced up from my packed lunch into three grinning faces: two female, one male. Although, no lie, my new coworker Billy Marshall sported more feminine qualities than JoJo and Amy combined. Not a bad thing, just the facts, and I freely acknowledge major envy with regard to the man's wardrobe.

Shoot, those slick kicks he was sporting had to cost more than my whole outfit *and* the one I wore yesterday, combined!

Smoothing a fuchsia-and-olive-patterned tie, No-Filter Bill leaned over like a giraffe, getting in my face.

"Well? Favorite food? Favorite song? Boyfriend? Girlfriend? Both?" He rolled dramatic eyeballs. "And with those sex-kitten looks, don't even *try* to tell me there's no one special, Goldilocks."

A vision of a big, bearded Viking bloomed in my brain and I quashed it to dust, dredging up a smile.

GRAVEDIGGER

"Grilled carnitas quesadillas with jalapeño salsa and dirty rice. 'Free Bird.' And sorry, but I'm as unfettered as the lyrics in that classic tune."

Billy shook his head, brows rising. "Shut the door! No main squeeze? What, have you been hiding under a rock all your life?"

Not until recently. But except for three dreamlike days since June the second? Why, yes, I have.

I tried for a laugh, picking at a romaine leaf peeking out of my turkey wrap.

"Just been busy, I guess."

JoJo poked Amy, chuckling. "Well, we'll have to remedy that, huh, Ames? Don't worry, Kent, we here at Professional Computers Inc. pride ourselves on sampling different happy hours at least thrice a week, including the menfolk that come with them. This summer, the pickins have been fairly dismal, but ever optimistic, we maintain that a positive attitude eventually produces positive results."

She pursed her lips, winking.

"Tonight, we're slumming… An honest-to-goodness dive way up in the seedier section of Main Street known as Mooney's Place. I'm certain you've never heard of it, but trust me, the old geezer owner mixes a mean drink. We oft hang there when the wallets are flat."

Amy chimed in. "Killer Buffalo wings, too. And, bonus… Son of Mooney mans the bar on weekends and Lordy, is the man *hawt*!"

Fanning his olive-green crotch, Billy smirked wickedly.

"Hot? More like summm-*moooooking.* Too bad for me that big stud plays for Team Snatch."

The girls tittered as I silently freaked.

Mooney's Place?

Good thing I wasn't chawing on Cajun-seasoned cold cuts at the moment, because I surely would've choked.

I stuck a regretful grin on my puss, gesturing to the sea of papers spread around my computer. "Uh. That sound's nice, but I really need to get my first project in the bag. And, er, my mom's expecting me home for dinner tonight, after I finish."

"Your *mom*? *Home?*" Billy scoffed, waving manicured fingers at the big picture windows.

"Are you nuts, lady? It's freaking Friday! Take a gander outside, at that splendiferous day. Damn, it's bad enough us tech geeks are trapped in this wall-to-wall-carpeted nightmare for eight hours straight. You can't be possibly go manga on meatloaf with your mama when happy hour beckons!"

GRAVEDIGGER

Wow. How the heck had he known it was meatloaf night?

Amy tilted her head, a puzzled frown crinkling her brow.

"Er. You don't actually still *live* with your parents, do you, Casey?"

I flushed, grabbing for my sweet tea. "Um, yeah. Just for the moment, though. Just until me and my sist... Uh, just until I save up enough for a condo in a new complex I have my eye on."

Billy sprang on my slip-up, waggling those expressive brows.

"Oooh, you have a *sister*? Is she as gorgeous as you?"

If that shit hadn't gone down with Gravedigger just when I was beginning to see light again, I honestly think I could've held it together. But because I was so despondent, in such a bad place, I blinked twice and burst into loud, messy tears.

"She's... She's DEAD!"

"Oh, *sweetie*..."

Next thing I knew, three pairs of arms were enfolding me, and I was rocked against two sets of squishy boobs and one set of semi-squishy moobs. I must have wailed for a solid five minutes until I eventually ran out of saline, rolling backward on rubber wheels and wiping my eyes.

"S… sorry."

Hiccupping out the apology, I squinted through swollen lids at the shocked and sorrowful expressions stamped on my coworkers' faces. Then past them, to the dozen other rubbernecking office heads turned my way.

Crap. I could only imagine the sight I presented. Red-nosed and streamy-eyed, cheeks all puffy and blotched. Fantastic impression for your first week on the job, Broom Hilda.

I fumbled for a tissue, blowing into it none too softly. Oh yes, we are talking a very unpretty crier here, people. I should know; I've had enough practice lately.

Billy moved first, rounding my desk in his shiny Salvatore Ferragamo loafers. Patting my shoulder like a dog, he made soothing shushing sounds, reaching across the desk for my tea.

"Shhh. Shhh. Shhh. It's okay. Take a sip, honey. Settle down."

He lowered to his haunches, hazel-hued orbs holding mine sternly.

"You listen to me, Casey Kent. You are going to give me your mother's number. I am going to call her and tell her to pack up your dinner for lunch leftovers.

GRAVEDIGGER

You are going to duck into the little girl's room and make repairs, while I go work my charms and get Mr. Simmons to give you the remainder of the day off."

His eyes slewed sideways and up.

"Well, give you, me, *and* these two hoochie mamas the remainder of the day off."

One eyelid dropped in a wink. "Boss Man owes my tight ass, after that sweet contract I reeled in for him last week. Once we're sprung, the four of us are going to squeeze into a rideshare and head on over to Mooney's, where we will partake in Hottie Bartender's heavy pours and ingest an obscene amount of fried chicken parts on his scrungy back patio. I'll even let you have all the drumsticks, a generosity I don't bestow even on my own wing-loving grandma."

Billy took a breather, tipping his coiffed head sideways.

"Sound like a plan?"

I sniveled loudly, fingers scrabbling for my handbag.

"O...Okay."

Shit, why the hell not? I was sorta sick of meatloaf, anyhow. Besides, after all the shot-drinking bonding that went down between Mitch Tirone and me two weeks ago, the man's sure to roll out the red carpet. Or, at the very least, slice me up a few extra orange wedges.

Peeping up through swollen lids, I smiled a watery smile.

"Yes, Billy. Yes, I'm in."

🪦 🪦 🪦

"Whew... These suckers are spiiiiiii-*ceeee!*"

Amy dropped another stripped chicken bone onto the graffitied picnic-style tabletop, wiping her shiny face. JoJo the Vegan snorted, her smooth Black skin unmarred by globules of greasy fat.

"Girl, you are inhaling those nasty things like a truck driver. Between you and Billyboy, you're gonna start sproutin' feathers. Save some for Case; she's hardly had any."

I scrunched up my nose, eyeing high-calorie morsels swimming in puddles of hot sauce.

"That's all right, Jo. I'm not really hungry."

On the other hand, I've been reeeeally thirsty.

Billy followed my gaze to the trio of drained glasses lined up in front of me. Tipping his chin, he chuckled, a half-empty Cosmo glass clasped in his hand. "Ready for another, my pretty?"

GRAVEDIGGER

I grinned back in the gathering dusk, sucking on a lemon rind. "Hmm, not sure. I've already had three…"

Slurping down a swallow, he snorted around pink liquor and ice cubes. "Big deal! What's three Cuba Libres in as many hours?" He motioned toward the wings. "Scarf down a few of those babies to soak up the booze. Hell, no one's getting behind a wheel, the night is young, and the joint's just starting to fill up."

Mischievous eyes darted around the crowded patio to the bar's back door, where more imbibers were jammed in the interior shadows.

"Who knows… Maybe we'll all meet our dream men before the clock strikes midnight!"

Amy guffawed, stabbing a carrot stick in blue cheese dressing. "You're a whore, Marshall. I'm thinking Timothy wouldn't be too happy with your indiscriminate ass right now—eyeing up every Tom, Dick, and Harry who walks by."

She bit down on the veggie, snapping off two-thirds.

"Emphasis on *Dick*."

Billy shrugged, not the slightest bit shamed.

"Pshaw. You know Timmybear and I enjoy an open and trusting relationship. And you should talk. Cast your mind back a few weeks to that nefarious biker bar, where you stuck your slutty tong—"

Flushing around her freckles, Amy cut him off. "Yeah, let's not go there. Didn't we agree what happens after one too many shots of Tito's stays with one too many shots of Tito's? Besides, we haven't finished grilling our adorable newbie yet."

She jabbed an orange nub at me, a raunchy smile creasing her face.

"I, for one, am particularly interested in hearing more tidbits concerning Ms. Kent's three unattached brothers. If they are even half as blessed by the Good Gene Fairy as her lucky butt is, I need to wrangle a meet 'n' greet, stat."

JoJo raised her arm, waggling it in the air.

"Me too. Me too!"

Billy joined in, those eyebrows of his all over the place.

"Me three! Me three!"

I had to laugh; the vision of my handsome, wholly hetero siblings squirming under Billy Marshall's lascivious stare quite the amusing one. Even as I pictured it, the man in question stood up, swaying slightly as he gestured to our dead soldiers.

"I'm heading in to beseech Stud Man behind the bar for another round and his private phone number. Ames, drop that wing, come up for air, and help me carry. Jo, you stay here and make it your mission to unearth more deets about Casey's brothers. Try to ascertain their shoe sizes, because you know what they say. Big shoes, big..."

"La, la, la."

Bleating out the syllables, I stuck hands over ears, fumbling to my feet.

"No, Ame, I'll go. And let me do the ordering, B. You saw with your own eyeballs that Mitch and I are thick as thieves. Didn't I tell you he'd treat us right?"

Yes, I had, right after we'd crossed Mooney's scuzzy threshold. And talk about surprising the troops... Not only could my brand-new buddies not believe I'd actually tied one on in this dank dungeon before, but that the well-built playboy manning the bottles had greeted me with a huge smile and a smack on the cheek. (He'd tried for the kisser, but I'd been too fast.)

Gawping with saucer-wide eyes, Billy had almost fallen out of his designer loafers!

"Come on. I've got this one." Grabbing two twenties out of my bag, I motioned for Marshall to make tracks. He did and I followed, the two of us weaving through the throngs, my Bacardi buzz rendering me pleasantly mellow.

Crazy times... If anybody had told me this morning as I donned duds for my just-secured computer programming gig that I'd be pickling my liver with a passel of foul-minded coworkers at the very ginmill where Clint "Gravedigger" MacGregor had dropped his creepy bomb, I'd have eaten my shorts.

Good thing I was sporting a thong.

Running fingers through uncombed curls, I locked my sights on Billy's fast-moving back, struggling to keep up. Struggling to exorcise that hateful name from my brain.

Clint.

Gravedigger.

Clint.

Gravedigger.

No!

I walked faster, the alcohol in my veins spurring me. Shorts or thong, I had to hand it to Billy; this drink fest was just what the doc ordered. At first, when the Uber had pulled up to Mooney's, I'd second-guessed my acquiescence. Questioned how wise it was to hang with folks I barely knew, sucking down spirits at a down-and-dirty watering hole that held both super sexy memories and a wrenching betrayal.

That dark, back-corner booth. Unloading to Clint, opening up my heart to a hunky, sympathetic stranger. Experiencing all those hot, burning glances and those even hotter kisses.

The parking lot, in his truck. The huge jerk slipping up, admitting he'd been spying on me for weeks. Had

GRAVEDIGGER

been perving on me every Saturday while I wept salty tears over my sister's grave.

"Damn, mama... Check out the goodies at nine o'clock!"

A lechy aside knocked me back to the present, and I followed Billy's gaze to a gaggle of guys leaning against the wall. They looked like rugby players or something, heavy into the brews.

Spewing out a series of lewd sounds, my companion screeched to a halt, causing me to crash against his lavender-shirted spine.

"Oooh, la, la, what a cornucopia! Okay... Buff and blond for me. Bespectacled and hot-nerdy for Jo. Irish tough for our redheaded, wing-hogging Ames. And tall, dark, and ha-ha-ha-handsome for my new bestie, the beauteous Casey Rae Kent!"

I rolled my eyes, shoving him forward.

"Dude. I hardly know you, but I have to agree with Amy... You are indeed a manwhore. I've half a mind to call your Timothy and tell him what a hound dog he's hitched to."

Billy smirked over his shoulder, fluttering unrepentant lashes.

"*Unofficially* hitched, until I get my big rock. And I say: if you've got it, flaunt it, sweet cheeks."

We rassled our way to the bar and I caught Mitch's eye, waving my moolah. Even though he was knee-deep in thirsty clientele, he buzzed right over, pissing off two girls squashed next to me who clearly had been waiting awhile.

"Hey, beautiful, what'll you have? The same? Extra fruit?"

"Yes, thanks. Also, another Cosmo, a Guinness, and a Sauvignon with ice."

Deep blue eyes caressed me, sweeping up and down. "You got it, darlin'."

"Oh, dear God. The man wants into your pretty panties so bad, it's not even *funny."*

Billy's unquiet bulletin tickled my ear, and I glared at him. This, while also trying to avoid focused death rays from the empty-handed brunette to my left.

Hissing, I set him straight.

"He does not! I told you when we got here that we're just friends. He helped me through a dark patch a couple of weeks ago, that's all."

"Riiiiiight." Billy shook his head, a superior look spreading over his face.

"Puh-lease, Casey. I may be gay, but I know a guy's lust for a lady when I see it. You're out of your mind it you think all that sexy thang wants to do is cut up slices of citrus for you."

GRAVEDIGGER

He paused for effect, mouth twitching.

"I'd say popping your cherry is a tad higher on his agenda."

"Billy!" I choked out his name, my cheeks aflame.

"What, I'm wrong? If so, you'd better alert Timmybear. He swears I can tell a virgin from twenty paces, be it male or female. So far, the stats haven't lied."

My skin burned hotter. "I...You... I..."

Mr. No-Filter smirked wider, licking his finger and jabbing it in the air.

"Oooh, yassss. And his streak continues."

"Here ya go, love." Moonlighter plunked down four glasses, smiling into my eyes. I handed him my twenties, and he took them slowly, his forefinger sliding over my palm.

"You need more fruit, you let me know." Winking, the handsome bottle man traced slow circles. "You need *anything*, you let me know."

"Uh. Thanks."

He released me and headed down the bar, hips rolling like he was auditioning for The Chippendales. I wiped a tingling palm on my skirt as Billy leered at me, nodding sagely.

"Mmm, hmm. Go ahead. Try and deny it, Kent."

A pissy voice cut in as the brunette next to me jabbed my arm, cheapo fake lashes narrowed.

"Just so you know, bitch, you freaking cut us. We were here first."

Her tall blond sidekick picked up the thread, sticking a pair of WonderBra'd tits in my face.

"Yeah, bitch. We've been standing here waiting on a refill for, like, ten freaking minutes."

Aiming for a look of sheepish contrition, I scooped up my drink and JoJo's wine, motioning for Billy to grab the rest.

"Er, sorry. 'Lighter asked for my order, and I…"

"Oooh, *'Lighter*, huh? Boinking the guy, huh? That's how come you get preferred service, huh?"

I gaped at WonderBra, my ears going hot.

"*Excuse* me?"

Billy shoved his nattily clad chest between us, getting in their faces.

"Tut, tut, tut. Ladies, let us not overlook the fact that, unlike you two, my friend here is a dick magnet with a capital 'DICK.' It's not her fault you got passed over. Consider this a life lesson learned."

Stunned, I watched him flick disdainful glances right and left, his eyebrows arched.

GRAVEDIGGER

"A little constructive criticism? Lose the drugstore lashes and the Walmart wardrobe. It could go a long way in helping you two—"

"Fuck you, Fruitcake!"

The taller one lunged for Billy, grabbing his tie. I yelped, sloshing the drinks back on the bar as I attempted to drag him from her acrylic-nailed clutches. Meanwhile, the brunette joined in, digging her claws in my hair and pulling, *hard*.

"Ouuuucchhhh!"

Tears of pain stung my eyes as I struggled to escape, windmilling backward. I landed against a huge, hard, granite-like wall, coming to an abrupt stop. Hair follicles smarting, I shoved my attacker away, feeling the wall behind me shift and heat up.

Wait a sec.

Shift? Heat up?

Holding my breath, I groped blindly. My fingertips met soft fabric and more heat, and I spun around, blinking at a muddy gray T-shirt hugging a taut, wide chest, heavy on the muscles.

Oh, Sweet Jesus. I know this chest.

Three voices sounded in my buzzing ears, vying for primacy. The first was feminine and shrill. The second, Billy's, dripped with ill-disguised innuendo.

The third was husky and growly and heart-stoppingly familiar.

"Get back here, bitch!"

"Oooh, la, la, la, laaaaah! *Hellooooo,* handsome!"

"Hey, Sunshine. Need some help?"

DIGGER: THIRTEEN

"Let's go somewhere else, man. It looks crowded as fuck here."

Two footsteps from Mooney's crappy door, Sledge shot me an "Are you serious," look over his shoulder, grinning like a pirate.

"All the better for checkin' out the scenery. This saloon may not be reeking of class, but my man Mitch has been known to draw in some decent booty on the weekends. Besides, it ain't like either one of us are exactly suited up for swankier environs, bro."

My buddy glanced down at his oil-stained shirt before quirking a brow at my equally filthy tee, splotched with cemetery soil and the same rancid furnace grease as his. White teeth flashed as he laughed, shoving the door open with a big mitt.

"Digger of graves and salvager of old houses... Damn, we make a real pretty pair, huh? Here's hoping Tirone's lights are half burned-out as usual, and the chicks are suitably lit."

Resigned, I followed Sledgehammer/aka Joe Jaggard into the teeming throng, squinting into the murk as I forced my eyeballs not to swerve to the far back corner and all its spectacular memories.

Me and Sunshine plastered together in that dark, secluded booth. Making out like mad, her juicy tits pressed against my heart, her sugar-sweet tongue licking mine…

My lonely cock twitched and I adjusted discreetly. Not that anyone would notice if I stuck my hand in my pants, pulled my prick out, and started playing with myself; the joint was that jam-packed. I gritted my jaw, trailing my companion as Joe made tracks for the bar. Fighting through a sweaty mass of bodies, second thoughts assailed me, stabbing in my skull.

Fuck. Why had I let myself get talked into a night out with my house-dismantling amigo? Allowed the Man with the Sledgehammer to wrangle me back to the last place I'd seen Sunshine in the flesh? Both of us unwashed and filthy, coming straight from that money pit he'd been tearing apart? Jesus, we look like a couple of homeless bums.

Reading my mind, Joe slowed down for a sec, socking my arm.

"Didn't I tell you? It's dark as hell in here. Trust me, nobody in this zoo can tell we've been goin' mano a mano with a century-old house part for the last two hours, nor do they care."

He jabbed me again, picking up the pace.

"Come on, man, make haste… A spot just opened up on the other side of the bar, and it's calling our

GRAVEDIGGER

names. And remember, MacGregor: drinks on me tonight, *all* night. If it wasn't for your additional manpower, I'd still be slaving solo on that cunt of a boiler."

I nodded, trying to get into the spirit. "Won't hear me complaining 'bout that."

Not hardly. I could use some liquid numbness, for sure. After the shitty, Sunshine-less two weeks I've suffered through? Hell, a whole fucking fifth won't be enough.

We plowed our way to the tiny patch of vacated real estate Joe had spied, the crowd parting for our six-foot-plus frames like we were two Moseses in a sea of lushes. Reaching our destination, I leaned sideways against the counter, acknowledging that sometimes, it really pays to be an oversized motherfucker.

"Right on! A perfect vantage point from which to view the passing parade, huh, Dig?"

Joe smiled rakishly, pulling out his leather as he flagged down the bar's second-gen namesake. Naturally, I recognized Mr. Happiness in his stained apron, me being somewhat of a regular. Not that 'Lighter and I were tight, not the way he and Sledgie were, being in the same line of work and all.

Personally, I considered Tirone a dick, a prick of the highest order. How a sourpuss like him ended up moonlighting as a bartender was a joke, family business or not. If you ask me, the guy should stick to hard-wiring houses or whatever the hell he did when he wasn't pouring. Or landing a gig in a graveyard, same as my unsociable ass.

I watched him from beneath hooded lids, recalling how he'd fawned all over Sunshine, loading her up with those damned orange rinds. My teeth gritted, molars gnashing.

Yeah. Not a prick to all of his clientele, though, is he? Not, for instance, to a certain rarity gracing his dive rocking sexy blond curls and pornworthy lips.

"Yo, Mitchie, how's it hangin'? Finish gutting out that barn on Sycamore yet, ya lazy fuck? Give us two Jacks, heavy on the hooch and easy on the ice."

After naming our poison and throwing down a wad of cash, Sledge swiveled his head like a hoot owl, eyes busy.

"Well, Clintie? See anything strikes your fancy yet?"

I grunted, shrugging. "Nah. And anyway, I'm not in the mood. I told you back at that money pit you're tearing apart; I'd have been happy to order us a coupla hoagies and a twelve-pack, put our feet up and—"

"Fuck that noise!"

Interrupting, he snorted, grabbing for the glasses Tirone slammed down in front of us. Shoving one in

GRAVEDIGGER

my face, Sledge sucked down a third of the other, wiping his mouth and smirking.

"You think I wanna be sittin' around some ball-busting rehab project with *your* nasty cemetery bones when there's fresh tail to be had? Shit, guy: it's Friday night, and you ain't my type."

A finger stabbed against my chest, poking twice. "And aren't you the man whining not so long ago over what a dry spell you've been havin'? Remember, chief? At this very bar, not three weeks ago, after you helped me haul away that beast of a bathtub?"

I flushed, vaguely recalling the boozy night of which he spoke.

Very vaguely recalling.

Damn, that's what happens when your buddy plies you with copious shots of Jägermeister... You let your guard down and start spewin' about your sex life. Or, lack thereof.

Shrugging again, I took a healthy glug of amber, avoiding said buddy's all-seeing eyes.

"Yeah, well, maybe that dry spell's over now."

Those green orbs widened as Joe's grin turned raunchy.

"Yeah? Do tell, friend. What, you hooked up and didn't let ol' Sledgie know? Who was it? A one-time thing, or you still banging her ass? We talking big tatas, small tatas, or in-between tatas? Come on, brother, spill."

My hand tightened around my glass as I gruffed out a reply, strangely enraged.

"Screw you. I'm not tellin' you shit."

Mainly because there's nothing to tell. Not anymore, there isn't.

The big perv didn't let up, elbowing me. "Ah, come on, Digger. Blond or brunette? Carpet match the drapes, or shaved to the skin?"

My eyes burned, his words bugging the shit out of me.

"Shut the hell up, Jaggard."

Exactly why I was so perturbed, I couldn't say. It's not like I'd officially hooked up with Sunshine, not after I'd blown it so royally in this hellhole's parking lot. But the way Hammer was sleazing on about a girl he had no idea existed was enough to make me want to bean my rocks glass over his thick noggin and demand he take those doggish words back.

Fuck me, I was fried. Intent on protecting the honor of a woman whose new name for me was Peeping fucking Tom.

"Hey, fellas. Mind if we sneak in to snag a couple of drinks?"

GRAVEDIGGER

A simpering voice had me pulling head outta ass, and I blinked down at a shortish brunette.

"Uh, sure."

I started to back away from the wood to give her access, and she giggled sloppily, pressing her hand against my chest.

"No, no, nooooo... I don' want to *displace* you, handsome! I can jus' squeeze in here and..."

Pronouncing 'displace' more like 'displashe,' she plastered herself against me none too subtly and I frowned, catching Joe's amused eye over her hair-sprayed mall bangs. One brow lifted as he assessed her cleavage, flauntingly displayed in a spangly, low-cut top. I looked, too, super-quick.

Hard not too, seeing her mammaries were propped on my tee like a pair of jiggly gelatin molds.

Ugh. Flabby and white. Nothing like Sunshine's firm, sun-kissed little beauties.

Flapping my hand, I took a step back, bumping against the clutch of bodies behind me.

"No, go ahead. I'll give you more room."

Another annoying voice hit my ears, this time from the other side.

"Hey, Stace! Leave it to you to find the baddest asses in the place the second I duck into the Ladies'. Introductions stat, you whore!"

A long string bean burst through the crowd, the chick's yellow hair all frizzed out and her puss slathered with more makeup than a circus clown's. The warpaint was obvious, despite the dim lighting and the fact that her rouged face was at the moment tipped sideways and south, checking out Jaggard's junk.

This time it was me who crooked a brow, enjoying the panicky look distorting my compadre's mug as he angled away from that avaricious stare. Without difficulty, I read Joeyboy's mind as he examined the cluttered bar top in tender, loving detail:

No. Fucking. Way.

I swallowed a wry laugh, half-tempted to whip out my cell and document the unprecedented occasion. Wow, talk about one for the record books… Joe "I'll nail anything with a twat" Jaggard actually turning down a green light come-on?

Must be those freaky-ass eyelashes.

Taking pity, I grabbed his arm.

"Let's leave these primo spots to the ladies, man, and check out the tables. I think I clock Scott Henderson over there, and his talentless ass is due for its monthly thrashing."

Clown Face protested, her sticky-looking lips turning down.

GRAVEDIGGER

"No, don't go! There's plenty of room here for a cozy foursome. Huh, Stace?"

Her runty sidekick nodded, slurring out an affirmation as her jelly molds quivered against my tee.

"Yeah, don' rush off to play shum schtupid game of pool. Let ush buy you guysh a wittle drinkie-winkie, instead."

Ah, Christ, this chick's more wasted than I thought. And now she drags out the baby talk? Save me, Jesus.

Sledge cleared his throat, sticking a regretful expression on his mug. "Sorry, girls. We'd love to, but we're already committed to the green felt." Throwing me a grateful look, he saluted the stewballs, tossing another tenner onto the bar.

"Have a coupla shots on us. Enjoy the rest of your evening. C'mon, Dig."

I didn't need a second invite and we swiftly took our leave, making tracks toward the back of the room and Tirone's trio of beat-up, uneven tables. As we shoved our way through the crowd, Joe blew out a breath, laughing.

"Fuck, what a coupla train wrecks. And all that makeup, shee-it! Thanks for the save, hoss... Fast thinking."

My reply was snarky. "Still surprised you didn't bite, ya dog." I smirked at him in the murk, ramping up the crude-dude bullshit. Not my usual style, but after those earlier comments of his, I was feeling sorta pissy.

"Dontcha keep a stash of wet wipes in your rig? You could've used 'em to scrap off the face paint before you banged Frizzy in the back seat. Dark enough outside now, anyway… You wouldn't have seen squat."

Hammer chuckled, simulating a shudder. "God no, man. Contrary to popular opinion, I do have a *modicum* of taste. That troller back there?"

He clenched his fist, miming a jacking motion.

"Slick, this is one of those rare cases when Rosie Five Fingers is preferable to the real thing. Not to mention, I just had my truck detailed."

I shook my head. "Fuckin' dog."

Our laughter intermingled as we hit the tables, but it died out fast when we discovered the wait list was a mile long. Sledgie attempted to bribe a few sharks we knew to cut in, but he was shot down by all and sundry. We stood there looking at each other for a few ticks before we shrugged, hoofing it back to the bar.

This time, to the opposite side of the wood.

Me? I could've happily hit the road and headed back to my crib. But seeing as how the drinks were on the

GRAVEDIGGER

house tonight on account of my helping hands, I decided to hang in.

What the hell. Sooner or later, the tables will open up and I'll kick Henderson's ass, score some sweet bread. And what's waiting at home anyhow, except a mountain of filthy clothes, a sinkful of crummy dishes, and a rumpled bed with no bright angel tangled in the sheets?

Naturally, there was no bar space to be had this time around; our last break an anomaly. Nope, Prickhead's clientele had now swelled to a good three-deep, and I sighed, labeling myself and Joe crackheads not to have snagged a backup when we'd had the chance. Eerily, my amigo voiced that very thought, letting loose a mighty barrage of F-bombs.

"Fuck, look at this fucking pack! Fuckin' shudda stayed where we were, fucking train wrecks or not. Look, man: let's split up and see who fucking lucks out first. You go back on the other side and see if you score faster getting that rookie's attention."

Sledge jerked his chin over at Tirone's backup, a frantic-looking college kid fumbling with the beer taps.

Suddenly he let loose a low whistle, following it up with a dirty chuckle.

"Whoa. On second thought, *you* stay here and *I'll* go. I'm seeing something I'm *definitely* willing to mess up my clean back seat for. Mess it up nice and nasty, oh yeah."

He licked his lips and I rolled my eyes, following his fixed, greedy stare. All I saw was a shadowy scrum of imbibers, indistinct in the haze.

The contractor made more sleazy noises, his tongue practically sweeping the floor.

"*Day-um.* Ya see her? The hot little blonde with the do-me curls? Never saw *her* in these parts before. Believe me, I'd have remembered. Dude with her is totally gay, so I'll just saunter on over and see if I can't turn on the old Sledgehammer charm and score me a pillow mate for the night."

The crowd shifted, and just like that I was gaping through the gloom at Casey Rae Kent—her beautiful face laughing and her sexy bod trussed up in a prissy blouse and dark, formfitting skirt. My mouth fell open and I grabbed Joe's elbow, shoving him back.

"No! I know that girl. I'm gonna go over and say hey. You stay the hell here."

Stay here is right. No fucking way do I want your lechy ass anywhere near my gorgeous angel.

Sledge barked out an incredulous laugh, brows high.

"Huh? You fucking *know* that fox, MacGregor? How, where? Holy shit, don't even *tell* me your lucky dick has nailed her fine—"

GRAVEDIGGER

I didn't hear the rest. I was already wading through the revelers, my heart slamming like a bitch. Good thing I hadn't heard the rest, either, because there was no doubt that roundhouse I'd been itching to throw earlier would've connected with Jaggard's jabbering jawbone, *hard.*

Swiping hunks of hair back, I circled the bar, confused as fuck. A medley of questions bombarded my brain, piling one on top of another.

Have I fallen and hit my head? Am I fucking dreaming? Sunshine is here, at Tirone's skanky hole-in-the-wall? Why? Can she possibly be hoping to see me again?

I bit back a bitter laugh, acknowledging how pathetic that pipedream was.

Yeah, right, fool. If that's the case, she would've returned any one of your two dozen calls, no? The lady's just slumming, returning to the joint where she corkscrewed your heart. Maybe her plan is to let that oaf behind the bar drool all over her ass and cut up oranges and lemons, so she can suck them off in his enraptured face.

As I neared my quarry, a heinous notion occurred to me, causing my chest to constrict.

Fuck my life, she called the guy good-looking. She damn well did. Holy hell, maybe Sunshine and Tirone the Clod are a thing now. Maybe she's hanging her sweet petunia around 'til closing time, so pretty boy can lock up and she can get busy sucking on something el—

Slamming that door shut before completing the hideous thought, I peered through the scrum at Sunshine's sidekick—a skinny fashionista-type dude decked out in a purple dress shirt, green stovepipe denim, and a pansy pink necktie. Running fast eyes up and down, I let my shoulders loosen a fraction as I mentally agreed with Hammer.

Yup, gay as Elton. No judgement, but thank you Jesus. One less man to hurt.

I was a yardstick and change away when a slurry, semi-familiar voice pierced over the classic Who tune pounding out the speakers.

"Just so you know, bitch, you freaking cut us. We were here first."

A second, slightly less bombed voice chimed in.

"Yeah, bitch. We've been standing here waiting on a refill for, like, ten freaking minutes."

Honing in, I spied the pair of trollers who'd been all over me and my bud a few minutes back, weaving like a pair of wobbly bowling pins next to Sunshine. Resembling Mutt and Jeff from the old comic strip minus the mustaches (I think), they were getting right in her angel face.

Sunshine tried to back up, an apologetic smile curving her luscious lips.

GRAVEDIGGER

"Er, sorry. 'Lighter asked for my order, and I…"

The blond one interrupted, her tone rife with scorn.

"Oooh, *'Lighter*, huh? Boinking the guy, huh? That's how come you get preferred service, huh?"

My fists curled as Ms. Huh voiced the sickening thought I'd just entertained. Sunshine gasped, hissing between her teeth.

"*Excuse* me?"

A small caravan of partyers shoved in front of me, and I lost sight of her for a second, half-hearing her rainbow-garbed companion spout something snarky back. The bits and pieces I could make out didn't sound too flattering, and next thing I knew, the frizzy-haired girl had hold of his tie.

"Fuck you, Fruitcake!"

I slammed forward, ending up directly behind Sunshine as the witch's wingwoman lunged for her own victim, sticking curved claws into a mop of messy blond curls.

"Ouuuucchhhh!"

Sunshine bawled, stumbling backward. She landed against me hard, little fingers reaching behind her hips to explore my waist. The sensation of those stroking digits was both pleasure and pain, and I held my breath, dying to grab hold of her and never let her go.

Instead, I cleared my throat, croaking out five words as she spun around, staring up at me with saucer-wide eyes.

"Hey, Sunshine. Need some help?"

"C… Clint?"

She sounded as dazed as I felt as we stood staring at each other, her fingers still on me. Dimly, I heard *GQ* Guy and the two bar hags squaring off, but all I could really hear, all I could really see, was *her*. My beautiful, golden angel, right here in front of me for the first time in two torturous, agonizing weeks.

I swallowed hard, trying like hell not to eyefuck her.

But Jesus, that tight little fucktease of a skirt she had on—!

My reply gruffed out like pea gravel squeezed through a rusty funnel.

"Yeah, it's me. Hey."

Christ. I sound like a goddamned half-wit.

Clearing my throat again, I gestured to her prim-but-sexy-as-fuck outfit.

"You, uh, you look different. The, uh, the way that you're dressed."

Sunshine's cheeks turned rosy as she glanced away, stepping back and regrettably removing her hands from my earth-stained shirt.

GRAVEDIGGER

"Er, yeah. I just landed a new job, a pretty good one, in computer programming. We, um, that is, me and my coworkers came here right after."

She jerked her chin at her colorful cohort, Mr. Green Jeans, deep into it with the skanks.

"That's one of them, Billy."

"Great." I nodded, happy for Casey that she was making what sounded like huge strides coming out of her grief, unhappy as fuck that I wasn't in her life anymore to share that healing.

An awkward silence commenced. Sunshine and I took this opportunity to try and catch the tail end of *GQ's* diatribe. Whatever the guy said, it worked, because Mutt and Jeff abruptly slammed their empties onto the bar, making motions to leave. The tall one grabbed her friend's arm, sneering in our faces.

"That's it. We don't *need* to stand here and get insulted. Come on, Stace... This place frigging sucks! Let's head over to Bud's Alley Bar, where people have some freaking CLASS."

Class? Yeah, you and Sloshy are full of the stuff, you cock-staring bitch.

Watching them lurch away, I could have laughed. Well, if I didn't have a raging hard-on that I was trying to hide, sprung from merely inhaling Sunshine's intoxicating, honey-sweet scent.

A self-righteous bleat blasted in my ear as her workmate swung a length of pink and green silk under my nose.

"Thank Baby Jesus in Diapers those nasty hoes are gone! Lord, just *look* how that Walmart-wearing nightmare mutilated my brand-new Missoni!"

Swiftly changing tacks, *GQ* Guy laid a palm on my arm, squeezing.

"So. You and Casey are acquainted, handsome? Rather well, if I were to guess. Mmm, hmm, isn't *she* the lucky one! Even with that messy mud smeared on you and all that shaggy hair, I certainly wouldn't kick your yummy bones out of *my* bed."

"BILLY!"

Squawking the name, Sunshine flushed, her cheeks as red as mine felt after hearing his "thanks-but-no-thanks" newsflash. Mumbling, she flapped a hand between my grimy getup and his mangled neckwear.

"Uh. Billy Marshall, Clint MacGregor."

"Oooh, what a manly moniker! *Cliiiint Macgregorrrrr...* Suits you to a 'T,' big boy."

Marshall chuckled, scooping an assortment of drinks off the bar.

"I'll just run along now, and deliver our concoctions to the troops out back. It may not be easy singlehandedly, but I knows sparks when I sees *'*em."

GRAVEDIGGER

He made a show of fluttering his lashes, pursing grinning lips.

"And mercy, lords and ladies, do I *see* 'em!"

With that, he exited stage left with hands full, throwing a parting shot over his shoulder.

"If you're not riding home with us, shoot me a text, Case. Trust me, bi-atch, I'll *tooooe-tally* understand!"

He disappeared into the crowd while Sunshine and I continued to make like a couple of department store mannequins, scores of oblivious A-holes jostling us from all sides. Her tight little tits lifted behind demure cream fabric as she sucked in a breath, the color on her cheeks deepening.

I held my own oxygen in seized-up lungs, terrified to twitch an eyelash in case she up and bolted.

Please don't tell me to hit the road, angel. Please, I'll never fuckin' survive.

Gaze fixated on my shoulder, she addressed dirty cotton, speaking stiltedly.

"Um, Clint… It's crazy-weird you're here tonight. I want to tell you that I, er, had a slight breakdown at work today. Well, more than slight. Everything sort of snuck up on me, and I seriously lost it for all and sundry to see. Billy and crew were great, but right after, on the way here, I started to think that maybe I was too harsh on you."

She bit her lip with those sexy-gapped teeth, the motion causing my Levis to shrink a size.

"I… I miss you, Gravedigger. And, yeah, I get that it's nuts and all in my head, but more than once over the past few weeks, I heard my sister ream me out for kicking you to the curb without a fair trial."

Sunshine's tongue appeared, making matters worse for me and my dick as she licked shiny pink lips.

"So, Clint…"

She stretched out a hand, stroking my burning forearm.

"Is it too late? Or will you take me back to your place, and we can maybe start over? Hash things out?"

Thick lashes flickered against flushed skin before slowly rising. I stared down, drowning in lustrous brown pools.

God, these fucking eyes.

Tongue to teeth, Sunshine lowered her voice to a teasy whisper.

"I can call my folks, and tell them I'm crashing at Laura Lynn Swanson's again."

CASEY: FOURTEEN

"Ah, girl, your mouth…"

Mumbling against my lips, Clint kicked my legs open, sandwiching me against the back of his front door and the front of his mammoth erection. A velvet-rough tongue performed a wicked dance and I speared my fingers into his hair, nails scratching.

The big guy liked that, groaning deeply. "Yeah, baby. Fuck, yeah…"

I squirmed in his arms, trying to get closer, although a sheet of paper couldn't have fit between us. Same scenario as our just-completed journey from Mooney's, grinding together in that cramped Uber. My pussy clenched, tingling as I recalled blushworthy highlights from the past twenty minutes.

Highlights? Who am I kidding? The entire trip was one gigundous highlight!

Crushed between two unyielding surfaces, I conceded that steamed-up back seats were becoming a thing between Gravedigger and me. A real hot, real sexy, real panty-wetting kind of a thing. And cripes, that poor driver… Incredibly, the same dude who'd chauffeured us two weeks prior.

Lord, the man was going to need hypnosis to forget the raunchy double features he'd seen!

And heard.

"Taste so fine… Skin like fucking silk… Gonna eat you alive, baby, every square inch…"

Fragments of uncensored comments seared my brain, causing my thong to dampen further. Dirty boy… Taciturn as he normally was, Mr. M. morphed into quite the chatterbox when gripped in the throes of passion. Didn't seem to give two figs who was listening in, either.

I'm not going to lie. With those kisses and caresses? Neither did I.

"Jesus, baby, my knees… Can't hardly stand. Gotta get you under me."

Clint husked out the update, gripping my skirted bum tight. His palms were two brands, singeing me through thin cotton sateen. Fingers digging into my ass cheeks, he spun us around, half-walking, half-dragging me to The Plaid Beast. I felt the bump of the sofa against my hip, and then he was kissing me again, bending me backward.

"Fuckin' hot little skirt…"

His hands smoothed over the fabric, restless fingers tracing its mid-thigh hem. I panted against his mouth; my own digits clamped to thick, straining biceps.

GRAVEDIGGER

"Ah Christ, Sunshine. We should stop. Talk, like you said…"

Dropping a string of kisses down my neck, Gravedigger groaned against my skin, pushing his pelvis against me. I shook my head, stretching up to cup the back of his neck as I whispered a negative.

"Later…"

Yes, we should talk. Need to talk. But not now. Not while I'm wrapped in your brawny Viking arms. Not when I'm back where I belong, after two endless, miserable weeks.

I licked his mouth and ran my tongue over his teeth, thrilled when another hoarse groan soughed out of his throat.

That's it, Lord Thor. Plenty of time to talk later…

"Damn, baby…"

Clint grabbed my face, angling it between his palms as his kisses turned wild, more desperate. Sexy-wet sounds ensued, exciting me, turning me on like a floodlight. My lips, already swollen from the car ride, stung under a focused assault and I tipped my head back, watching the face so close to mine.

Spiky lashes flicked against my skin as our gazes locked, a flush mantling Clint's cheeks. Growling, he moved one hand to trail slow fingers down my throat, five tips of live flame.

"Baby, Christ. C'mere."

He dragged his lips away, stumbling us around the sofa's arm. Collapsing onto the cushions and pulling me on top of him, he spread his thighs wide, leaning back and positioning me over what felt like an angry anaconda trapped behind his fly. With one forearm wrapped around my waist, he ground me down on it, grunting as it jerked against my behind.

"Feel what you do to me, girl? How hungry I am for your sweet sugar?"

Not waiting on a reply, he pushed my head against his chest, bending for another messy sideways kiss while his palms smoothed down my sides, clamping my hips. He crushed me to him, both of us moaning as that pulsating pole bucked harder.

"Jesus, you make me insane…" Gravedigger groaned the admission, his hand sliding to my stockinged knee. Nudging it, he draped one of my legs over his quad, fingers fiddling with my skirt again. He eased the hem up a few inches, pausing to ask permission in a thick, impeded tone.

"Baby. Baby, can I—"

My heart banged behind my blouse like a wild thing.

You sure can, big guy.

Silently, I lay my hand atop his, pushing crumpled fabric up. Cool air hit me as the top of my thigh-highs made their appearance—the ebony lace trim stark

GRAVEDIGGER

against my paler skin. And then there were my panties...

"Holy *fuuuuuck...*"

The man beneath me drew out the curse, grabbing my chin and staring into my eyes. His own orbs darkened as he licked parted lips, a silver-black gaze darting to my crotch and back.

"Fucking thigh-highs. And a tiny fucking thong, soaked through. You trying to kill me here, woman?"

I blushed top to tail, glancing away from that rigid, ravenous face.

"I, um, with my new job, I figured stockings were more professional. And I, er, I don't care for pantyhose so much, with their waistbands..."

Trailing off, I bit my lip, equally turned-on and embarrassed.

The thick cock tickling my cleft throbbed as Clint pulled my chin back to him.

"Don't look away from me, Sunshine, not ever. I need to look into these beautiful eyes when I tell you I've never seen anything so fuckin' sexy in my entire life."

He scrubbed a hand over his mouth and beard, fingers shaking.

"Can I... Can I touch that pretty lace, baby?"

I'd downed three rum and cokes earlier this evening, but the buzz rendering me dizzy had nothing to do with the diminishing ABV in my bloodstream and everything to do with a burgeoning sense of feminine power as I nodded to the manic-eyed man grinding his jaw and waiting on my blessing.

You've been on me for weeks, so here goes nothing, Bethie.

Recalling all those freakish "forgive him" messages delivered telepathically from my departed twin, I smiled and added the words.

"Yes, Clint. Please."

"Beautiful girl..." His chest expanded, heaving against me as he sank teeth into bottom lip, his unsteady hands lowering to my legs again. I quivered when calloused palms landed on me, half-on and half-off the tops of my stockings. He held them there unmoving, his voice hoarse.

"Baby. You sure you don't wanna talk first, hash shit out? Ream me a new one for spying on you? 'Cause you need to know, the second I move these mitts one centimeter higher, I'm a dead man."

Those stilled hands twitched in tandem with the mighty erection pulsing beneath me.

"Seriously, Sunshine. Maybe we should—"

"Gravedigger." I turned my head, flicking the tip of my tongue against his steaming neck. "I told you,

GRAVEDIGGER

talking later. And, yeah, 'reaming out' is on the agenda. But, right now, I'm not in a chit-chatty mood."

I licked again, nipping the underside of his beard.

"Truthfully, I'm more in a get-ravaged-by-a-Viking kind of a mood."

That was all it took. As soon as the tease was delivered, Clint's mouth was back on mine and his hands were moving on my skin, stroking up splayed thighs to brush against my thong. I shivered, seduced by the wonder of his tongue, his teeth, his greedy, biting lips.

His thick fingers, sliding under delicate lace.

"Aw, baby…"

Growling, Gravedigger jostled his knee as he tipped me further back, shoving me wider. I lay across his lap like a boneless doll: breasts full and achy under my prissy blouse, pencil skirt bunched around my waist, high-heeled pumps dangling.

"Skin like fuckin' velvet. Mouth like honey…"

A hesitant forefinger flicked against a drenched slit, and my mighty Viking shuddered, his entire body quaking.

"Goddamn, so juicy for me." Rough skin slid over my waxed pussy, tracing circles. "Sweet little pussy—pink and bald and fuckin' soaked."

Oh my God, this man and his dirty, dirty mouth.

I moaned as Clint added a second finger, shifting, turning us deeper into the corner cushions. Kicking out his legs, he slid lower, his cock a long, iron ridge against my almost-bare butt. His whiskers tickled my neck as he buried his face against it, breathing hard as tentative fingers worked me.

Then, not so tentative.

"That feel good, babe? You like my hands on your sweet cunt? Fuck me, I know I do. Can't wait to get my tongue in on the action."

"Clint!" I gasped, cheeks burning, and he abandoned my neck, drawing back a few inches to smirk in my face as his diabolical digits continued to wreak havoc below. Glittering eyes held mine as he slowly licked his lips, the action swooningly sexy.

"What? You think I'm not gonna make a meal of this fine, tight pussy?"

His fingers slid through my wetness, exploring soft and deep.

"Think I'm not gonna condition my beard with all this delicious cream?"

"Clint!"

I sputtered out another shocked gasp. Skin aflame, I squirmed on his lap but the devil held me fast, a beefy forearm locked against my belly. Lowering his head,

GRAVEDIGGER

he crooned against my cheek, his breath an intoxicating mix of whiskey and mint.

"Well, I got news for you, baby. I plan on having me a sweet, sticky appetizer before we get to the main course."

"Oh, God, Clint, no…!"

Seriously… My skin could not *possibly* get any hotter.

"Oh, God, Clint, yes. But first, I need this mouth again."

He took his other hand, tilting my face as he kissed me savagely, his lips harsh. Helpless to resist, I wrapped my arms around his neck, the strong column damp with sweat. We made out for long, dizzying minutes, one of Clint's hands taut on my jaw, the other buried beneath my saturated thong.

"Fuck!"

Barking the curse, he shifted and slid me off him sideways, laying my boneless bod flat on itchy upholstery. He loomed large, shoving his hair back, his darkened eyes lasering my lips, my boobs, my…

"Oh!"

I yelped as a thick wrist twisted, tearing my thong from my hips and tossing the scraps to the carpet. Gravedigger stared down, breathing like a dying man as he gritted a warning between clenched teeth.

"Last chance, angel." He scrubbed a hand over his mouth. "Talk, or ravage?"

"No brainer, Sissy. Door number two, all the way!"

Beth's sly tones whispered in my ear and I smiled up at six-foot something of sweaty, agonized-looking male. Moving my fingers to the tops of my thigh-highs, I watched Clint's face tauten as I traced minute circles, taking my sweet-ass time in answering.

"Um… Let's see."

Like a seasoned minx, I drew one stocking a few inches south, at the same time subtlety widening my legs.

"I think… Ravage."

A strangled sound choked out of Clint's throat, his wide eyes gobbling up my exposed, glistening pussy. Cheekbones ruddy, he stared fixedly, hissing out two words.

"Fuck meeeee..."

Scarcely believing my boldness, I licked my lips, tasting Essence of Hot Gravedigger.

"All righty, sounds good. I thought you'd never ask."

Those sexy silvers stretched wider as my meaning sank in. To make certain there was no misunderstanding, I leveled a gaze at the huge bulge riding down his thigh, my fingers continuing to fiddle with black lace.

GRAVEDIGGER

"Unless you want to play Hearts, or something?"

"Little witch…" In a swift motion, Clint jackknifed up, crouching low to snatch me off the sofa. Clasping me high against his muddy shirt, he strode out of the living room and down the hall, muttering unintelligible garble as he headed for his bedroom. I uttered not a peep of protest, nuzzling his neck as he kicked open the door and flicked on the light.

Two seconds later, I was tossed onto a big unmade bed, the sheets all rumpled and deliciously scented. Bouncing once, I lay panting in the middle of the mattress, staring up.

Oh, my.

Big, dark, and bearded, Gravedigger was the very epitome of a marauding Viking, complete with dirty duds and wicked ink. Breathing hard, he ran incendiary eyes up and down my bod, lingering on heaving breasts and a bunched-up skirt. Deliberately, I made a show of kicking my heels off, sending them airborne to land on the clothes-littered carpet.

Those glittering eyes narrowed, fixating on my stockinged legs. Jerking his chin, Clint gestured to my skirt, gritting out a command.

"Push that fucker up again, baby. Lemme see that slick, shiny pussy."

I hesitated, heart booming behind my blouse.

A feral smile creased his face, teeth flashing between black whiskers.

"Unless you changed your mind, and I should go dig out the cards?"

Over my dead body, Thor!

"Nope. No mind-changing here." Trying to act like I knew what I was doing, like I seduced oversized Viking Lords daily, I shimmied back against the heap of pillows, half-sitting. Ignoring his request, I started with blouse rather than skirt, my unsteady fingers flicking open buttonholes.

"Fuck, yeah."

Gravedigger's growl of approval was encouraging as I drew cream cloth off my shoulders and my lacy La Perla made its debut.

Boy, never did I dream while donning my just-purchased lingerie this morning that somebody would actually see the stuff. I'd just figured: new job, new undies, and I couldn't very well show up at the office in the braless state I usually rolled with.

"Jesus. So fucking hot. Now the skirt. Leave the bra and the stockings on."

Prowling closer, Clint's knees bumped the edge of the mattress as he stared down, a thick ridge hugging his thigh.

"Yes sir, Gravedigger, sir."

GRAVEDIGGER

Holding his gaze, I lifted my hips, easing my skirt off and dropping it to the floor. Destroyed thong back in the living room, my pulse skyrocketed as Clint's eyes shot south, the evidence of my excitement blatant against bare, pulsating folds.

No hiding that shit, mama.

"Ah, Christ, baby."

He groaned long and low, a big hand stroking his cock through his jeans.

"So gorgeous and wet. So pink and juicy and perfect. Gotta have me a taste…"

In a swift motion, he grabbed my ankles, dragging me down to the foot of the bed. At the same time, he dropped to his knees, and next thing I knew, a shaggy head was between my thighs, anvil-like shoulders forcing them apart. Panicking, I tried to wriggle away.

"Clint, no! No, wait, I've never…"

He laughed darkly, licking the skin just above my stocking.

"Never? Fuck my life, am I a lucky man."

With both hands, he spread my legs wider, turning his head to run a slow tongue above the lace on my opposite thigh. Transfixed, I stared down, whatever Bacardi buzz lingering in my veins instantly erased by his focused, wicked caress.

Oh God, this is really happening. And here lie I, more clueless than an infant.

I jumped as that meandering tongue slid higher, hoarse praise husking out of Clint's throat as his fingers tightened.

"Smell so sweet. Like fuckin' honey."

Jesus, Mary, and Joseph… Probably a good time to inform Gravedigger MacGregor he's got an honest-to-goodness virg in his bed. Full-fledged, and not just when it comes to oral. Seriously, the man has a right to know, even if it means—

"O- oh!"

My head fell backward on the pillows as Clint licked straight up my soaked slit, burying his face deep. It felt amazing, heavenly, wicked as sin, and he did it again.

And again; his burning eyes watching me from under a clump of damp bangs.

"Feel nice, baby?"

He rumbled the question against my pussy, his tongue tracing leisurely figure eights. I bit my lip harder, fists clutching wads of wrinkled cotton as I jerked out a nod.

"Y…yes."

The virgin thing? I'll confess in a second. Or maybe a few thousand seconds. Not right freaking now!

GRAVEDIGGER

After I stuttered out the go-ahead, Clint set in with a vengeance, and any functioning gray cells snapped off like switches. Bucking under his stiff-pointed tongue, I moaned, my toes curling, my neck taut.

"Sweet as fucking sugar…"

He spread me wider, muscly shoulders pushing my thighs apart. His fingers got in on the action, parting me, petting me. The dual sensations of those slow-probing digits combined with a mega talented tongue were like nothing I'd ever experienced—light years away from the pleasures attained from my own hand or my trusty, battery-operated boyfriend.

And I'd spent beaucoup bucks on the buzzy little sucker!

Clint added a third finger, licking around it and its two active pals, and my hips shot off the sheets.

"Oh, God, oh, Jesus!"

Mercy, I was close. So deliciously close…

Sensing it, Gravedigger shoved me up the bed, crawling up onto it himself and flinging my stockinged legs over his shoulders. Delirious, I squeezed the shaky limbs against his neck, thrashing and panting as he zeroed in on my clit and sucked hard.

"Ahhhhh….!"

My orgasm hit like a tsunami, shattering me, remaking me. Stars exploded behind my shut eyelids as I cried out, sweat prickling my temples and upper lip. Beneath a swirling tongue, my pussy clenched and spasmed, causing my thighs to tense further, nearly strangling the man trapped between them. Another strong aftershock hit me and I whimpered, slitting pleasure-drunk eyes open.

"No more. Clint, no more…"

He laughed, nuzzling his wet beard against me. I moaned again, meeting a glittering stare and a taut, flushed face.

"Yes, more. Gimme another blast, babe, before I bury this hungry fucker balls-deep in you for the rest of the night."

Clint reared back for a moment, going up on his knees as he stroked the massive ridge distorting his jeans. Hissing, his palm ground down hard, the red on his cheekbones deepening to brick.

"Oh yeah, girl. All. Fucking. Night."

I blinked at his hand and the throbbing bulge beneath it, semi-freaking at the thought of that monster jammed inside of me.

Tell the man, Kent. You need to tell his ass, get him up to speed. Tell him, right now.

Gravedigger drawled out more words. "But, first, like I said…"

GRAVEDIGGER

Swear to God, I was about to spill. But before I could croak out a Virgin-Alert syllable, Clint's face was back between my thighs and his lion-rough tongue was spearing deep. Additionally, not only did he add his fingers to my pussy, this time around the demon brought his other hand into play, messing around with my butt and the rosette hidden between twin cheeks.

"Oh! *Cliiiiiint...*"

He grunted against my sopped slit, mumbling filthy fragments of praise.

"Tight little hole. Gorgeous, tight ass. Sugar-sweet cunt."

Lord, that dirty mouth. So flipping hot!

Mindless, I writhed beneath wet lips, soft whiskers, and thick fingers, their combined forces heart-stopping.

Oh my God, this man... Every lick and every caress felt so exciting, so off-the-charts incredible. In a matter of moments, I was wound tight as a top again—another fast-building orgasm set to shatter me into dozens of tiny, rapturous pieces all over Gravedigger's rumpled sheets.

"Oooh, yes, Clint. Yes, right there. Oh, right *therrrrrrrre...*"

I screamed, grinding a pillow over my face as I detonated. A series of gibbering gasps sobbed from my throat before my noodle-soft legs fell to the mattress and Clint's sweaty shoulders worked free of them. I felt him prowling up the bed, and then he was plucking the pillow away and heavy, hooded eyes were burning into mine.

"Ah, you sweet, sweet thing. C'mere…"

He grabbed my cheeks, planting small, biting kisses on my mouth as he ground his bod against me, its crushing bulk fiery as a forge. I tasted myself on his lips and blushed, digging my nails into his skin as I kissed him back. His beard and mustache were drenched, and I whimpered against them, scarcely aware what I was saying.

"Thank you, thank you. Mmm, felt so good. So unbelievably good…"

Gravedigger drew back, wiping his mouth, teeth glinting in a smug smile.

"The pleasure was all mine, baby. All fucking mine. And now…"

He jackknifed up, brawny arms crossing over one another as he yanked his dirty tee off. I licked my lips, salivating as a wide, cut chest filled my vision, heavy on the muscles and ink. Flinging the shirt to the floor, Clint's hands went to his zip, seemingly on the verge of busting clean open and scattering metal teeth all over the ding-dang place.

GRAVEDIGGER

I blinked at tented denim, at a zipper being yanked down hard.

Tell him, Little Miss Virgin. Tell him NOW.

"Clint. Uh, Clint, there's something you need to… mmmpfff!"

Again, I tried. Sort of hard to impart a message when someone's tongue is halfway down your throat, though, and ten wicked fingers are wreaking havoc left, right, and center.

Inwardly shrugging, I opened wide beneath ravaging lips, sighing my bliss into Clint's mouth.

Ah, well. The man's going to find out soon enough.

And aren't most surprises a good thing?

DIGGER: FIFTEEN

I fell onto Sunshine, fly gaping and belt loosened, my dick a bar of iron behind its barrier of denim.

One more kiss. One more taste. Then, it's Showtime.

Crushing her mouth beneath mine, the essence of my baby's sweet snatch intermingled between our lips—an intoxicating blend of honey, salt, and pure, liquid Sunshine.

Fucking delicious. Her cunt… Most scrumptious little pussy I've ever had my tongue on.

"Angel..." I licked deep, rigid with excitement.

Ever had my tongue in.

I opened her mouth wider, unable to get enough. Just like I couldn't get enough down below, buried between her slick, creaming thighs. Both of which were a first for me. Being a straight-up "let's fuck," type of a guy, I went through the motions of kissing and oral only because a woman expected it, not because I got any big-time enjoyment out of it. Not really. Not with the casual, one-and-done chicks I was accustomed to.

It was different with Sunshine, way different. A whole 'nother motherfucking league kind of

GRAVEDIGGER

different. *The things the woman did to me, the way she made me feel...*

"Christ, baby, you taste so fine. You taste yourself on me, girl? Taste how fucking sweet you are?"

She moaned under my lips, scratching at my scalp with restless nails.

"Mmm. Yes. Yes, Clint."

After another filthy kiss, I drew back, heart pounding, dick set to detonate. Rolling sideways, I stumbled off the edge of the bed, almost face-planting on my cluttered carpet as I whipped belt out of its loops.

Damn. Legs shaky as a just-birthed colt's.

"Don't. Move. A. Fucking. Inch."

Biting out the command, I stabbed a finger at the pocket-sized concubine sprawled atop tangled sheets.

"'Kay."

Whispering her assent, Sunshine licked puffy lips, eyes glowing between half-mast lashes. One boot off, I paused staring. Fuck me, what a vision—a veritable wet dream with arms flung wide and stockinged legs parted, the dew of her excitement glistening on a sweet, waxed slit.

Christ, this beauty. Fucking unreal.

Grinding a palm over tortured flesh, I reconsidered that last directive, jerking my chin.

"On second thought, lose the bra, babe. Nice and slow, while I fight my way outta these fuckers."

Sunshine smiled dreamily, tiny fingers fiddling with brassiere clasp as I toed my other shitkicker off. Breathing hard, I shoved down jeans and boxers, two about-to-burst balls screaming for release. *Jesus—!* I cupped their ponderous weight and gave a squeeze, silently pleading with the come-laden devils.

Hold it together, boys. You're almost there.

A trail of sweat slid down my temple as my cock bucked, not happy with the delay. Freaking, I transferred my grasp from nuts to prick, pinching the leaking tip, hard.

That goes for you, too, honcho.

Owwwwww.

Fuck, maybe a little too hard! But shit, what doesn't kill you makes you stronger. Isn't that how that wailing chick tune goes?

My Levis were at my ankles when Sunshine's bare tits hit the air.

Goddamn! Not only did I stop undressing, I more or less forgot how to breathe. *Oh, holy hell…* Throat seizing and eyeballs boggling, I slurred out reverent praise, addressing the pair of luscious, rose-red nipples jutting my way.

"Ah, look at you... Gorgeous little tits, so taut and round. Fucking perfect."

The petite temptress tossed two cups of lace aside, studying her chest with a cute frown.

"Really? They're sort of on the small side, don't you think?"

"You fucking kidding me?"

I licked my lips, voice wrecked.

"Touch 'em, baby. Play with those fat, sexy nipples."

Sunshine blushed ten shades of pink but sensationally did as requested. Convinced I must be dreaming, I scrubbed a hand over my pussy-wet beard, watching her caress dual handfuls of ripe flesh, pluck at a pair of stiff points. My gaze sharpened on those sun-kissed, strawberry-capped mounds and I moaned.

Fuck me running. No tan lines. Does my naughty angel sunbathe topless?

She tweaked her nipples again, watching me from under sweeping lashes. I swallowed thickly, more turned-on than I'd ever been in my life. Jiggling in her palms, her tits flushed to match her face, the sweet peaks clasped between her fingers lengthening and darkening. A rush of saliva filled my mouth—

my lips, tongue, and teeth dying to taste those rosy beauties.

Bite and suckle and savor and...

It could've been ten seconds or ten minutes that I stood drooling at the show, but once Sunshine threw back her head and sighed, once I saw more cream seep out of her sleek folds, I cursed, coming to fast and furious life.

Yanking my jeans loose, I flung them across the room, toppling back onto the bed. Hooking my angel around the waist, I reared over her on bended knees, my cock stiff as a flagpole. Big brown peepers dropped, latching onto the beast tapping an insistent beat against my clenched abs, and I bit back a caveman smirk.

Like what you see, love? He's all for you. All for fucking you.

Her cheeks pinkened some more as I took a hand and stroked myself, tip to balls.

"You want this big boy crammed nice 'n' deep inside that tight, dripping snatch, baby?"

Pink turned to crimson as Sunshine's eyes widened, her tongue darting out to slick kiss-swollen lips. Watching a pulse in her throat jerk and beat faster, I was swamped with another tsunami of excitement.

My dirty talk turns her on. Sweet.

GRAVEDIGGER

She stammered out some shit, still eyefucking my cock.

"Y... yes. But, Clint, there's something I need to tell—"

I laughed, stroking again.

"Time for talkin' later, babe." I cut my eyes south, biting my lip. "Not lyin'... If I don't get this fucker into you in the next twenty seconds, we're gonna have us a real mess on our hands."

Letting go of myself and grabbing her ankles, I spread her wide, fingers smoothing over sheer thigh-highs.

"Christ, these stockings... hotter than fuck. Loved 'em wrapped around my neck while I was eating you out. Need 'em locked around my back while I'm fucking you blind."

I stared down, something moving in my chest as silky lashes flickered and Sunshine chewed her lip, glancing away. Frowning, I captured her chin between forefinger and thumb, turning her face to mine.

Damn, was I wrong about the graphic play-by-play?

"What is it, girl? Does my nasty language distress you? Shit, baby, I'm sorry. I can dial it back, if you—"

Sunshine shook her curls, stuttering.

"No, it's not that. I… I like the things you say to me, love them. It's just that, that…"

My heart leapt to my throat, panic seizing me.

Fucking A, kill me now. Don't even tell me the lady's gone and changed her mind. Jesus, me and Clintie Junior will never survive it!

"Just that what, beautiful?"

I held a tight breath, my dick harder than Carrara marble, my mashed-together molars about to crack into a thousand porcelain shards.

Lustrous orbs blinked shyly up. Clearing her throat, Sunshine whispered a reply I strained to catch.

"Just that I've never done this before."

Clueless as to what she was attempting to convey, I strove for patience, tracing the cockjerking bow of her upper lip.

"Never did what before, baby? Never got it on with a dirty gravedigger in his trainwreck of a bedroom?"

Sunshine's tongue snaked out to lick my finger, causing my cock to bounce like a baton.

"No, not that. Well, yes, that. But, uh, what I mean is…"

Her teeth nipped me as she sucked in a breath, disgorging an astounding APB in a torrent of rushed-together words.

GRAVEDIGGER

"What I mean to say is, I've never done THIS before. Never been with a man before. Never, er, never had sex before, any kind of sex. You... You're my first."

I fucking stopped breathing.

Holy shit. Holeeeey shit. Sexy-as-sin Casey Rae Kent is an innocent, a virgin?

Shaking my heads stupidly, I struggled to compute, but all that buzzed in my brain were those same two words:

Holeeeeeeeey shit.

I stared down into big eyes, my heart swelling within my chest like a circus balloon. Sunshine gifted me a tremulous smile, and testosterone-driven possessiveness gripped me by the short hairs—the discovery that no other guy had breached her perfect pussy making me high, euphoric. Making me want to pound my pecs like a fuckin' Neanderthal.

Never did a virgin before. Never wanted to. Now? Now, I want to brand this goddess with my fucking initials, make her mine forever.

Dizzying emotions slowly morphed into something else and that internal balloon expanded, pressing against my throat.

Ah, fuck... I sank slowly back onto my heels, my thighs shaky and sweaty, my horizontal dick flapping like a flag of hardened, veiny flesh.

Dismayed, I assessed its obscene girth. Then, my big, grimy mitts, permanently etched with graveyard clay.

Sunshine, a goddamned virgin.

Right then and there, I knew I couldn't do it. Knew I couldn't be the one to desecrate this innocent angel, this unreal, unbelievable gem. No fucking way. Casey Kent deserved someone far better than a messed-up slob of a soil slinger to be the recipient of such a sacred and special honor. My pulse pounded sickly, the thought of my unworthy paws tainting Sunshine any further than they'd already done an anathema to my soul.

Fuck, fuck, *fuck!* Should've known this dream was too good to be true.

I averted my eyes from a pair of nervous-looking brown ones, teeth lacerating the inside of my cheek as I choked down a curse—torn between slamming open a window and howling to the moon, or dropping to linty carpet fibers and weeping like an infant.

Saving either or both options for a later date, I jackknifed off the bed, scrabbling on the floor for a pair of discarded sweatshorts.

Jesus God, I needed to cover this monstrous motherfucker, and fast.

GRAVEDIGGER

Hauling raggedy gray cotton over the stiffest hunk of wood this side of Yosemite, I slicked back my hair, addressing framed military crap on the wall opposite.

"Put your clothes back on, baby. We're not doing this."

A sharp indrawn breath sounded and then Sunshine was speaking, her tone incredulous.

"What? Are you serious? You're stopping *now*? Why, just because I'm a dweeby virgin?"

Not turning, I sucked in my own lungful, hissing through clenched teeth.

"There's nothing 'dweeby' about being a virgin, Sunshine. Nothing to apologize for, or to be embarrassed about. The fact that you're still untouched is beautiful, sweet as fuck. Shit, baby… One day, some lucky-ass guy is going to—"

Sunshine interrupted, her retort dripping with sarcasm.

"'Some lucky-ass guy?' But not *your* lucky ass, huh, Gravedigger?"

I curled my fists, eyes burning. "That's right. No, not mine."

Behind me, I heard the mattress squeak and the thud of two small, stockinged feet hitting the floor. Those tootsies zoomed over and Sunshine grabbed my arm, whipping me around. I blinked down at an angry angel face and a scrumptious, curvy bod, clad solely in a pair of fantasy-inducing thigh-highs.

Ah Jesus, those sexy fuckers.

Narrowed eyes pinned me as Sunshine stuck hands on hips, looking majorly bent.

"Explain yourself, Clint MacGregor. Explain why you're shutting this down the instant you find out I still possess my V-card. What, boffing a unicorn freaks you, turns you off?"

Her gaze dropped to my crotch and the obscene erection tenting my sweats, and a red lip curled.

"No. No, that doesn't appear to be the problem, now, does it?"

I shifted, my neck roasting.

"Fucking cover yourself."

Bending, I scooped up a soiled Oaklawn shirt. Tossing it toward Sunshine's trembling tits with one hand, I ground a palm over my cock with the other, laughing without humor.

"You know damned well how you affect me, baby. Pretty tough to hide." I stroked myself roughly, watching her eyes widen. "Yeah, this beast is hard as fuck anytime your fine ass is within viewing distance, and that includes spying on you in fucking cemeteries."

GRAVEDIGGER

I snorted, correcting myself with a savage squeeze to the nuts. "Viewing distance, my ass—every time I think about you. Regardless, he's not getting anywhere near that untapped pussy. Not after what I just heard."

Sunshine dragged her eyes from my hand to my face, an exasperated expression scrunching up her brow.

"Why, Clint? *Why?*"

Simple, baby. You're far too precious to be defiled by the slovenly hulk before you.

Not voicing the reply aloud, I gestured to the rag crumpled at her feet.

"Put that thing on and we'll talk, out in the kitchen. I'll see if there's anything in the fridge to heat up, and we can—"

A doll-sized foot kicked the work shirt, sending it sailing across the room.

"I don't want to heat anything up from the fridge!"

Sunshine pointed a finger at my bulging dick, then down at her shiny, puffy pussy.

"I want THAT in THIS."

She tossed her head, plush mouth pouting. "And if you're not gonna give it to me, then I may have to resort to nefarious tactics."

With that, she balanced on one leg, slowly drawing off a lace-topped stocking. I groaned, gripping handfuls of hair.

"No, don't. Leave those on. And your skirt, your blouse… You need to get them, baby, and…"

"'Fraid not, big guy."

My voice petered to a second moan as Sunshine zinged a length of silk at me, shifting to her left gam to remove its hot-ass mate. Once both her lovely legs were bare, she sauntered back to my bed naked as a jaybird, heart-shaped ass swaying.

"Baby, no. No, wait."

Ignoring me, she swan-dived onto the sheets, twisting to land onto her back. Shoving a bunch of pillows under tangled curls, she kicked one leg wide and bent the other, a pink-nailed foot planted next to her butt.

Motherfuck me…

I gawped at the taunting beauty gracing my bargain-basement Serta. At the delectable, fully-exposed pussy staring me in the kisser—all slick and bald, its plump folds glistening with mouthwatering dew.

Command shaky, I flapped a hand at a hunk of black cloth lying near the nightstand.

"Get off that bed and put your skirt back on. We need to talk. You can't—"

GRAVEDIGGER

Sunshine's little fingers slid to her cunt, and she started petting herself, sighing.

"I'm getting sick of you bossing me around, mister. If *you're* not going to help with this…"

Her fingers moved faster, one dainty digit disappearing into her slick slit.

"…then *I'm* going to have to do all the work myself."

My cock lurched, straining against constricting cotton. "Ah, God. Don't, baby. Jesus Christ, I'm on the razor's edge as it is."

Lambent eyes caressed me from across the room, sliding over my mouth and chest before zeroing in on the state fair-winning zucchini pulsing between my thighs. She grinned, her gaze tracing desperate inches.

"Yeah. As mentioned, I'm getting that. Loud and clear, Mr. M."

Scarcely aware I was moving, I prowled closer, collapsing against the footboard.

"I'm not gonna fuck you, baby. I'm not. I… I can't. You need somebody better than me, somebody more deserving."

"Pshaw." Sunshine snorted out the sound, moving her other hand to a bare breast. "For real, Clint? That's the dumbest excuse for not banging a virgin I've ever heard."

She sighed again, naughty fingers pinching her pointy nipple, and we moaned in tandem, our eyes locked.

Voice slurry, I jerked my chin at the hand between her legs, losing the battle but not the war.

"Keep going, baby. Lemme watch."

Those chocolatey orbs sparked, glittering as they dropped to my distended crotch.

"You… you, too."

I groaned, powerless to look away, powerless to refuse her. Shoving my sweats under swollen balls, I pulled myself out, the friction of fist on dick brutally intense.

My audience of one mewled, Sunshine watching avidly as I started jacking. Lashes dipping, her own hand picked up speed—thrumming over her slit, fingers sliding through a pocket of creamy juice. A growl rumbled from my throat as I watched, enthralled by the orchestra of wet, sticky noises filling the room.

Jesus fuck. So goddamned hot.

"Another finger, babe. Stick another finger in that tight, dripping hole. Then, another. Pretend it's this big fucker in you, cramming you full."

The plea husked out of me, filthy and raw as I pistoned my prick. Making a dirty show of it, letting my angel see how thick I was for her, how long and hard and hungry.

Dying to leap onto this bed and fuck you in half, girl.

"This... this isn't over. I'm still going to win."

Sunshine gasped out the challenge, flopping her bent leg back onto the bed and spreading wide. Fuckin' hell... I savaged my lip, sweat dripping in my eyes as they gobbled up her beautiful, writhing form. Demented, I fixated on those small, wet fingers, their motion a blur.

"Not gonna fuck that sweet, virgin pussy. Not gonna dirty you up."

My vow hissed between clamped teeth, cock a spike in my fast-moving fist.

"We'll... see... about... that..."

The demoness panted out the words, blond curls thrashing. I leaned harder into the footboard, my knees mush as I worked myself.

"Almost there, baby? Come on, angel. Bring it home for me. Hurry it up... I got twenty seconds 'til I blow to kingdom come."

Heavy eyes glowed between fluttering lids as Sunshine whimpered, her dazed face sweat-slicked and gorgeous.

"Yes… Yes, Clint, almost there. Almost— *aaaaaahhhhhhh…!*"

She blasted off like a cord of dynamite. Keening wildly, her stiffened legs splayed and her flushed, hard-nippled tits quivered. Eyes burning, I stared down at four drenched fingers and the slick folds beneath them, at the copious juices gleaming on pussy and thighs.

"Fuuuuuuck…."

My balls drew tight, intense prickles gathering in the small of my back. I tried to hold back, but it was impossible—my eyes locked on Sunshine's dripping honeypot, my fist furiously jacking. Next pounding heartbeat, I was spewin' all over my sheets, arcing scalding ropes of spunk over rumpled blue cotton and choice portions of Sunshine's golden skin.

Struggling to breathe, my dazzled eyes traced a come-stained belly and hip, the sight of my ejaculate decorating velvety flesh getting me hard all over again. Cursing, I slapped a palm over my twitchy dick, but it was too late. Sunshine had already seen.

She blew out a sated-sounding sigh, her eyes gleaming wickedly, a pink tongue snaking out to lick curling lips.

"Oh, yeah… Forget about it. Prepare for defeat, because I'm telling you true, mister; you are going *down.*"

GRAVEDIGGER

Two fingers moved languidly through luscious trails of cream, causing my traitorous cock to jerk anew.

The witch tangled in my sheets wiggled, grinning with adorable gapped teeth as she threw down the gauntlet.

"Mmm, hmm."

"Only a matter of time, MacGregor."

"Only a matter of time."

CASEY: SIXTEEN

"Seriously, Sunny? *Seriously?* You're not telling me you're actually *seeing* that big slob of a fucker who was spying on you from behind a tree? Are you fricking nuts? Well, you'd better be doing nothing more than *seeing* the tool. Swear to God, if you so much as think of screw—"

Mom plunked a bowl of strawberries on the table with one hand, cuffing my brother's head with the other.

"Christopher, please! No trash-talking at the table. If you can't keep a civil tongue, go wait in your car until your sister's ready. And I think it's nice that our Casey has found herself a new friend."

Brown eyeballs a shade lighter than mine bulged.

"Jesus, Ma, that guy's not a 'friend!' He's a big, dirty motherfucker who only wants to get into her—'

"Christopher! Enough! That 'big, dirty motherfucker' just so happened to save your sister from being raped!"

Whoa! Way to go, Mom.

Betting the farm I'd never before heard that particular word voiced in Delores Kent's ladylike tones, I nodded, chiming in.

GRAVEDIGGER

"Yeah, bro... That's right, he did. And what's the big deal, anyway? If I thought making mention of it would get your panties all in a twist, I would've kept my mouth shut. And quit telling me who I'm allowed to date. You've been pulling that crap ever since you put the kibosh on me and your buddy Moose back in high school."

Chris snorted, pinning me with slitted eyes. "Yeah, and good thing, too. For your information, missy, Moose Sinclair is currently residing at Southern State Correctional for five to ten, thanks to his penchant for carjacking and dope."

Shaking his head, he pulled out the martyr card.

"Shit, Case... Can I help it if I know what guys are like? Help wanting to protect your naïve butt? Hell, you should be *happy* your brothers aren't letting a bunch of degenerates and hoods sniff around you and Be—"

He cut the name short, and a heavy silence descended. Six downcast eyes stared at the cheery sunflower tablecloth, Beth's absence throbbing between us.

Dad entered stage right just then, throwing golf gloves and a marked-up scorecard on the counter.

"Honey, I'm hoooooe-um!"

He grinned over at Mom, a smug-ass expression creasing his face.

"Behold, wife… The champ arriveth! As predicted over our sunrise java, your man beat the pants off Charlie Whittaker. Eighteen holes, eighteen pathetic excuses. It's going to be a while until that blowhard challenges me to an early morning game again, let me tell you! Any sausages left? I'm starved."

Flinging open the refrigerator and pulling out the juice, he paused, blinking across the room.

"Hey, how come everybody's so quiet?"

Checking things out, Pater Familias got his answer, sorrow shading his baby blues. Biting my lip, I traced a sunflower with the tines of my fork, its outline blurring.

Beth. Beth. Beth… The crushing aftereffects of my twin's death may have eased up ever so slightly in the Kent household since June the second, but her family still had an Everest to climb before any of us could speak her name without spiraling into the abyss.

Lord knows I had my black moments. Too many of them, too often. Lacerating, gutting, unbearable moments. I glanced over at the wall clock, the pressure in my chest ramping when I read the numbers.

An hour's worth of those moments set to start shortly, as soon as I drop to my knees in front of her pretty carved stone.

GRAVEDIGGER

Suddenly, a floating hologram of Clint materialized, transposing itself over Mom's corny rooster clock. The tension locking me loosened as I shut my lids and savored the hunky mirage, mentally tracing black whiskers, silver eyes, and a brawny, to-die-for bod.

Yes, the hour between noon and one was going to suck, as always. Even more so than usual with Chris the Watchdog crashing my "alone time" with Beth. But immediately following a somber, notebook-scribbling session, I had a hunch that the *rest* of this fine summer Saturday wasn't going to suck at all.

A secret smile curved my lips, bare thighs tingling under my sundress.

No siree, it sure was not. For, instead of me heading straight home from Oaklawn to hide out in my bedroom with a box of lotion-enhanced tissues, the cemetery's main man was punching out early, and Gravedigger and I were going to spend the reminder of the day together.

I reopened my eyes, grin widening as I gazed out the picture window at acres of cloudless blue sky.

The remainder of the day, *and* the remainder of the night.

Popping a berry in my mouth, I shot Mom a glance, a twinge of guilt prickling me for blowing off tonight's meatloaf supper again. Unlike last time, however, I wasn't skipping a homemade meal to slurp down happy hour specials with my new work buddies. Nope, a scuzzy gin mill with regrettable wall décor was not this evening's destination.

Rather, Clint MacGregor's grubby batch pad was, and devilishly, I'd toted out the same subterfuge story I'd dreamed up a few weeks prior to appease my hamburger-happy mother.

Thanks, Laura Lynn Swanson, wherever you are. One day soon, who knows… Maybe I'll call on you for real, my friend.

Another tingle twitched my thighs and what lay between them—my pussy pulsing beneath its extravagant, just-purchased thong.

Mmm. Hope Lord Thor's partial to high-priced ivory lace. Because tonight, the big guy was in for another surprise show, and my skimpy undies were getting top billing.

Well, until they landed on his carpet.

Recalling the saucy stripper routine I'd rehearsed all week via YouTube, I flushed, squirming in my seat.

Heck yes, was my Viking man getting a surprise. And this one was going to end with a "BANG."

Literally, if me and my virgin hoo-hah had any say in the matter.

GRAVEDIGGER

🪦 🪦 🪦

"You think she knows that we're here?"

I arranged my weekly bouquet against Beth's stone, making sure the petals didn't block her name.

Hovering above me, Chris grunted, dropping a palm on my shoulder. "I dunno. I'd like to think so, but that's a mystery no one has the answer to, Sis."

My reply, as I dug in my Burberry for gardening shears, was hushed. "Yeah, I know."

Do you ever hear her voice in your head, bro?

I almost asked it out loud, but same as all the other times I've been tempted to query the rest of the fam, I kept my lips zipped. Mostly because I figured it was a "twin thing," and that I—and I alone—was the recipient of Beth's phantom messages.

And, also, because I wasn't keen on the parent folk and my trio of brothers deeming Casey Rae off her flipping rocker.

Right, there was that.

"BLANGBLANGBLANG..."

Chris's heavy metal ringtone blasted in the silence and I grit my teeth, mightily annoyed. Lord, the guy was as clueless as Mike and CJ when it came to cemetery etiquette. The frigging three of them...! Since 'The Incident,' and my sibs taking rotating turns playing graveside sitter, my aggravated ears have learned just how cell-addicted each of the clods was.

Did the sanctity of these tomb-studded lawns mean nothing?

Disturbing the peace, Christopher's voice blared out.

"Hey, boss. Whasssssssup?"

I groaned, savagely snipping stray blades of grass. Great... Sounds like Butchie Bostwick on the horn, Chris's yakety supervisor at the plant. Newsflash: I wasn't a fan. For one thing, the blowhard always uses fifty words when five would do, never coming up for air except to nudge his underlings for another helping of brown-nose praise.

For another, whenever our paths crossed, I swear his married-man eyeballs left scorch marks on my ass.

Glaring up, I made shooing motions for Chris to take a hike and leave me and Beth in peace, but he ignored them, a frown furrowing his brow.

"Mmm, hmm. Uh, huh. Craig G., huh? That skinny fucker... measles, no shit? Wow, thought only kids got that crap. Ya sure there's no one else to cover?"

Why don't you talk a little louder, foghorn? I don't think that old geezer visiting his loved one three hills yonder caught that.

GRAVEDIGGER

I endured another dozen "uh, huh's," and a few more "ah, shit's," before Chris pocketed his phone, bopping me on the head.

"Sorry, Sun, but we gotta cut this short… I have to take you home and head into work. One of the guys on my line is down with the fucking measles. Can you even believe it?"

"What? No!" I bolted up, brushing clippings off my knees and checking my watch. "I can't leave; we've barely been here ten minutes. You know this is my thing, mine and Beth's."

Bending, I scrabbled in my knapsack, yanking out my journal. "I haven't even written to her yet!"

Christopher's eyes were sad as he shook his head.

"Yeah, it sucks, but I'm not leaving you here alone. No way. Not after what that asshole pulled a few weeks ag—"

I interrupted, talking fast.

"Bro, be realistic… I can't never not come here without having you or CJ or Mikie in tow. That's going to get old quick, and pretty soon you guys will be making excuses to skip a week. Believe me, I was freaked over what happened too, but I'm hyper-alert now, not to mention better prepared."

"Hello…!" My fingers went to my neck, fumbling with a long string. Grabbing the twine, I stuck the police whistle-slash-mace spray necklace Dad had fashioned for me in his basement gadget room under my brother's nose.

"You yourself gave approval to this bad boy, no?"

Chris curled his lip, eying it dismissively.

"Only to shut Pop up. Get real, Sun… Who's gonna hear that thing in this deserted place? And what happens if that sicko sneaks up on you from behind, like last time? There's no way you're going to be able to get a decent blast in."

He stretched out an arm, waggling impatient fingers. "Come on. Let's say goodbye to Beth, and then we gotta make tracks."

I avoided his grasp, consulting my wrist again.

May as well tell Brother Dearest now, rather than just before the hour strikes one, as originally planned.

"You go, Chris. Go: I'll be fine. I, er, I wasn't going to have you drop me back home anyway. I, uh, I actually have a date, starting at one on the dot."

Christopher's jaw gaped. "A date? What? A date where? Who with?"

"Um…"

Getting the picture, he swore, sneering. "Oh, shit, no. Not that gravedigger fuck."

GRAVEDIGGER

I made a foul face back. "Yes, that gravedigger fuck. And the man's name is Clint, Clint MacGregor. You'd better get used to it because, as I said, we're seeing each other."

"Seeing each other!" A dramatic eye roll. "Puh-lease. Question of the ages... What in God's name can my beautiful baby sister possibly see in that big, muddy oaf?"

Hmm, waaaall... Besides his smokin' badass looks, his bravery, and his sweet, gentle giant side that refuses to plunder eager virgin soil? Okay, how about his huge, hard, throbbing—

My skin turned hot and I put salacious thoughts on pause, flopping back onto the grass and flipping my notebook open.

Can't be thinking that naughtiness in front of big brother, hornball! Best drag your mind out of the gutter and pen a few pages of bottled-up emotions to your dearly departed instead.

Chris loomed over me, breathing hard and grumbling expletives.

"Case, come on. You know I can't leave you here by yourself. Shit, Mike and Ceej will have my ass!"

Not looking up, I spoke to messy lines of prose. "They won't know because we won't tell them. Chill, bro... Clint is meeting me here in less than forty-five minutes, and he's likely somewhere close by besides, armed with his trusty shovel. I told you; I'm fine. Go on, skedaddle… Those sweet overtime bucks are calling your name."

Grumpy gave it one last try before I heard the jangle of his keys.

"All right, you mule. But I'm not liking this, not at all. Stay sharp and keep that damned mace at the ready." He tipped my chin up, jerking his jaw at my journal.

"And put that thing away until next time. You're not gonna catch a psycho creeping out of the bushes by channeling Virginia Woolf."

I obeyed, but only because for the first time since I began my ritual before Beth's stone, I didn't feel an urge to purge on paper. No. Instead of dwelling on death, my mind was preoccupied by life. Life as in the form of a muscly, hot-as-hellfire gravedigger, and the Pop the Cherry game plan I'd spent the better part of the week perfecting.

Who wudda thunk plotting out Best-Way-to-Seduce-a-Stubborn-Viking would help so much in tamping down a sister's grief?

"Okay, brat. Against my better judgment, I'm out. Remember to keep those big eyes open. *Wide* open."

Hinging at the knees, Chris pecked me on the cheek before pinching the skin between finger and thumb, none too gently.

GRAVEDIGGER

I yelped, swatting his hand away. "OW! What the hell was that for?"

His reply was grim. "For not listening to reason and leaving with me. Additionally, consider it a brotherly warning to keep it G-rated with that dirty fucker Mac-what's-his-name on your damned 'date.' I find out he's messing around with you, I'm going to mess *him* up."

Watching his tense frame walk off, I bit back a smirk.

Suppose you could try. But built as you are, bro, Gravedigger's bigger. And wouldn't you be surprised to hear the man's been a veritable gent each time we've gotten together since Friday last—sticking solely to swoony make-out sessions all four frustrating evenings, not venturing a muddy footstep off first base?

God's honest, we're talking Boy Scout Handbook, despite this gal's desperate desire for him to knock it out of the ball park.

"Clint, please. Pleeeease..."

I played with blades of grass, recalling my breathless pleading as I lay clasped in strong arms, listening to Gravedigger's groaned, hoarse refusals rasp against my lips.

"No, baby. Goddammit, no. Not gonna do you. Not gonna be the one to christen that sweet, tight pussy with this hungry-as-fuck dick."

Mercy, so hot.

Chris's Audi took off down the path and I relaxed, smoothing palms over my sundress. My brand-new, pale green, thigh-grazing sundress with the deep, square neck. The smirk on my face widened as I stroked the fabric caressing my braless boobs and skimpy lace thong, picturing Clint's face when he got a load of my recent purchase.

Not gonna be the one, big guy? We'll see about that, later on, in your bedroom.

Leaning forward, I traced Beth's name with light fingertips, murmuring out loud.

"You hear me, Sissie? We'll see who's going to be crumbling to his hunky knees in a few hours, right after I fall to mine and unzip his fly. We'll just see, won't we?"

"That's the spirit, Lil' Miss Sunshine. Failure is not an option. Tonight, he's yours!"

By now, I was sort of used to my twin's voice in my ear, but I must say it did still freak me out.

I patted her stone, eyes stinging. "Thanks, Bethie. I think so, too."

Which was true. Even without the sexy dress and panties, my confidence was mighty. After Thursday night, and all those passionate kisses in Clint's truck, parked a block over from my parent's house? Shoot, my ravenous Viking had been so worked up, I'd

GRAVEDIGGER

barely been able to understand a fraction of the filth husking from his mouth into mine as he ate me alive under a burned-out streetlight.

"Sweet little baby. Want you so bad. Open wider, babe. Ah, fuck, can't get enough of my beautiful girl…"

Oooh, I adored it when Gravedigger called me "his girl"—the words making me yearn to be his in every way that there was.

I stared into space, my gaze dreamy.

Mmm, hmm, every way. Every last, delicious, "see ya later, cherry" way the man could dream up. With my eager assistance, of cour—

"Remember me, bitch?"

A low hiss was my only warning before a pale, skinny arm wrapped around my throat. Crushing my windpipe, it pressed in hard as a hand slapped over my mouth. Panic paralyzed me as I was dragged to my toes and pushed against sun-hot granite, knees scraping.

"Saw your bodyguard drive off, bitch. Just when I was gonna throw in the towel, too, after the last coupla weeks and your ass never alone."

No! God, no!

Coming to life, I struggled madly, biting foul-tasting flesh and kicking out behind me.

My attacker laughed, the sound manic, his voice hideously familiar.

"Good things come to those who wait. Today's my lucky day, cunt. Yours, not so much."

He butted his chest against my back, sending me stumbling past Beth's headstone. I tried to dig my sandals into the grass, tried to lunge for my bag and phone, but both efforts were futile.

"Come on, cunt, *move*." Snarling, he pushed us toward a thick fringe of tall bushes. "We're heading to my home-away-from-home, where we'll be nice and alone. No big hero runnin' down the hill to save your skin this time, not where we're going."

Hot bile flooded my mouth as visions of a Jame Gumb-style basement complete with gaping floor pit and night-vision goggles bombarded my brain—Jodie Foster's character in *Silence of the Lambs* replaced by rookie understudy Casey Rae Kent.

Oh, dear Jesus. Oh, holy Lord in Heaven.

Beth's voice rang in my ears, urgently strident.

"The mace, Sunny. The whistle!"

Petrified brain cells registered her alert and my fingers fumbled, but my wrist was wrenched away and the cord ripped from my neck. The man behind me giggled like a girl, sending Dad's creation sailing through the sky.

GRAVEDIGGER

"Nice try, bitch."

We got to the bushes, and he shoved me through a veil of prickly leaves, sticking something sharp and metallic between my shoulder blades.

"Feel that, tasty cunt? That there's a piece, something I forgot last time. Not gonna make that fuckin' mistake again."

A gun!

My eyes bulged and I struggled harder, trying to scream around disgusting-flavored flesh. Jame Gumb chuckled again, pressing his palm against my teeth before removing it and spinning me around.

I fought to maintain my balance, opening my mouth to shriek bloody murder, but his arm flashed out and he was grinding a snub of steel under my chin.

"Not a sound, bitch. Not a single sound, or this fucker's gonna blow your pretty head to vapor. Nod if you understand."

Staring into a pair of cold, colorless eyes, I obeyed jerkily, scarcely recognizing the guy as the same cretin who'd attacked me four weeks ago. If not for that dead gaze and the weapon kissing my jaw, he now resembled your average schmoe, albeit on the scrawny, vitamin D-deprived side.

Reading my mind, Jame grinned, gesturing with non-gun hand to his preppy polo and tailored shorts.

"Look different, don't I? Like a real upstanding citizen, just payin' a visit to his poor Ma, buried six feet under. That sweatshirt and jeans were all wrong—made me stand out, gave my ass away."

His pale eyes narrowed as his mouth went flat.

"Made me a sitting duck for that big cocksucker hero with his motherfucking shovel."

Clint. Oh God, Clint, where are you?

I forced out a string of lies, my throat tight and raw.

"He, he's meeting me, any minute. And he packs a gun, too. Really good with it. You should leave now, while you still—"

"Bullshit, he is."

That snub pressed harder and I whimpered, trying another tack.

"Please. Please, don't hurt me. My… My sister just died recently, my twin, and I… I have money. Lots of it. You can go get it; it's in my knapsack."

His expression didn't alter, and I babbled faster. "Listen, I swear, I won't say a word to anybo—"

"Shut it, and start walking." The man glanced around before grabbing my arm, plastering me to his side. "You're gonna stroll next to me nice and easy, like we're fucking Dick and Jane on a picnic, got it? You ain't gonna make a peep, and if we pass anybody, no eye contact."

GRAVEDIGGER

He hauled me past a trio of matching tombstones with winged angels perched on top, and I shuddered, shooting off a fevered prayer to three weatherworn faces.

Help me, somebody. Help me, God. Help me, Gravedigger.

Eerily, the sicko saw inside my head again, his voice bored as he imparted a newsflash.

"Yeah, don't be counting on hero man to be comin' to the rescue today. Nah, I planned things out nice…. Started me a little bonfire clear on the other side of this boneyard just before I hightailed it over here. Odds are good that big fucker is busy puttin' it out, getting himself another gold star. It's just me and you, bitch, and the surprise I got planned for you."

My heart thudded in my throat, the heavy beats choking me. I strained to hear Beth, to try to think of a plan, but all that echoed in my ears were buzzing bumblebees and tweeting birdsong, and all that filled my head were heinous visions of a dank and barricaded basement.

Jame Gumb walked faster, dragging me alongside him like a sack of garbage. One of my sandals slipped off and a sharp briar poked my instep, but I scarcely felt it. Not with all the undiluted panic rendering me numb, I didn't.

Fragments of distraught half-thoughts slid in and out of my head as claw-like fingers dug into my skin.

Two stood out, repeating themselves on a loop:

Oh, God… Christopher is going to kill me for not listening. That is, if some skinny psychopath doesn't beat him to it first.

And:

My noble Viking Lord is saving Casey Rae's stupid cherry for this?

DIGGER: SEVENTEEN

"Goddamnedmothersuckingsonofabitch…"

I stomped on a smoldering pile of evergreen branches, hollering over at Albert down on the path.

"Can't you handle this? We agreed I'm off-duty at one today."

The head cheese made a prissy face, watching my muddy boot fly.

"You're certainly not suggesting *I* crawl in all those dirty leaves? I have a bereaved family to sign shortly! It's not even a quarter past the hour, man… Another few minutes won't kill you, just to make sure all the embers are out."

A vision of a pissed-off Sunshine vacating the grounds flashed in my head and I stomped harder, enraged by the delay some bored punk had instigated.

Probably the same degenerate who'd fucked up the gating a few weeks back.

"Cudda called the fucking hoses."

Albert shot that down fast, flicking nothing off an immaculate suit lapel. "Not necessary, since you spotted it so fast. You did right, Gravedigger, alerting me and not them. We don't need a bunch of ear-piercing fire trucks disrupting our Elysium, especially not on such a glorious Saturday. Lord, think of the negative publicity!"

Shuddering with sound effects, he fluttered two fingers sideways.

"Over there to the left: I think I spy a small spark still burning."

Yeah? Why don't you climb up here so I can shove it up your white-collar ass?

Eight minutes and change later, boss man finally satisfied that the mini barbeque was vanquished, I leapt into my ride, throwing it in gear. Eyeing my sweaty reflection in the rearview, I groaned, furious as almighty fuck.

Christ. The one goddamned day I ask to cut out early, some lowlife decides to play pyro in my backyard.

I floored it, sending gravel shooting as I sped down narrow winding paths.

Please, baby, don't have left yet.

Naturally, the bullshit I'd just dealt with occurred diametrically opposite Oaklawn's confines from Sunshine's sister's grave, and it seemed to take half a century to get there. My journey wasn't expedited when I hit the babbling brook and the approximately fifty fat ducks waddling their way across the road.

GRAVEDIGGER

Motherfuck me!

A wizened old bat brandishing a loaf of Wonder Bread smiled at me from the edge of the grass, cooing into my window.

"Darling, aren't they?"

I bared my teeth at her, gritting out a terse lie as my jittery fingers thumped the wheel.

"Totally."

Once the last green-feathered tush had cleared the path, I roared off, leaving Granny and her crusts in a cloud of truck exhaust. Rounding the final curve, I jerked it into park, my feverish eyes flicking up the hill in quest of a bright beauty in a sexy sundress. Clocking the distinctive pink granite of young Beth Ann Kent with nobody kneeling before it, I cut my gaze left and right, heart sinking when all I saw were endless blocks of stone.

Shit, she's gone!

I slammed out of the cab, shading my eyes against the sun as I spun around then around again, no living and breathing angel in sight. Shoving back sweat-damp hair, I swore, kicking my front tire.

"Godfuckingdammit!"

Remembering all the evenings this past week Sunshine had squirmed and moaned on my rock-hard cock as we made out like maniacs, I slapped the hood savagely.

Jesus… Between those dick-weeping suck-face sessions and our mutual blast-off bonanza in my bedroom last Friday, the woman can't have possibly have thought I'd stand her up!

Diving through the open window, I snatched my cell, stabbing in her number. It rang and rang, no answer. I cursed again, recalling Sunshine telling me she always muted the mother when she entered the cemetery gates, out of respect.

Great. Fuckin' fabulous. Either she was still here and had forgotten to crank the volume back up, or she was deliberately avoiding my call.

Fuck!

I threw the thing down and stomped up the slope, figuring an elevated view might yield pay dirt in the form of a disgruntled sexpot stalking down gravel paths.

Hadn't Sunshine said her brother was leaving her here? That she'd be without transport until I showed my ass up?

A few yards from her sister's stone, I stopped dead in my tracks, a sickening sensation icing my veins.

Wha…

GRAVEDIGGER

A familiar plaid knapsack sat in front of the Kent marker, a water tumbler and notebook lying in the grass beside it. I lunged forward, almost bashing my noggin on the granite as I scooped up the bag, fingers shaking. Pawing through the contents, my heart nosedived as I pulled out Sunshine's sparkly wallet and her similarly themed phone.

No, do not think what you're thinking, man. You're fucking paranoid. Maybe she just had too much water and needed to pee or something. She's probably just crouching behind that big obelisk over there, and any second her pretty head will pop out.

"Sunshine? BABE?"

I shouted and then ran around a bunch of the taller monuments like a nutjob, but it became swiftly apparent there was no one on this hill but me and a shitload of dried-up corpses.

Sweating like a sonofabitch, I jabbed at the phone, but its screen was locked and black. Riffling through her wallet, I saw nothing amiss—a modest amount of cash organized in ascending order, a couple of credit cards, some photos stuck in plastic sleeves. Chest tight, I stared at a smiling shot of Sunshine's doppelgänger, except this girl's hair wasn't so tousled and she didn't have my baby's enchanting tooth gap.

Must be her poor, dead twin. What a shit-ass deal Miss Beth Ann got. Same as my man Kev and his blown-up body parts, buried seven sections over.

Eyes stinging, I stuffed the leather away, grabbing water and notebook and shoving them in, too. Barreling down the slope, I threw myself behind the wheel, chucking Sunshine's bag next to me. I performed two accelerated loops around the hill before tearing up and down a clusterfuck of intersecting paths. Pouring sweat, I passed not a (living) soul, highly unusual for a sunny Saturday. Finally, on a skinny and shady lane, I almost took out three mom power walkers, striding in rigid formation.

"YO!"

I screeched on the brakes and stuck head out the window, trying to moderate the panic in my voice.

"Afternoon. I lost my… my girlfriend. Did you see a curly-headed blonde around here? She'd be on foot. Five-foot-four-ish, wearing a sundress and sandals?"

Educated guess there, based on Sunshine's prickjerking MO.

The trio peered at me suspiciously from under matching baseball hat brims, taking their time deciding whether I was a psycho killer or not. I stuck a fake smile on my puss, jerking a thumb at the Oaklawn crest decorating my breast pocket.

GRAVEDIGGER

"I'm, uh, I'm the head groundskeeper here, and I was supposed to meet her at one, but I'm running late. She, er, she probably thinks I stiffed her. But, see, there was this little fire I had to deal with, and, er, never mind."

After checking out the identical logo painted on the side of the truck, the pickle in the middle lady piped up, taking pity on my stammering and, no doubt, the frantic look in my eye.

"There's been a handful of cars, but other than that, we've only passed a teenager on rollerblades and an elderly woman feeding the ducks."

She stuck hands on hips, a know-it-all expression on her mug.

"Oh, speaking of that… Perhaps you can settle a bet, seeing you work here. Tell me… Isn't feeding the fowl frowned upon? Especially with spongy white bread? All those empty carbs can't be good for their constitutions! I'm certain there used to be signs posted, stating under no circumstances should anyone—"

I cut the bitch off, interrupting her motormouth ass.

Fuck those goddamned quackers. Their webbed feet cost me precious time.

"That's it? That's all you saw? Nobody else? No girl in a dress?"

No sexual deviate camouflaged in winter black?

Wildlife Mama shook her head, but one of her buddies took to the airwaves, pointing up.

"No… no, you're wrong. We *did* pass a blonde in a dress, Sylvia, not too long ago. Remember, she was in those thick trees with her boyfriend?"

She shot me a coy look, smirking. "It couldn't be *your* girlfriend, handsome, because the pair of them looked really lovey-dovey. Walking together so close, they may as well have been glued together!"

A hideous premonition gripped me and I cleared a jammed throat, my voice rasping like sandpaper.

"Oh, maybe that was her. Yeah. With her, uh, with her brother. Was he skinny, wearing jeans and a dark hoodie?"

The lady laughed, looking at me like I'd sprouted another head.

"A *hoodie*? In this heat? Lord, no!" She fanned herself, pursing her lips as she played star witness. "Skinny, very. And pale too. He was sandy-haired and nicely dressed, wearing a navy shirt with a collar and tan shorts. And as I said, he seemed most attentive. Ah, young love…"

She fluttered stubby eyelashes. "I remember when my Darren used to be so—"

"Okay, thanks."

GRAVEDIGGER

Deaf to the rest of the crap she was spewing, I floored it, gifting the women my dust as I sped off, inwardly freaking.

Oh, Sweet Christ, it's that same twisted bastard. Goddamn my life, it's him, in a new guise. He's taken Sunshine, taken her off that hill by force. Jesus God, I'll stake my fucking life on it.

I tore up and down well-traveled paths I could maneuver in my sleep, driving like a lunatic, white knuckles pulverizing the wheel. Checking the dash's clock, I tried to talk myself off the ledge, tried not to have a fucking heart attack as my eyes darted to and fro—up monument-stuffed slopes and down sun-splashed lanes.

Chill, man. It's only one-fucking-forty. This boneyard's many an acre. No way has that sick fuck exited the main gates.

Passing the forest of fancy mini mausoleums, cold sweat soaked my tailbone.

Not unless he's got a vehicle this time.

That possibility sent my panic skyrocketing and I fumbled for my cell, stabbing in the admin speed dial. Albert's gal Friday, Ursula, answered on the first ring, her voice anxious.

"Gravedigger. There isn't another fire, is there?"

"No, not that, something else. Listen, Urs: lock the gates and call the cops, right now. I'm headin ov—"

A flash of blue in my peripherals had me flinging the phone down, my eyes straining. Dimly, I heard Urs squawking from the passenger seat, but all my senses were fixated on the grand VanEvery crypt, and the two figures I saw struggling beside its rusty, iron-grilled doors.

Sunshine!

I cranked the wheel, skidding half-on and half-off the grass, narrowly missing mowing down a century-old headstone. Hauling ass outta truck, I grabbed my sharpest spade from its bed and charged forward, bellowing as I ran.

"HEY! HEY, LET HER GO, ASSHOLE!"

Two pale faces turned, and it was déjà fucking vu all over again. Same as three weeks ago, I was drowning in Sunshine's big, terrified eyes before switching my death glare over to a pair of weaselly, beady ones.

The cocksucker belonging to those fugly eyeballs swore, his claw circling my baby's neck.

"You again! Fuck me, do ya have a tracker attached to this bitch?"

I was a few yards shy when he shoved Sunshine away, sending her bashing against Victor VanEvery's pretentious homage to himself. Leveling his chicken-bone arm out straight, the psycho bleated high and shrill.

"Stop, Hero Man! Stop right there! Ya see this?"

GRAVEDIGGER

Ah, shit!

Slamming on the brakes, I hovered between two tombstones, clocking the snub-nosed piece shaking in his grip. He waved it back and forth between my angel and me, metal glinting. Catching my expression, he laughed smugly.

"Yeah, big man, not this time."

Keeping that bead on me, he hauled Sunshine up, yanking open one of the mausoleum's creaky double doors and shoving her through it. She shrieked, resisting.

"NO! What are you do—"

My girl was struggling like a hell-cat, but that twisted fuck had her in a tight hold, wrenching her sideways.

"Zip it, cunt. You stay in there and wait for me. I'll join ya shortly and we'll have us some fun, just as soon as I make hamburger out of Hero Man here."

"No! No, wait!"

The door slammed in her face and the fuckhead turned a big, ancient-looking key in the escutcheon before dropping it in shorts' pocket. My mind ticked frantically as I tried to compute, his action flipping me right the fuck out.

Custom mausoleum key, circa 1870. Oaklawn property, stored in the suit's back offices with all the other hardware. Scarcely ever used, rarely needed.

How in Satan's name had this prize gotten his hands on the thing?

Frenzied fists were banging against the grillwork doors, and Sunshine peered through thick, hazed glass, hollering shit I couldn't hear. I held her gaze for half a heartbeat, keeping my expression neutral. Attempting to convey calm, despite the fact I was losing it epically.

Cutting my eyes back to El Fucko, I half-believed I was back home tossing in my sheets, mired in the middle of some surreal nightmare—this one taking place in a serene Vermont necropolis, as opposed to the usual blood-splattered terrain of Kabul, Afghanistan.

He was watching me, grinning, stroking the gun with his left hand. This would be the mitt not aiming the barrel straight at my left aorta. Jerking his chin toward Sunshine's macabre jail, the douche's smirk was creepier than hell.

"Check it, Hero Man… My home-away-from-home. Got it tricked out real nice—blankets, candles, skin mags, even a little propane heater. Wait 'til you see. Been crashing in there for months now, bunking between the Mr. on the left and the Mrs. on the right."

Smile vanishing, he clucked his tongue. "Ritzy fucks… You wouldn't believe the amount of room."

I stared at him, speechless. Dimly, I recalled that weird flicker of light I'd seen through the grills a few weeks back, and how I'd dismissed it as an optical illusion.

This Class-A sicko is shacking up in the VanEvery death house? Taking cozy catnaps on a limestone floor, sandwiched between two marble sarcophagi? Lying in wait for innocent victims like my Sunshine? And I, main man on campus, hadn't had a holy clue?

My fists curled into rocks as red-hot rage rolled through my veins like lava.

Told you before, fuckwad. You picked the wrong place to play. This is Gravedigger Territory.

Injecting a note of awe into my voice, I made my eyes go all wide, fawning in his rat-like face.

"Wow, really? No shit! Have to hand it to you... I had no idea, and I'm up and down these roads ten times a day. You must be really stealth."

The asshole puffed out his scrawny chest, looking like I'd just awarded him The Silver Star.

I kept talking, inching forward in undetected baby steps.

"How in hell didja you get the key? From what I understand, the whole family died off years ago. Shit, I'll bet nobody's set foot in that rock this century."

He scoffed, sneering. "Are you serious? A kid could sneak in those offices and grab whatever the fuck he wants. Back in May, I pretended I was into buying a plot for my folks—as if—and while that sanctimonious fart took an age getting a bunch of paperwork together, I grabbed a few keys from their fancy little drawers. I knew those losers would never even miss 'em."

Waving his free hand up and down Mausoleum Alley, he bragged some more. "I lifted three others, besides. Once in a while after dark, I switch it up for shits and giggles, but this sucker's the most spacious, and all my stuff's inside."

He smacked a palm on VanEvery limestone, so full of himself he didn't notice I'd cleared the stones flanking me. I took another tiny step, sweat soaking my shirt.

A few more feet. Keep going, soldier. Then it's time to break out those tactical moves you can execute blindfolded.

Sunshine pounded on the doors again, the sound muffled like she was underwater, and Psycho Boy raised his voice without taking his eyes, or his piece, off of me.

"Quiet, cunt! Nobody can hear you; that fucker's built like an armory."

Manic eyes gleamed in his milk-white mug.

"Did you know that, Hero Man? Know how solid these fancy digs are? Damn, they don't build 'em like

GRAVEDIGGER

this anymore. Thick-ass marble, limestone, iron doors…"

He shook his head, rueful. "Shit, I was nuts not to drag that last girl in the thing. Cudda had me lots more time, instead of having to rush, do her out in the open."

Bile filled my throat as I crept onward. "Last girl…?"

The whoreson was back to stroking his gun, giggling gleefully.

"Yeah, hotshot, last girl. The bitch they didn't get me for. I covered her eyes, did my business real quick. Cunt didn't see jack shit. In an' out, know what I mean? Stupid pigs had no fricking clue. The morons tried to pin that last attack on me, the one crosstown near the tracks, but I had nothin' to do with that. Think it mighta been my competition, Crazy Jess from the trailer park."

His piehole crinkled like he'd swallowed a lemon.

"Dude's always trying to one-up my ass."

That bile choked me, rancid and bitter.

Fuck my life. Rapists have running scorecards?

I was closing in, tensing my right leg for a full-body roundhouse kick when my boot hit a root and I stumbled. The twist instantly stiffened, gripping the pistol handle with both hands.

"Hey! Hey, stop right there, dickbag! Did you just fuckin' move?"

Raising innocent mitts in the air, I shook my head. "No, sorry, I just shifted a little, and—"

"Liar!"

His eyes turned wilder, that metallic snub shook, and before I knew what was what, a searing sensation ripped through my left shoulder, sending me crashing to the ground.

Goddamn… The scrawny cocksucker shot me!

"MOTHERFUCKER!"

I roared, the pain agonizing. Nauseous, I clamped a hand over my skin, fingers coming away sticky and red. I blinked at them, a thousand and one shitty PTSD memories crowding my skull. Dully, I heard those iron doors thud again, and I tried to raise my head to find Sunshine, to let my baby know I was alive, at least for now.

Before I could focus, my line of vision was blocked in the form of Psycho Rapist.

"How's it feel, Hero Man?"

A dorky tasseled loafer stomped on my wound, grinding into exposed tissue and bone as I writhed and howled.

"Mother… *FUCKERRRRR*…!"

GRAVEDIGGER

"Yeah, you already said that."

The bastard stood smiling down at me, scratching his jaw. "Hmm. Wonder how hard it'll be to drag your oversized ass over to one of my other stone abodes, while me and your hot girlfriend get better acquainted."

He squinted up at the sun. "Still a lot of time left until dark, but hopefully, if luck's on my side, nobody'll pass by until you're locked up nice 'n' tight. Hope you can handle roughing it with a pile of bones 'til somebody finds you, *gravedigger*."

His shrill cackle had me shuddering.

"Or, until somebody doesn't."

I gritted between my teeth, pain making the words jerky and disjointed.

"You...insane? All kinds... people...around. You'll never—"

"YOU, SIR! DROP YOUR WEAPON THIS INSTANT!"

An outraged, strangely familiar voice had Psycho Boy and me whipping our heads around. Squinting through the hair flopping in my eyes, I stared at three pairs of upside-down legs, sporting striped socks and color-coordinated Nikes.

The storm troopers!

The douche standing on my shoulder snarled, flailing his piece.

"Fuck off, cunts, and disappear. Unless each of ya wants a bullet in the—"

KA-BLAM!

Gun Guy dropped like a stone beside me, shrieking like a schoolgirl as he clutched his leg, a big stain of red blossoming over his kneecap.

"Ahhhhh! You evil bitch!"

Meanwhile, face-planted on the grass, I watched six spiffy sneaks zoom over, one laced leather boat kicking the weapon away. A gaggle of female hands pulled on my uninjured arm, dragging me to a semi-sitting position and propping me against an ivy-covered cross.

Someone whipped out a clean hankie, someone applied ruthless pressure, and someone else stuck something behind my dripping shoulder to cushion the wound.

Felt like a baseball hat.

Day-yum. It's like they've done this shit before.

I blinked up at the trio of mom walkers, the one in the middle slipping a pretty little piece back in her fanny pack and hauling out a cell.

She scrunched up her face, talking to herself.

GRAVEDIGGER

"Oooh, my Darren's gonna *kill* me! But I didn't take all those expensive lessons at the range for nothing! And I *did* aim for the knee, just like they taught us in defense class."

Punching in three numbers, she zipped her Saturday Afternoon Special away and barked out a few orders.

"Sylvia, keep applying that pressure. Greta, you go and try to get that poor girl out of that tomb."

Annie Oakley smiled down at me, fluttering her stubby lashes.

"Me? Me, I'll take care of handsome here, and see if he's in need of any CPR."

CASEY: EIGHTEEN

Mom's voice startled me as I stood over my bed, stuffing crap into a duffle.

"How's Clint doing, honey? Have you spoken to our wounded hero this morning, or is he still zonked out?"

I glanced over at the doorway, pausing in my packing. The matriarch's eyes flicked to the pair of barely-there boy shorts dangling from my fingers, but to her credit, Mom held her comments.

And why not? She's seen plenty of sexy lingerie coming out of the clothes dryer lately… My racier numbers making up the bulk of Gravedigger's requests regarding his temporary nurse-slash-chief bottle washer's wardrobe.

Flushing, I dropped peach lace into the bag, clearing my throat.

"Um, yeah. He buzzed me ten minutes ago, just after my shower. Said he's craving Chinese for dinner."

I fiddled with the zipper, eyes down. "I figured I'll head over to his place straight from work with a smorgasbord from Golden Wok. And we're going to binge on some *Ozark*. So, I, uh, I'll probably crash there again, seeing it'll be on the late side."

GRAVEDIGGER

I smiled down at my bedspread, adding an internal addendum.

And seeing, dear Momma, that, by hook or by crook, tonight's the night I plan on getting Mr. Thousand and One Excuses to deflower me, right after I misplace the remote.

Flaming tidbits from the past three evenings zinged through my brain, turning my skin hotter.

The first night. Clint home from his overnight stay in the hospital, woozy from surgery and pain management meds, but demanding I sleep beside him. Me, sporting a skimpy tank and bikini bottoms. He, bare-chested and gauze-wrapped, his brawny bod clad solely in a pair of raggedy gray sweatshorts.

Mmm. Those thin, can't-hide-a-thing rags...

The second night. Same scenario, except a lot less drugs in the big guy's bloodstream, as per his command. Me, garbed in another tiny tee and panties, he, rocking a different pair of sweats.

Indigo-blue this time, soft and worn, tented like a teepee over his bulging parts as we rolled around the sheets.

"Ah Jesus, baby... your mouth. Goddamn, I'm hard as fucking granite. One more kiss, angel. One more taste, then we gotta stop."

The third night, last night. Clint back to the raggedy grays. Yours truly bare-ass naked, save for a darling blush-hued thong courtesy of Vickie's Secret; me and my unbound girls trying our darnedest to make things happen.

"Please, Clint, please! I want you, so bad. I'll get on top—you can show me what to do. Why are you being so stubborn, denying us this? Let me take you out, put you in my—"

"Sunny, are you all right? You're awfully flushed."

I blinked at Mom, who had come to stand beside me while I'd been busy fantasizing about shoving a huge, fat cock inside my hoo-hah.

"Oh, I'm just a little warm from the shower." Sputtering, I forced out a laugh, fluffing my still-damp curls.

She nodded, looking far from convinced.

"Well, okay. But take an Emergen-C before you leave. We don't need you coming down with a summer cold, not with your new job and taking care of Clint."

Straightening a pile of pillows, she spoke to Myrtle, my ancient stuffed turtle.

"Er, honey… I thought that maybe today, I'd start clearing out a few things from Beth's closet. If it's okay with you. Not anything I think you'd want, some of the older stuff. And her shoes, seeing you're a size smaller. There's a big block sale next weekend, and I thought all her pretty sandals…"

GRAVEDIGGER

She trailed off, rearranging Myrtle's stubby, bright pink legs.

I swallowed around a ball in my throat, reaching out to squeeze her hand.

"It's okay, Mom. The shoes, that's a good idea." Another canned laugh as I shook my head. "Darn, why'd the girl have to go and have such big clodhoppers? It would bug me to no end, how I couldn't steal any of her sweet heels."

We gazed at one another sadly, our eyes moist.

"Greetings, womenfolk! Is this a private party, or can anyone join in?"

Dad stuck his head though the doorway, morning newspaper in hand.

"Scram, old man, we're having a girlie moment." Mom made shooing motions with four fingers, pinning him with a stink-eye. "I hope you're not planning on getting cozy with that paper anytime soon. Remember, you promised you'd fix the birdhouse and prune the rose bushes. And those breakfast dishes had better be in the drainer, mister."

A dramatic groan rent the air. "Slave driver! *This* is early retirement? I *knew* I should've gone golfing!"

"Come on, you fool..."

I chuckled for real, watching my mom drag her protesting spouse down the hallway.

All right. Better make tracks.

Rechecking that my duffle contained everything I'd need for an inspired night of past-due cherry-popping, I zipped up the nylon and grabbed my cell and handbag. Passing the mirror, I eyed my image with satisfaction.

Not bad, lady…

Hair, semi-behaving. Stylish skirt and sleeveless blouse, spiky heels. Sheer stockings gleaming. *Thigh-high* stockings, just purchased, topped with frothy cream lace. With two free fingers, I pushed my skirt up, admiring the delicate threadwork.

Mmm. I know somebody who's going to like these babies, a LOT.

I smiled, winking at my grinning reflection, itching for it to be six o'clock already.

Eager to be in Clint's arms, taking care not to maul his poor, shot-up shoulder.

Excited for him to check out my new outfit, to watch his silver eyes narrow and darken.

My pulse sped up as I pictured that hungry stare.

Oh yeah, my Viking loved my sexy-yet-tasteful work duds, no question there. Snatching me close the instant he flung open the door, hauling my bod to his. Crushing my mouth with ravenous lips, shoving his fingers in my hair. Running hot hands over my clothes, growling against my neck about how strongly I affected him, and how much he'd missed me.

How much he needed me.

I sucked in a breath, giddy anticipation cresting. Lord, today was going to be endless before I was back where I wanted to be.

Back where *I* needed to be.

Tingling all over, I floated out the door.

Back with big, bad, gun-shy Gravedigger, the man I'd fallen ass over teakettle in love with.

"You're looking especially scrumptious today, Goldilocks. Having another sleepover at Hunkalicious's, are we?"

Billy's tone was coy as he parked his rump against my desk, slurping an industrial-sized coffee and waggling his brows. "Lucky youuuuu. Inquiring minds need to know… Is there perchance room for three in Master M.'s bed? Consider me a package deal… I could take notes, join in, and play backup nursie all at the same time."

I flushed, scowling. "Leave me alone. I'm wrapping up a troubleshoot here."

Not only did the layabout *not* disappear as directed, but he was immediately joined by Amy, brandishing her own foul-smelling hazelnut blend.

"Hey, Florence Nightingale, how goes it?"

Setting the mug on important paperwork, she looked me up and down, focusing below the ankles.

"Nice shoes. Plan on wrapping them around a certain someone's neck in the next couple hours?"

"Amy!" I glared at my twin nemeses, teeth gritting. "Don't you guys have anything better to do other than to harass me and see who can come up with the lewdest comments?"

Billy scratched his jaw, yawning. "Speaking for myself, frankly, no. I finished today's project ages ago and am going out of my gourd staring at the second hand. Better to wander over here and discuss how my pal's gonna say 'buh-bye' to her hymen than to atrophy on my ergonomic throne."

I gaped at him, cheeks aflame. "Billy, my God!"

Amy piped up, grinning raunchily. "Hear, hear. I too am all caught up and in need of some almost-quitting-time-distraction." She nudged Billy's elbow. "Can Marshall here and I help it if we're bonafide software whizzes and get our shit done in half the time allotted?"

GRAVEDIGGER

The pair of them high-fived and I seared them with beady-eyed death rays.

"Bully for you; your medals are in the mail. Now go take your huge egos and goof off someplace else. I need to get this crap finished by five." Dismissing them, I hunched over the keyboard, transmitting silent messages.

Go. Vanish. Get lost. Scram.

Naturally, No-Filter Uno and Dos ignored my brain waves, both of them continuing to loom and guzzle from their matching troughs.

It didn't take long for the man decked out in head-to-toe shades of chartreuse to pose a thoughtful question.

"So. What's tonight gonna be? Attempt number four, or is it five? I dunno, Case… Maybe your god-like gravedigger is in the closet. I'm starting to think that must be it, resisting a fox like you getting in his boxers."

I threw him a baleful look, ruing like mad my loose lips earlier in the deserted break room.

Why, why, why? Letting slip my virgin angst to these clowns over a fattening raspberry Danish?

Billy read my mind, tutting as he patted my arm.

"Now, now, don't go beating yourself up, chick. All *I* did was ask if you've done the nast with Mr. Hung-

Like-a-Horse yet, and all *you* did was moan back, 'I wish.'"

His sidekick chimed in, Amy's expression positively prurient.

"'WISH' voiced in capital letters. And you forgot the, 'I must be the last twenty-four-year-old virgin in this doggone town, and not for lack of trying,' part."

I choked, remembering how Beth had always said my mouth moved faster than my common sense.

Note to self: in future, affix duct tape to lips before entering the workplace.

Realizing the odds of me wrapping up my project in the next half hour were zilch to none, I pushed back on four wheels, raking fingers through my hair.

"You idiots are impossible. If I had any sense, I'd unfriend the two of you this instant and go find Mr. Simmons and get him to can your lazy asses."

The tech geniuses guffawed at the empty threat, and I wrenched open my bottom drawer, pulling out my purse. "I'm going to the restroom to freshen up. When I return, this desk had better be clear of any caffeine-happy deadbeats."

Billy eyed me top to tail when I stood, pursing his lips.

"May I make a suggestion, hotstuff? Lose the undies before you come back out that door. Hell, if finding

GRAVEDIGGER

you all commando under that sexy little skirt doesn't get our Clintie wanting into The Promised Land, nothing will. And if you *do* strike out, hand the man my number, because he is most definitely playing for Team Marshall."

Lips clamped and cheeks burning, I ignored him, striding down the hall.

Outside, I was keeping it together. Inside, I was freaking—silently answering that skinny, green-garbed mind reader with something close to awe.

Lose the panties? Plan to, bucko. Tell me, William… At what point did you hack into my mental playbook and guess Miss Casey's first plan of attack?

Clint growled against my skin, his soft whiskers nuzzling my neck.

"Jesus *fuck*, babe, was this day torture. Not able to work, sittin' around doin' jack shit, waitin' for your gorgeous ass to show…"

"Mmm."

Purring, I snuggled deeper into his lap—one heel on, one heel off, my mouth already bruised. A foot away from the Plaid Beast, cartons of cooling Chinese sat on the coffee table alongside a lingerie-stuffed handbag. Eyeing said bag from under heavy lashes, I ground my skirted bum against what could pass for a lead mallet, and the man attached to that mallet cursed, arms tightening.

"Damn, girl…"

"Clint, take it easy… your shoulder!" I pushed against his uninjured side, tapping a steamy, shirtless chest. "And where's your sling? The doc said you should be wearing it as much as you can, to offset the pressure."

Gravedigger snorted, making a face.

"Fuck my shoulder, and that uncomfortable bitch. Don't need it, all it does is make shit harder." Tilting up my chin, he stared at my lips. "Tell ya what I *do* need. Need another kiss, angel, right the fuck now."

I happily complied, lolling my head against an uninjured shoulder.

"Me too."

We kissed passionately—mouths fused, tongues twining, breaths out of control. It was heavenly, seriously panty-melting. Well, if I happened to be wearing panties. When the oxygen eventually ran out and we were both damp messes, Clint drew back with a full-body shudder, eyes glittering.

"God, baby, the way you taste."

GRAVEDIGGER

Licking swollen lips, my reply was shaky. "Back atcha, big guy. But, this…"

I stretched out a hand, running my fingertips over swathes of white gauze, stark against sun-burnished skin.

"…Does it hurt terribly, baby?" I flushed, the endearment sounding strange and awkward coming from my mouth. Clint didn't seem to think so—his cheeks reddening, those silver orbs darkening.

"Call me that again."

I whispered it in the quiet room, holding his gaze. "Baby."

"Ah God, yeah. *Yeah…*"

He squeezed me harder, and this time, I truly was concerned for his well-being.

"Clint, come on, be careful! You're not supposed to—"

A rough laugh barked out of his throat. "You think what that sick twist did with his little pop gun is gonna keep me at arm's length, babe? Think fucking again." He angled my head sideways, spearing ten fingers in my curls as he flicked hot eyes over my lips, throat, breasts.

They honed in on the girls, narrowing.

"You wearin' a bra, baby?"

I was, but it's currently residing next to its matching thong, stuffed over yonder in saddle-stitched leather.

Biting lower lip, I shook my head, excited by the look on my dark Viking's face.

His fixated expression turned fierce. "Can't say I like that, babe… Those sweet nipples on show for guys you work with. Isn't that sort of—"

"I took it off just before I left, baby. For you, only for you."

And that's not the only undergarment missing around here, handsome.

Clint's eyes sparked at the admission, and I suspected at hearing that second "baby," as well.

"Beautiful Sunshine…" He sucked in another uneven breath, removing his hands from my hair. One palm stroked over my neck before he nudged me off his lap and onto itchy upholstery.

Clearing his throat, he jerked his chin at the takeout containers, slashes of red painting each cheekbone.

"The food… We should eat; you must be starving."

My eyes skittered to the mega bulge throbbing under his sweatshorts and my pussy tingled, scandalously bare beneath a layer of snug navy gabardine.

Starving? That I am, sirrah. That I most certainly am.

GRAVEDIGGER

Boldly, I threw out a suggestion, hell-bent on keeping "Operation Seduce A Reluctant Gravedigger" chugging along at a decent clip.

"This sofa is so scratchy. And your kitchen table... It's back to being an unholy shambles. How about we nosh in bed, where we can be nice and cozy? I can stuff a bunch of pillows behind your shoulder and set everything out on a baking tray. Dish you up like a regular king."

A look of panic clenched Clint's face as his gaze trailed up and down my bod, lingering on select sections. He took a finger and traced my collar, shaking his head.

"Uh, uh. Not a good idea, babe." That digit dipped an inch, smoothing over pale-yellow silk. "No way. After last night, these tight little tits under my tongue? Fuck me, I could barely keep it together. Could barely stop myself from..."

He removed his finger and looked away, balling his fists.

"No. We'll eat here. I'll go get some plates."

Beth's voice murmured in my ear, egging me on.

"Your Viking's on the edge, Sun. Time to show him what's missing under that classy pencil skirt."

Silently, I answered her back.

The very thing I'm thinking, Sissy.

I blew out a sigh, pretending to acquiesce. "All right, party pooper. If you say so."

My heart pounded like a wild thing as I slumped lower into the cushions. Clint lurched to his feet, wincing as his wounded shoulder flexed. He grunted, snatching his sling off the table and wrestling into it, talking to the kitchen archway.

"Might as well put the fucker on while we're eating."

"Mmm, hmm." Humming, I eyefucked his muscular, Paul Bunyan-sized back, wantonly widening my legs as far as constricting fabric would allow.

"Clint? Baby?"

I waited until he was just short of the threshold before I called him back, my tone as beguiling as this fledging seductress could manage. Two mismatched shoulders tensed, the bandaged one twitching. Without turning, Gravedigger gruffed out a reply.

"Yeah?"

"To drink… Could you bring me a… um, a…"

Deliberately, I let the sentence hang. He stood there a second, waiting, before swiveling on a heel. Instantly, his eyes dipped to my spread thighs and stretched wide as headlights; a pair of silver laser beams clamped to my naked pussy.

"Jesus fucking *Christ*, babe!"

GRAVEDIGGER

He stumbled against the jamb, scrubbing a gaping mouth.

"What... Where..."

I smiled, running slow fingers over the lace capping my thigh-high.

"Where are my panties?" I slid teasing eyes to my purse, tracing tiny circles. "Same place as my bra, big guy."

"Jesus!"

Clint's chest expanded like a bellows—the brown flesh sprinkled with a smattering of hair, wicked ink, and an eyepopping display of cut, sinewy muscles. Struggling not to dribble, I licked my lips as I traced broad pecs, corrugated abs, and a delectable happy trail.

I need to follow that trail, stat. No GPS needed.

The landlord of all that tantalizing testosterone scowled, raking his hair back.

"Sunshine, angel... What the living *fuck* are you trying to do to me? Shut those legs and get your damn underwear back on, girl! I told you: I can't. We can't."

I didn't move an inch. If anything, I spread a wee bit wider.

"And why's that?"

Groaning, Gravedigger slashed a hand in a sweeping gesture before smacking palm over heart.

"Christ, baby, I've told you a thousand times 'why not.' Hell, look at this fucking place! Look at *me*!"

I licked my lips again, tongue pointed. "Believe me, mister… I am looking."

Clint made a strangled sound as he tried, and failed, to keep his eyes off my pussy.

"Ah, God. Be serious, babe, I mean it. You're way too special to let a big, dirty fucker like me take your sweet—"

"He's weakening, Case. Almost there. Keep it up, Sis."

Listening to the voice in my head and interrupting the man searing eyeholes in my crotch, I pled my case, tutting.

"Clint, Clint, Clint… You need to stop this crazy talk. What is the big deal, here? Seems pretty cut-and-dried to me."

I moved hands to my hair, ruffling it as blazing orbs clamped to two outthrust tits. Lowering my voice, I softly cajoled.

"Come on, baby, it's simple. I want you; you want me. What's with the kid gloves? I'm not a little girl, I'm a grown woman, and I know what I want. Know *who* I want. Honestly… I never thought I'd be begging to have a man divest me of that which I'm most willing to give."

Gravedigger shook his head again, looking miserable.

"You don't understand, angel. You think you know me, but you don't. I'm all kinds of messed up—a slob of a laborer with a shitload of war noise rattling around upstairs. You need a dude who's got it together, babe, somebody with class. A guy who'll treat you right, a guy who'll…"

"How about a brave Viking Lord who saved me from being attacked?" I interrupted again, scooching off the sofa and standing up. "Huh? How about that?"

My hands slid to my back zipper, fingers fumbling with the clasp.

Clint swallowed, his eyes tracking the movement, his thick throat working. He looked away and then back again, grinding out a rationalization.

"Anybody would have done that, if they'd been around. And fuck, Sunshine, I was *spying* on you. Have you forgotten how fucked up that shit is? How pissed it got you?"

I slid the zip down, wriggling my hips. "Yes, I was pissed. Catastrophically pissed. I can't deny it. But once I saw you again at Mooney's, all that outrage floated away, Clint, and I realized how much I missed you. How excited I was to see you again. And that night, at your place…"

Need I remind you, Mr. M.? Surely you haven't forgotten our super-hot, mutual masturbation extravaganza?

My eyes dropped to a masculine crotch, and the humungo bulge tenting soft gray cotton.

Doesn't appear forgotten, no siree Bob.

Sweeping my gaze north, I smiled at the flush staining his skin as Gravedigger attempted to subtly adjust. Quite the joke, considering the size of that torpedo under his palm.

Wickedly, I embellished, pushing skirt past thighs as I whispered.

"I haven't stopped thinking of that night, baby. Your hand on your big cock, your eyes on mine. My pussy, how wet it was, how empty…"

Clint moaned, pressing that palm tighter.

"Baby, don't. Stop. Pull that thing back up, now. Please, I'm on the fucking brink here!"

That's what I'm a' hoping, hotstuff.

Beth chimed in again, offering a most splendid suggestion.

"Prick the devil's jealous side, Sun. It'll send him over the cliff; I'm sure of it."

GRAVEDIGGER

Wishing I'd thought of it myself, I threw her a mental salute, kicking my skirt aside. Clad in a pretty blouse and a pair of lacy thigh-highs, I smoothed one hand up my flank, brushing a finger over damp folds.

"Fuuuuuuck me…"

Ignoring that protracted groan, I repeated the motion, sighing.

"Well, okay. If that's your last word on the subject."

Another sigh, dramatic as they come. "Guess we're at a stalemate then. I'm *certainly* not going to spend another night under this roof getting all frustrated, begging the man I'm in love with to initiate me into the pleasures of the flesh."

A harsh gasp burst from Clint's throat. "In… in love with?"

Ignoring that as well, I added a second finger, leisurely circling my slit.

"Guess I'll get dressed and head on over to Mooney's Place, take a seat at the bar."

I fluttered my lashes over at a pair of slitted eyes.

"Are you aware that Mitch Tirone handed me his number that day I left you in the lot? With great enthusiasm, might I add. Quite the good-looking guy, that Moonlighter. Not to mention a seasoned pro when it comes to fruit-ish matters. Mmm, hmm, I'm sure he'd be *more* than happy to discuss cherries rather than orang—"

"Goddamn you, you evil witch!"

Gravedigger lunged, propelling himself across the room and crushing me close, gripping my naked bum with savage fingers as he ground me up against him.

Ooooooh….

"You win, baby. You fucking win; I can't take it anymore. I'm yours, as long as you'll have me."

Silvery eyes seared into mine, backlit with demonic fires as Clint's big bod juddered.

"Another guy touching my girl? I'd fucking castrate the motherfucker in half a heartbeat. Better get used to the jealousy, babe, 'cause when it comes to your sweet ass, I'm drowning in the poison."

I smiled against a marauding mouth, zinging off a silent thank you.

Good call, Bethie. Good call.

My possessive Viking drew back, brushing my lashes with two shaky thumbs.

"I'm in love with you too, Sunshine, fuckin' crazy in love. Have been, from the first time you clocked me at Oaklawn with these big brown eyes. Jesus, one look and I was fried… Complete and utter toast. Burnt to a fucking crisp."

GRAVEDIGGER

I squirmed closer, heart melting, practically crawling up his heaving torso.

"Great. Then we're good. Can we hit the sheets now, pretty, pretty please?"

Kissing his neck, I whispered against sweaty, pine-scented skin.

"I'll grab a few fortune cookies, so we have some sustenance until our Chinese leftovers breakfast."

DIGGER: NINETEEN

Thrown-off clothes ringing the bed, I knelt above Sunshine, shaking like a leaf.

"My angel…"

I bracketed her head between my palms, staring into wide, chocolatey eyes.

"You're so beautiful, baby. Jesus God, do I love you."

Licking my lips, I tasted the sweet cream I'd just spent delicious minutes savoring, my shoulders wedged between a pair of wicked silk stockings. The left bastard ached like a sonofabitch, and my baby may have dislodged a bandage or two during my appetizer, but ask me if I fucking cared.

Yeah, like a pain-in-the-nuts gunshot is gonna shut this fantabulousness down.

I outlined Sunshine's mouth with a gentle finger, my command hoarse.

"Tell me if it hurts, babe. If it hurts, I'll stop."

Might howl like a gutted grizzly, but I'll stop.

My cock smacked my belly, stiff as steel as I crossed imaginary fingers.

GRAVEDIGGER

I hope.

Sunshine smiled up at me, that tiny gap between her teeth making my heart clench. She whispered back, her own voice husky after all that protracted screaming.

"No stopping. Do your worst, Lord Thor; I'm ready."

I sucked in a shuddering breath; my hand palsied as I moved it down to my dick. Fisting rigid flesh, I lined up at her entrance, painting my about-to-blow head up and down a soaked slit.

Holy fuck, so juicy and sticky and slick.

Transferring my weight to uninjured arm, I ground my knees into the mattress, nudging forward a fraction. Hell, not even a fraction. Sunshine bit down on her lip as I split her, just the very tip of me inside. *Ah, Jesus...* I shook hunks of wet hair back, rivulets of sweat stinging my eyes as I gauged her reaction.

"Hurts? Or okay?"

The words gritted out between clenched teeth, and I held my breath.

Sunshine's forehead crinkled as she wriggled underneath me.

"Hurts. But... okay."

I sent a quick prayer off to The Man Upstairs, pushing in a smidge more. *Christ, so tight, so right, so perfect.* Watching my girl closely, I fed myself into her clenching channel in excruciatingly slow increments—each half-inch breached the most exquisite, mind-blowing torture a man could endure.

Wanna shove myself in to the balls. Wanna pound this cherry cunt like a madman. Wanna slather this angel with my seed, douse her in my come, make her leak for a fucking week.

Locking my jaw, I did none of these things, grunting out a few more sounds.

"Too. Much?"

Sunshine shook her head, a riot of blond curls kissing my pillow. Her eyes glowed as she dug ten fingers into my biceps, short nails stabbing.

"No. Keep going. Stings… but feels… nice."

"Nice?" "Nice?" I can think of a few better words than "nice," darlin'.

I was maybe a quarter in by now, shaking, sweating, poised on the cusp of insanity. But I maintained my pace—determined to go slow, determined to make it as good for my girl as I could. Not that I knew what the actual fuck I was doing. Having never made it with a virgin before, I was flying without a guidebook; figuring "slow-as-molasses" was the standard protocol.

Doubts assailed me as I slid in another half-fraction, my heart slamming like a mofo.

GRAVEDIGGER

Maybe I should go a little faster, get the pain over with, so we can get to the good part? Maybe I should flip her over, have Sunshine up on top? Maybe I should—

"Baby? I think you should go faster, get the pain over with, so we can get to the good part."

I blinked down, freaking at how a squirming, buck-naked beauty had just peeked inside my cranium.

"You…you sure?"

Sunshine jerked her head, nails scoring my flesh.

"Yeah, I'm sure. Stick that beast all the way in, big guy, so we can start rockin' and rollin'."

Hell, who was I to refuse the lady? Especially seeing if I didn't do as requested, I was headed straight to Blue Ball Academy to pick up my diploma for "Hugest Pair on Campus."

Taking hand off dick, I slapped a palm next to Sunshine's shoulder, bracing myself. Then I threw my head back and shoved my hips forward, driving nine rock-hard inches into the sweetest, tightest, most phenomenal pussy on the planet.

Ah, my fucking God…

"OWWWWW!"

Sunshine stiffened beneath me, arms and legs flailing as I pinned her to the sheets. Hazily, I thought of slowing down, or even (Jesus help me) pulling out, but that train had left the station. Lord, there was no fucking way. Drawing out to the tip, I pushed carefully in again, the unholy tightness enveloping me making my eyes cross. Then I repeated the motion, a tad faster.

Then again, a mite faster still.

"Mmm… Clint…"

Okay. That sounds encouraging.

My eyes locked on her face, I watched Sunshine's lovely visage slide up and down the pillow as I worked my angel, her fluttering lashes and bouncing tits making me high. I bit my lip before bending for a filthy kiss, mumbling against parted, panting lips.

"Is it getting better, baby? Are you starting to feel… 'nice' again?"

Thick lashes rose, chocolate orbs glittering.

"Y…yes. Yes, Clint, yes. F… faster."

With that green light, I picked up the pace, flinging saturated hair back. Over and over, I sawed in and out, taking care not to lose control, not to give in to temptation and fuck this unbelievable creature in two. But goddamn, was that shit the work of the devil.

"Baby. Aw, Jesus. Your little pussy, so fuckin' sweet. So fuckin' *tight*…"

GRAVEDIGGER

Sunshine moaned, her curvy hips starting to buck. "More, Clint. More, harder."

Fuck, yeah!

"Oooh, it feels *niiiiice*. Again, baby, again."

Damn straight, again.

I sank into her, cramming that delicious, dick-sucking channel. Lowering my hand, I parted drenched pussy lips, flicking a gorgeously distended clit with light fingers. That set Sunshine off and she bucked harder, her ass rising up off the bed.

"Clint!"

Petting that pulsating pearl, I drew back, gazing into her eyes as I wheezed out a hoarse truth.

"Love you, girl. Love you, sweet angel."

Not sure if it was the words, the clit action, or my fat cock pounding into her, but thank Mother Mary and all her sisters Sunshine blasted off just then, long and hard and wild—her stockinged legs wrapping around my soaked back, her slim arms strangling me. Feeling like a fucking king, I let her ride it out until I couldn't take those diabolical python-squeezes a second longer.

Spine tingling, I looked down at us joined together, my baby's abundant juices saturating my hair and my balls and my pistoning prick.

God bless it. Fuckin' hottest sight in the world.

I started slurring guttural nonsense, barely aware what I was saying as I straightened into a plank, balancing on toes and palms as I went to town. Stung my inflamed shoulder like a sonofabitch, but like I said: tough goddamn titties.

"So beautiful, so tight. Fucking feel so fine. Fucking love you, angel, so much."

Swearing, I threw back my head; shaking, sweating, insane.

"Ah, Jesus, I'm there, babe. I'm fucking *therrrrrrrrrre…*"

People, there are no words.

No words at all.

Sunshine and I ended up doing it again that first, fabulous night, which I thought was totally pushing it, but little Miss Sex Maniac insisted.

And like I could say no to those tiny fingers, stroking here, there, and everywhere?

Hey, at least I got her primed up good and proper again with tongue and fingers before I brought it home, growling more besotted babble to my brand-new fiancé as she bounced on top of me—her lovely face tipped to the ceiling, her red-nippled breasts a dream.

Yeah, you heard right. Fiancé.

I didn't mean or even plan to ask her, at least not without a shiny rock to present, but the words blurted out just before Sunshine gushed all over my dick. I think it surprised her as much as it did me, but my baby didn't hesitate, didn't even take a breath before accepting—falling forward for a long and luscious kiss as her pussy spasmed wildly, over and over and still over again.

"Yes, Clint. Yes, I'll marry you, my handsome, brave, slob of a Viking. Oh… Oh, *Ohhhhhh!*"

We stayed in my trashed bed until morning, not budging from the thing except for quick bathroom breaks and for me to grab that tasty chow and a couple of brews. Gorging straight from the containers, we laughed like kids, legs entwined. When our bellies were full, we swirled close, Sunshine's curls tickling my chest.

Touching. Kissing. Planning our future.

It was fucking awesome, every second of it. Well, except for the part about soon-to-be Mrs. MacGregor overhauling my crib once she moved in next week, alluding as to how she was going to "whip this pigsty into order like nobody's business."

Pigsty! Now, come on. Maybe this place is a little disorganized, but shee-it... I'm a hardworking stiff, woman!

The best part was the fortune cookies. There was a shitload of the suckers in the bottom of the bag, but Sunshine only allowed us to draw out one each, shaking the sack a hundred times like it contained fucking Powerball numbers.

My girl went first and I went second, reading tiny slips of paper out loud in the lamplight.

Hers sucked, lame as all get-out:

YOU LOVE EGGROLLS

Sunshine went ape, pinching the scrap into a miniscule ball.

"Really? *Really?* This has to be the worst fortune ever. I demand another!"

I smirked, shaking my head.

"Uh, uh. You made the rules, gorgeous. My turn."

Crumbling the cookie and extracting its message, I squinted, the made-for-me missive making my chest swell.

And okay, making my eyes well up, too.

Big-time well up.

GRAVEDIGGER

KEEP YOUR FACE TO THE SUNSHINE AND YOU WILL NEVER SEE SHADOWS

The craziest thing? After I read the last word out loud, voice catching, I swear to Christ I heard Kev drawl in my ear, his Vermont-rural accent unmistakable as he quoted his beloved *Star Trek*.

"Live long and prosper, dude. I've got your back."

I blinked fast, reaching for my bright angel and smashing her to my heart.

Plan to, good buddy.

Plan to.

CASEY: EPILOGUE

I stood close to my husband in front of Beth's stone, leaning against his muscly bulk. The May sun reflected off my diamond as I stretched out a hand, tracing my twin's name and the dates beneath it.

"Next month will be a whole year, baby… I can hardly believe it."

Gravedigger squeezed me tight, no doubt getting mud all over my pretty cream sundress.

"You know she's at peace, angel, same as Kev. And like I've said how many times: I wouldn't be surprised if those two are an item up there, making whoopie in the clouds."

I snorted, the sound echoing over rows of carved tombstones.

"Fat chance. You've shown me plenty of photos, and I told you… Bethie was into a lot more refined than Kevin Stanley Kerkowalski."

A deep chuckle rumbled from my spouse's throat. "Yeah, well, maybe that fast-talking Trekkie got your sis to change her mind. The man's powers of persuasion were legendary."

GRAVEDIGGER

We sobered and grew quiet for a moment, each of us locked in our own thoughts.

Abandoning pink granite and grabbing Clint's hand, I ran a thumb over his ring. This, the oversized gold band with a corny fortune cookie saying kissing his third digit, its inner message etched in teensy-tiny letters.

KEEP YOUR FACE TO THE SUNSHINE AND YOU WILL NEVER SEE SHADOWS

The huge softie.

I smiled, remembering how I'd threatened to do the same—walking around with I LOVE EGGROLLS scrolled within the most precious piece of jewelry I possessed.

Naturally, the big guy had shot that suggestion down stat and pitched another, so *my* band's inscription featured our initials, intertwined around a pin-sized heart rocking angel wings.

The huge softie.

"Baby?" My voice was soft as I interlocked our fingers, not giving a hoot if mine got smeared with cemetery soil.

"Yeah, love?' Gravedigger looked down, his eyes adoring as they searched mine.

I nodded toward Beth, speaking low.

"Why do you think I never hear her voice anymore? It's been ages and ages; I can't even remember the last time."

Clint turned me to him, taking his free hand and stroking my cheek.

Whoa, mud city. Good thing I have wet wipes in the car.

"I told you why, angel. It's because when she passed, she knew you were alone and that you needed her. Until you knew that she was okay. Until *she* knew that *you* were okay, and had a big slob of a gravedigger to love on you for the rest of your natural born life."

Silver eyes glowed, turning darker.

"And beyond."

I swooned inside, smiling up at my solemn, brawny Viking.

Gad, am I bonkers about this man. And his demons are almost conquered, thanks to bi-monthly sessions with Mom's trusted guru. And my Gravedigger loves me, so damned much…

"Ah, angel…"

Licking his lips, Hubby stared at my mouth and I had a hunch someone was jonesing for a kiss or ten. But rules were rules, and I've told the Mister countless times that the sacred environs of Oaklawn are not the

GRAVEDIGGER

place for hanky-panky. Usually, the sex maniac extraordinaire abided, but every so often I got ravaged under cover of a tree or beside that charming creek, when our occasional snatched lunch breaks got the better of us.

Speaking of snatched lunch breaks...

Glancing at my wrist, I made a face, untwining our hands. "Shoot. I've gotta run, handsome... It's back to the grind, and I have a mountain of work waiting for me on my desk. Please say a prayer that Billyboy leaves me alone so I can make a dent."

Clint blew out a sigh, shoving dirty fingers through his hair.

"Only if *you* say one back that the rest of my dig goes smooth, and that I don't encounter any huge-ass roots or rocks the size of my head."

"Deal."

We fist-bumped, and I slung on my knapsack. The thing was a shit-ton lighter than it used to be, seeing it no longer housed gardening shears or a fat notebook. No... Gravedigger took special care of the grass weekly, no charge, and my journal was full, sitting on Beth's bookshelf back at the homestead. Maybe down the road I'd start another one, but for now, I considered the tear-stained prose I'd needed to disgorge to my sibling in those early, hell-dark days complete—a healing homage to a beautiful soul taken far too soon.

And anyhow, these days, I didn't use a pen... I rolled with verbal communication whenever I had something to say.

Whenever, such as now.

"Bye, Sissy. Try to send Dad a sign from above on his b-day, okay? That would be the best present ever. Love you, see you soon."

I smoothed a hand over her stone, patting the shiny dime resting on top that my husband switched out for a new one whenever his silver talismans got tarnished.

A big palm blanketed my knuckles and Clint pressed down, his calloused flesh hot and comforting as he gruffed out his own goodbye.

"See ya, Beth. You're gettin' some fresh seeds and the watering can bright 'n' early in the morning, so look sharp."

We smiled at one another and I snapped my fingers, remembering something.

"Oh! Your fan club prez Christopher asked if you could bring a twelve of that craft beer you turned him onto at Mooney's to Dad's bash tomorrow night. He said you'd know the brand."

I eyed him askance. "And don't let me forget to give you clean clothes to stick in your truck so you can change before you show, you filthy beast."

GRAVEDIGGER

White teeth glinted through his whiskers as Gravedigger ran a hand across his grimy chest.

"I thought you liked me all down and dirty, Wifey?"

Tossing my head, I tried not to melt all over the grass.

"You know I do. Just not in front of fifty-some birthday guests, including four prim and proper aunties who consider 'mud' a four-letter word. And don't forget: your best buddy Sledgehammer and your new pal Moonlighter are going to be gathered around that cake, too. You don't want those stud muffins to show you up, do you?"

Clint scowled, hissing through his teeth. "Don't call them fuckin' studs. And remind me again why Hound Dogs One and Two are invited, anyway. You know it drives me nuts how Jaggard drools over your ass, and that whiskey slinger is even worse with the googly eyes."

He shook his own head, mumbling to himself.

"Why the fuck I let Sledgie talk me into hangin' with the prick…"

Stretching up, I rubbed his soft beard, soothing the savage beast.

"Amy and JoJo, that's why they're invited. The girls insisted on some beefcakey eye candy, and since you're already spoken for, I threw on my thinking cap. You should be glad your friends accepted, babe… Now you'll have a few more dudes besides my brothers to suck down nasty dark hops with."

Groaning, Gravedigger was back to studying my lips.

"Jesus. How many times, baby? How many times do I hafta tell you not to say that word, not unless we're tangled in the sheets?"

I flicked a look at a rigid face from under cover of my lashes, repeating it in drawn-out whisper.

"What word? *Suuuuuck*?"

Pewter eyes turned black and I dropped my gaze to a pair of disreputable khakis showcasing a severely tented fly. My pussy tingled beneath the sexy silk "I'm Taken" panties Clint had recently gifted me as I whispered, holding that turbulent stare.

"You know what, lover? My work is still going to be there in an hour, and you said yourself that grave is already halfway dug. It's been a month of Sundays since I've had a tour of your spiffy, shovel-stuffed garage…"

I licked my lips, peeking south again.

"Care to reacquaint me with some of your long, hard… *tools,* Gravedigger mine?"

More by JC

Readers, I hope you enjoyed Casey and Clint's tale as much as I loved dreaming it up. Please consider leaving your review on the platforms of your choice... Positive feedback is so appreciated. Got lots more dirty boys on tap, so lock the door and dive on in...

Bad Boys Abroad
Ravenous on the Riviera

Dirty Boys Do It Better Trilogy
Gravedigger

Sledgehammer

Moonlighter

Breakaleg Trilogy
Need It Now

Feel It Fierce

Want It Wicked

My Sinful Santa – Three Naughty Tales

Moody Under the Mistletoe

Contact JC

Newsletter
Sign up for bi-monthly teasers and announcements.
subscribepage.com/jcjaye

Amazon
Check out my smexy covers and peruse
the blurbs on my Amazon profile.
amazon.com/author/jcjaye

Goodreads and BookBub
Add my titles to your TBR list
on your favorite book discovery site.

Facebook
Find me posting here…sometimes
@jcjayeauthor

Email
Drop me a line anytime!
jcjayeauthor@gmail.com

Website
Everything JC,
including the occasional personal absurdities.
jcjaye.com

About the Author

It's all Rhett and Scarlett's fault.

(Talkin' the grand staircase scene, people.)

Stung by the literary lovebug at a tender young age, JC has been devouring steamy romantic fiction ever since. Seriously… What could possibly be more delectable at the end of a rough day than a big, bad, moody male brought to his alphalicious knees by a gorgeous, sassy-talking heroine?

Well, besides Tom Hardy showing up shirtless on your doorstep with car trouble.

Penning "I wish" fantasies while slogging through the woefully Rhett-scarce world, JC invites readers to indulge in decadent escape through her foulmouthed and passion-saturated tales.

Uh. You did hear foulmouthed, right?

Printed in Great Britain
by Amazon